# MONSTER EARTH

*Edited by*
JAMES PALMER

# CONTENTS

## BOOKS BY JAMES PALMER

Slow Djinn

Four Terrors: Weird Horror Tales

**As Contributor:**

Gideon Cain: Demon Hunter

Blackthorn: Thunder on Mars

Mars McCoy: Space Ranger vol. 2

This is a work of fiction. All the characters and events portrayed in this book are either products of the authors' imagination or are used fictitiously.

No giant monsters were harmed during the making of this book.

MONSTER EARTH



ISBN-10: 0615753469

ISBN-13: 978-0615753461



A Mechanoid Press Book

www.jamespalmerbooks.net

❀ Created with Vellum

# INTRODUCTION

Welcome to Monster Earth.

It is a world like our own, except here, giant monsters appeared around World War II. They were put into the service of the countries that discovered them, and used as living weapons as well as threat deterrents. On Monster Earth, there are no nuclear weapons. The Cold War was fought instead with giant monsters.

Many of these tales deal with war and conflict. The classic Japanese monsters, including Godzilla, were born out of the bombings of Hiroshima and Nagasaki, and our collective fear of atomic power and its ability to heal or destroy us.

With these tales, we highlight the human element, to show how ordinary people live their lives in the shadows of these colossal beasts. That's what the best of the Toho giant monster films that inspired us did. In these pages you'll meet a young boy whose birthday happens to coincide with the Japanese attack on Pearl Harbor; you'll witness how a creature on the loose entangles the lives of a bank robber, a cabbie, and a young woman; you'll see ordinary people called into service to fight against the onslaught of these gigantic horrors.

Some of these monsters came to us via unknown yet scientifically knowable means, while others have a mythical origin that ties in with the mythologies of the world. However they got here, they are ours to command, lest we be destroyed by them.

We know you will enjoy these tales from Monster Earth!

James Palmer
Jim Beard

1

# THE PARADE OF MOMENTS

JIM BEARD

*Central Intelligence Agency file #0-345-40548*

*HIGHEST SECURITY LEVEL*

*The following was transcribed from recorded audio tapes found in the effects of Donald Allan Witnes on August 2, 2001 in Boulder, Colorado. Tapes estimated to have been recorded between May 2001 and July 2001 by Witnes himself, alone. No other person or persons connected to or unknown to Witnes believed to have knowledge of tapes.*

*Transcription:*

[*Several false-starts by subject, amounting to only a few words or phrases with no real bearing on the bulk of the following content.*]

WITNES: Guess I'm just gonna *tell* this thing and not worry about making it flowery. The world already knows so much of it...but there's a part or two of it I've never told anyone. No one at all. Now I'm gonna tell it and the world can do whatever the hell it wants to do with it. Or nothing at all.

[*Long pause.*]

Doesn't much matter anymore to me. I'm so goddamned old, never thought I'd live this long.

[*Long pause with periodic sighing.*]

The world changed on that night in China, July the Seventh, 1937.

Everyone knows that. It's in the textbooks and on the TV shows and probably right outside your window every single goddamn day, but like I said there's a part of it they don't know. That the world doesn't know. *I* saw it and *I* know and it's all true.

I was sent to China in June of 1937 by my bosses at the studio. Boy, was I a twenty-one-year-old cocksure bastard, all full of vim and vigor and "gonna make waves" and "better get out of my way, sailor" and all that. It took exactly three days there to put me in my place, to get on with the job. Little did I know then I would be seeing history unfold before my eyes and my camera. Don Witnes of "The Parade of Moments," before he became a star. Before the world went to hell in a thousand handbaskets.

That one goddamn night in China, in Beijing. July the Seventh, 1937. Before the war? Hell, before *anything*. Nothing that came before that really mattered, not to me, not to anyone.

We didn't have *monsters* before that night.

"Parade" had sent me to China to cover the "plight of the common person," as they said. The newsreels tried to take at a look at *everything* back then, not just the big events, but the "human interest" stuff, too. We got a bit more then we bargained for in China, I'd say.

The country was being torn apart from the inside in those days, back in the thirties. It was the Confucians, the old guard, trying to hold off the Communists from taking over. Mao was giving the government all kinds of fits with his crazy new ways and ol' Chiang Kai-Shek was at wit's end trying to hold it all together and not allow China to slide into something he thought it wasn't, just because Mao wanted it that way. On top of all that, the Japanese sure weren't helping anything. The bastards had been *waiting* for an opportunity to march in and take over the whole ball of wax, and the thirties were just full of *incidents* that helped their cause. Boy-oh-boy, did the Japanese *love* their incidents. And hell, they had a goddamned foothold in China already in 1933 when they took over all of Manchuria and put that idiot Kang Te on the throne there... I once read something somewhere that said that the Japanese had "never emerged from feudal barbarism," and that was why they wanted to invade everything, every place they could. Wanted to take over the world. Tried a few times, didn't they?

So, anyway, here's me in 1937, not speaking a word of Chinese – still don't – and being plunked right down in the middle of all that and told to stick my nose and my camera into the lives of the "common person." Like I said, it took me all of three days to realize that the common person in China was something I hadn't expected. These people were proud and they were strong and they were dignified, but they were living dirt poor and they'd been beaten around and pulled from all sides [*pause*]. But they were humble, too. God, were they humble. Most of 'em, anyway.

I was pretty much just a cameraman in those days, but being sent to China in '37 was my big break, or so I imagined, in showing my bosses I could run the whole show. I was going to give 'em everything: film, narration, a real *look* into the country and its struggles. I got off the plane all by myself, "stranger in a strange land," and thought *I* was going to conquer the world! After looking into the *faces* of the Chinese people, the *real* people, into their *eyes*, I saw something that the Communists and the Japanese could never conquer [*long pause*]: heart and soul.

My translator, assigned to me by the Chinese government, was a guy named Cho. Good ol' Cho. He was a smiler. But he was also a Nervous Nelly, a real shaky type. His English was pretty good, actually, and he was my lifeline while I was there, before the... getting ahead of myself. Hang on, have to get a drink.

[*Tape machine shut off, then turned back on at a later, indeterminate time.*]

WITNES: This old thing still works, dammit. Made to last. Wish I had it in China back then; we would have had the sounds to go with the images. Ah well [*ice cubes clinking in glass*].

Where was I? Oh, yeah, Cho. Cho was a godsend because he got me out of the city, out of Beijing, and into some of the outlying areas. [*Pause*] Wait, I mean Peking. [*Pause*] Or is it still Beijing? We called it Peking back in the day. Anyway, the people in the city seemed more nervous, like Cho, but on the outskirts they just went about their business, not overly worried much about the Communists or the Japanese or whatever. They just lived their lives. I began to...began to learn a lot from them. Through Cho, of course. Good ol' Cho.

In early July I found myself in the little town of Wanping, outside of Peking, talking to the people there, filming and generally making myself a nuisance. But, the Chinese seemed to accept me after a few days and went along with it, for the most part. I think it...helped in a way to keep their mind off of what was going on around them. The Japanese had been puffing out their chests and rattling their sabers at that time, trying to bully the Chinese into clearing out of the area. Militarily, that is. Wanted to build an airfield there or some such. Chinese said go soak your heads and, well, the tension was pretty high.

Cho liked to take a few snoots now and then and on the night of July 7th we had had a few shots of some kind of native wine – rice wine, I think – and we had settled in and were waiting for the maneuvers to begin. Japanese maneuvers. Had them every night and the locals were pretty frazzled from it all, even though they were allowed to the Japanese by some stupid treaty rights. Still, Cho told me that everyone was expecting something to happen, and happen *soon*.

[*Coughs*] I don't think anyone expected what they got that night [*coughs repeatedly*]. Jesus, I get the chills even thinking about it now, all this time later.

I found out later that the Japanese were supposed to tell the Chinese *in advance* before their maneuvers, you know, so that the locals could prepare themselves. I guess that didn't happen that night, 'cause everyone acted pretty shocked when the those soldiers started moving around and doing their stuff. Cho and I couldn't understand that ourselves – weren't they marching around *every* goddamn night?

Anyway, there we were, feeling kind of right and a little bit tight and we hear shots. Now, until that night we had never heard shots. Wasn't those kind of maneuvers. Me, with a little rice wine in me, I get up and look around. Cho laughed, told me I was crazy. Then all hell broke loose.

Shots. Lots of shots. I could tell right away that it wasn't just ceremonial or whatever. It was fire and return fire. I got cold, very cold. You know how they say the blood drains away from you? That's how I felt when I heard those shots. I didn't sign up to be in the middle of any goddamn war zone, no matter how cocksure I felt. But, I was a cameraman and something like a reporter, so I thought, and I finally remembered all that and grabbed my camera, grabbed Cho and off we went. The Green Hornet and Kato...

I had gotten to know – through Cho, of course – a few of the Chinese brass stationed in and around Nanping. I was authorized, allowed to be there, and the army...okay, they didn't *embrace* me, but they didn't really impede my work. Got to know a few of them, even drank with them, and they were all right. Pretty stand-up guys. Don't ask me how, its all kind of a blur, but I managed to get a word with one of them that night. Cho translated for me and I found out that the Chinese believed a Japanese attack was going down.

Mother of God, things went sour pretty damn quick after that. It was as if all the tension and ill-will and aching to get something started flowed right to that little town outside of Beijing and exploded. Talk about a match to the tinder. The Japanese, for their part, didn't help anything when they called up the Chinese and demanded to be let into the town to – get this – look for one of their people that had gone AWOL. Craziest damn thing we'd ever heard, and believe me, I had heard a lot of crazy stuff between the Chinese and the Japanese up to that point.

Missing soldier? I mean, how do you *lose* a soldier? The Chinese didn't really believe it either and they told the Japanese to go suck eggs. I think literally, too. Then, around, oh, must have been just before midnight, General Qin Dechun of the Chinese said he'd conduct a search himself – I mean his soldiers would do it – for the Japanese grunt and he'd get right back to them with the results. That seemed to throw a wet blanket on the whole thing.

[*Chuckles softly*] Yeah, for about a minute or so.

Japanese were talking out of both sides of their mouths. They attacked! For real this time – some infantry soldiers tried to break down the door, so to speak, and the Chinese threw 'em back, good for them. Japanese then tossed out an ultimatum, said they'd get their soldier back no matter what and the whole country be damned if they didn't like it. General Qin called in reinforcements and Cho and I knew the stuff had really hit the fan. We knew it was war. You can just tell these things sometimes. That was one of those moments.

[*Pause*] Good God, were we stupid. Everybody there on that night was so goddamn stupid.

It got quiet, or what passed for quiet when you're sitting in a little walled city with a bunch of nervous Chinese soldiers fingering their rifles and waiting to be attacked again. Then, around 3:30 in the morning, we could see the Japanese pulling up some big guns, what they called mountain guns, huge artillery pieces, and a whole clutch of machine guns, too. Cho and I looked at each other, dumbfounded. An hour later, General Qin let some Japanese *investigators* in the town – I say it with scorn because if those little twerps were investigators there to find an allegedly missing punk soldier, then, well...I doubted that's what they were. Didn't really matter, because their own people didn't think much of them either. They were cannon fodder, just like the rest of us.

[*Long pause*] Have you ever seen the Marco Polo Bridge that was at Wanping? I mean, in an old photo?

Beautiful, and when I say beautiful I mean completely different from anything you've ever seen before. True to the Orient, it was... alien. *Unique.* Stretched over the river, the Yongfu? The Yingding? Something like that. Regardless, the bridge was hundreds and hundreds of years old; I think they started building it in the 1100s or around then. Marco Polo mentioned it in his book and even though it has a real name of its own – don't ask me to pronounce *that*, either – *his* name stuck to it and the rest is history. It had these incredible stone lions all up and down it, something like five hundred of them. Someone once tried to count them all, but for whatever reason they could never pin it down. Cho told me all about it back then, but that's too many years ago.

I hope you've seen a photo of that bridge, 'cause its not there anymore. For me, I see it too much in my dreams to ever forget it.

So, the Japanese armies opened up on their end of the bridge with those machine guns at five in the morning and I thought my ears were going to bleed from the sound of it. You're talking about a kid with snot still practically dripping out of his nose, still brushing the dust off his boots from Durango, Colorado, who'd never been near anything bigger than a double-barreled shotgun. I had tears in my eyes. Cho grabbed my arm and pulled me away from the Chinese soldiers, looks for a safe place. "Safe place," ha-ha. When we saw the armored vehicles coming, I knew there wasn't any such thing.

That was a cake walk compared to what came next [*loud, sustained coughing*].

The Japanese had more than just guns and tanks. They brought in something else.

Listen, you've seen the...photo of it. The one real photo we have of it, beyond my other film. I'm looking at it right now on the computer. I know there's not much there to see, really, and it's grainy. It's also... Jesus, I don't know what to say about it that hasn't been said a hundred times already, but you have to know that back then, in that little town, it hurt our heads to look at the thing. Couldn't wrap our heads around it at first. To see it come up out of the river and just [*long pause*] ...it came up and *scarred* us all, in every way imaginable.

The Japanese began advancing across the bridge, encountering some resistance from the Chinese on our side, but they weren't slowed down much. When General Qin sent this colonel and, I dunno, maybe a hundred men across to shore up the sieve that it was quickly becoming, that's when the Japanese pulled their dirty, stinking trick.

And I filmed it. Not sure how, but I did, for what it's worth. You know those goddamn idiots today that film or take pictures with their cellphones of everything around them, all the accidents and fights and whatever? Like, the world's falling apart around them and they just need a picture of it? That was me. I was the first one to do it, maybe.

So, this-this *thing* comes up out of the river, and there's me with my camera and Cho screaming at me to run. Just drop it all and *run*. But I didn't. Nope. No one's ever seen that footage, not even my wife, God rest her soul, but it's there on the film.

[*Note: See disc marked "Witnes-Lugou Bridge-7/8/37"*]

At first all I saw was a Chinese soldier lift up off the ground like he'd suddenly grew wings and could fly, but when he screamed and then his body split in two I figured something wasn't right. There were these *tentacles* everywhere, slipping up and over the bridge and grabbing men and...and...slicing them in two. Beheading them. Killing them. I cranked my camera like my life depended on it, though really I was probably risking it by doing so. If you were to watch the film, well, it's pretty shaky, like all those damn movies and TV shows today. Heh, maybe I was the first to do that, too...

I remember how *dark* it was, the night, the air, and thinking that the dawn couldn't have been too far off, but it was so damn *dark*. The skin of that *thing* was black, black like pitch. Like tar. It blended in with the night – if it weren't for all the men being killed by something that clearly wasn't bullets or bayonets, you might not even have seen it. Hours later, I couldn't have told you exactly what it looked like; that came later. Then, it was too dark, too quick. Just a killing machine that seemed to *hate* everything.

And *big*. Boy was it big.

[*Laughs softly*] See? Listen to me, how it's all just flowing out of me now – could barely talk at the beginning but now I'm just running my mouth, trying to get it all out...

Where was I? Oh, yeah; listen to this. Never told *anyone* this part: *they couldn't control it.* Not really.

The Japanese brought that thing at us, at the Chinese. There isn't any doubt about that, is there? Where they got it, well, I don't know if we ever found out for sure; maybe our military knows. But if they do, they never told me. And I never told them that it killed the Japanese soldiers, too.

The thing...I sensed that it was hard to keep a leash on it, or whatever. Nothing concrete, mind you. I don't have any hard evidence. But

I saw it cut down a Japanese private and I thought to myself, "What the hell? Why is it killing its own guys?" But I saw it and if you were to look real close at my film, you might see it, too. That son-of-a-bitch was *mean*. It oozed meanness. If they told it to only kill the enemy, the Chinese, it didn't listen so well. Or maybe the Japanese commanders just figured that as long as the bridge was taken, and the town of Wanping with it, what was the loss of a few men of their own?

All's fair in war, right? A few Japanese soldiers, a hundred or so Chinese...and a seven-hundred-year-old, beautiful stone bridge... what the hell does it all matter?

So, the Japanese crossed the Marco Polo Bridge and engaged the Chinese deeper into Wanping and I got the hell out of their way. Cho finally broke my stupor, my automatic filming reflex, and we retreated.

And in some back alley somewhere in the town we ran into a Japanese soldier. Cho...ran into the guy's bayonet. Or the bayonet ran into him. Never been sure. Cho...tried to talk, plead with the soldier, even as he was...trying to pull himself off the bayonet. He knew a little Japanese, not much but more than me, but the soldier just *stared* at him like something he'd just happened to find stuck to his rifle.

[*Long pause*] Like a piece of garbage.

I ran. Yep, that's what I did. To some building somewhere, a little hotel, I think? Got up on the roof and watched as the Chinese soldiers drove their opponents back to the bridge and pushed them back over it. Then the Japanese had their big buddy destroy that beautiful structure, five hundred lions and all. Thing broke up like... like a sand castle and made the most horrible noise as it crashed down into the river. Couldn't film it because I had run out of film and my spare reels weren't with me. My dumb bad luck. That big, black whatzit slipped back into the river and the dawn finally broke.

[*Heavy* sigh] I miss you, Cho, buddy. After all these years, I still miss you. But I'm glad you didn't have to see that.

[*Tape machine shut off, then turned back on at a later, indeterminate time.*]

WITNES: Okay, [*clears throat*], so, when I pulled myself up out of the bottle I found out that the Japanese had the *balls* to say that they were *indignant* after the *attack on their soldiers.*

Let that sink in. And by the way, that Japanese soldier that was missing? He wandered back on his own. Not kidnapped or abducted, just too soused and heady over prostitutes to bother to check in with his regiment. I knew how he must have felt.

I stumbled around the area, asking people if what had happened was real or if I had dreamt it, maybe. Didn't help that I couldn't speak Chinese, so I think they all just thought I had gone loopy from the sun or the, you know, fighting. I held on tight to my film reels and I packed up to go, just as the shelling came around the 20th of July – there was supposedly a cease-fire, but nobody gave a damn about that and they all just went on scuffling and shooting and stabbing each other. That *thing* didn't show up again in Wanping, thankfully, but it didn't have to; the Japanese were mean bastards all on their own.

By the beginning of August I had had a stomach-full of all the back-and-forth between the Chinese Communists and the old Imperial leaders and their concessions to the Japanese and I moved along. Couldn't get in contact with my "Parade of Moments" bosses back in the States so I picked Shanghai on the Yangtze to try and set up a new center of operations for myself, such as they were.

Big mistake. The old dumb bad luck at work again.

I made my way down the coast to Shanghai in an old truck that I had paid the owner just about every damn bit of Chinese money that I had left on me. I had hoped that the farther I got from Beijing...*Peking*! The better the air would be, you know? It wasn't really any farther away from Japan, geographically speaking, but I guess I figured then that they just wanted the north of China...and I'd be okay if I moved south. Well, it was a good thought, but it didn't really work out that way.

Something...something just struck me. A thought. Dunno why I never thought of this before, but it occurs to me now that that *thing* was *fueled* somehow by the Japanese's rage – their anger that night. I said the tension could have been cut with a knife? Right? Yeah, and that monster was a very sharp knife.

In Shanghai, in August of 1937, the world as we know it today was created. Was *founded.* [*Coughs softly, sounds of ice in a glass*] Everything before then, even the crap that went down at that bridge – maybe that *was* nothing. *Nothing.* Now, you can stop listening and go and look it up in your history books or on the Internet or whatever, but you won't get it like I can give it, right here and now. So *listen*, dammit.

Chiang Kai-Shek – remember him? – by the end of July he had had it and was bound and determined to "drive out the invaders." Rest of the world either was just watching or simply didn't care. Don't think imperialistic Chiang cared either, I mean about what the rest of the world thought, 'cause he had Japanese all over him and a big old hoodoo coming out of that river to help them. I bet he was messing his pants wondering if that thing was going to appear again. And if so, where.

It appeared August 13th, in Shanghai, just like your history books tell you.

Now, where is that...? [*sounds of paper shuffling*] Here it is: one-hundred-*thousand* Japanese soldiers invaded China on that day. One-hundred-*thousand.* And covered by battleships sitting out there in the water off Shanghai's coast, at the mouth of the Yangtze River. The Chinese, they put up a helluva fight, looked like it was going to go on for a long, long time. Me, I was stuck there; no way out. I found some nerve in me and set up to film. Found a spot about a half-mile from the beach and pointed my camera, turned the crank.

Okay, I admit it – I think I had a death-wish by then.

We saw it clearly on that day. After a full morning and early afternoon of fighting in and around the city, it came up out of the East China Sea around four p.m., right between two Japanese battleships. Easy-like, so as the wake from it wouldn't capsize the ships, I'd guess. I thought it was big before, back at the bridge in Wanping, in the river, but I was off by a tad. It was huge, *immense.* And black, even in the daylight, with water streaming off it, it was deep, dense black, as if the sunlight just sunk right into its hide, completely absorbed. Ah, those Japanese – they knew how to make an entrance. I can't imagine that entrance wasn't choreographed.

So, it wades up onto the beach, step by step. I know, I know – my film's shaky at that point, too. I watched it just now on YouTube and it doesn't capture a tenth of how it felt that day. I remember it was like we were all given an electric shock, every one of us on shore, when we first saw that monster. Like the electricity jumped from one man to the next, completing an arc. Maybe it was something in that creature, something that came *from* it...I don't know.

It had a thick hide, like armor, like armor plates – have you ever noticed it looks like a samurai? Yeah. That's what it was: like a *samurai.* I watched a TV program once where this scientist or historian or whatever she was speculated that, somehow, the Japanese had patterned their samurai armor – I mean long ago, of course – on that monster. I think the historians found some old Japanese paintings or something of the creature. Look at the damn thing's head...that's a samurai helmet. Don't tell me it isn't. Maybe the effect doesn't come through my film, I admit that, but if you were *there* you would have seen it, too. A big, coal-black samurai, rising from the sea, with glowing white eyes shining out from slits in its armored head.

Don't tell me you wouldn't have pissed your pants if you had seen that.

Well, it hit the shore after only a few short steps and these tentacles come out from under the armor, around the shoulder areas, and I realize that was what I saw at the Marco Polo Bridge, and that was what passed for *arms* on the thing. Like big bunches of gigantic, engorged snakes wriggling around. I wonder now how much of it came up out of the river that night in July, how much of it was there but we couldn't see. Still, I would have remembered those eyes if they'd been above the water...I guess the Japanese were still *testing* their monster that night.

The tentacles grabbed a Chinese army truck and crushed it like a soup can. We were the first people to ever hear what that sounds like. And the screams. The screams of human beings dying from being crushed by a monster. We were the first to hear that, too. Lucky us.

The thing itself didn't make any sounds, which made it all the more horrifying, I think.

[*Extended coughing*] We never gave it a name back then. Nobody did, not even the Japanese. Later, after the war, US intelligence said that even in the Japanese records about the monster they never named it. Just "the subject" or "the creature." I think they were afraid of it, too. Saw on one of those TV shows – might have been that same one from before – that some "monsterologists" look at that thing and say it was "Ground Zero for monsters in the Modern Era." So they call it "Monster Zero."

[*Coughs*] I guess that's as good a name as any for it.

Where was I? My mind is wandering...oh, so the one-hundred-thousand Japanese soldiers follow the creature onto the beach and then the shelling began. From both sides. I saw two, maybe three shells hit the monster and then I got out of there. Shrugged off those blasts like it was a light rain. I didn't stick around to see more, "Parade of Moments" be damned. But where could I go? There was fighting *everywhere*, and over it all, like...I dunno, God's vengeance on us all, there was Monster Zero, big and dark like the mother of all storm clouds.

But, give the Chinese credit, they did their best. By nightfall it was an all-out official fracas between the two countries. Big ol' China, divided by what amounted to civil war, beset by little Japan, the world's rat terrier, nipping at everyone's heels. But they had a monster to give them the edge.

The rest of that day and the many that followed are a blur to me now. Guess because I got old. But wherever it was that I holed up – some corner somewhere, in a room – I can remember the *sounds* and the *smells*. The din of the screams, the yelling, stamping of feet...and the pounding advance of that thing the Japanese brought. Each step was like a little earthquake. I tried to figure out where it was, though I couldn't see it, but the thunder it made when it walked seemed to come from...all over. Yeah, all over the place. Ask someone who would know about that sort of thing how much it probably weighed; all I know is that there in Shanghai I thought it was shaking the whole world. And its smell? Like cabbage. Cooked, almost-rotten cabbage. *That* seemed to be everywhere, too. You just wanted it to stop, you know? Just *stop*. All of it.

It didn't stop. Kept right on going. I learned later that the Chinese tried to push their opponents into one of the other rivers there – not the Yangtze, one of the other ones – but it was just chaos. I don't know how there's even a city still standing there today. Monster Zero was chewing it up and spitting it out. Do you know what a building sounds like when it's torn off its foundation, lifted up into the air and then thrown back down again? I do.

Something finally clicked in me at some point, a vision of Cho appeared to me or whatever, and I got up and made my way outside. Still had my camera with me. The dust in the air was so thick it almost blotted out the sun. Looking around, trying to get a fix on where the heavy fighting was and really wanting to stay away from wherever that was, I heard something *new*. It was...it was a...*roar*.

Why did I climb that tower? You've heard the story, haven't you? How intrepid "Parade of Moments" newsreel reporter Don Witnes mounted a radio tower in the middle of the worst fighting in the city of Shanghai and scooped the entire world on what happened there on that day, August 23rd, 1937. Yeah, you heard me right: that adds up to ten days. I was cowering in a corner for ten days. In the middle of a war zone.

So, I climbed that tower dragging my big, bulky camera with me – Don Witnes Gets His Shot! Don Witness, Our Man in China! – and went as far as I could. Felt the damn thing swaying, but I didn't stop, just kept on going. Started strapping the camera to a strut with the belt from my trousers and another strap I had. I think it was from the film reel bag. Anyway, got it in some semblance of a stable position, where I could turn the crank, and pointed it towards the roar.

[*Long pause*] One gigantic, impossible creature is one thing. *Two* is one whole other thing.

A lot has been said about the other beast, creature, monster that showed up in Shanghai that day. About how it saved everybody or it made everything worse or even that it never really was there at all.

That my film of it is a fake. That the dust in the air created a mirage or an illusion of some kind. I won't address those opinions; that's just what they are and everybody has 'em. I know what I saw. I know what I filmed. I know what I saw later, too. I'll get to that.

I pointed my camera at the thing's roar. It welled up and out of it like a challenge, like the call of a wild beast in the jungle to another. "Here I am. Turn and face me." It got real quiet when it appeared. Fighting died down and all. A stillness in the air that was almost as frightening to me as the sounds of war.

The Chinese monster – that's what it was – is reported to have followed the Yangtze into the city. I'm telling you here and now that it didn't follow any damn river. It *came* from the river. And you can quote me on this: it came from the Marco Polo Bridge.

[*Loud and sustained coughing*] I saw it. Maybe no one else there did, but I *saw* it. It… it *formed* itself out from the river and it was solid when it hit the ground. They say it came up *out* of the ground or it trotted in from the hills or some other goddamn foolish thing, but I know what I saw. The river *created* it.

It looked like the lions, the stone lions from the bridge back in Wanping. It was as big as the Japanese creature – I mean almost literally the same size. It also kind of looked like a dragon, or what amounts to a dragon in China. You know what I mean, except this creature was dusky grey all over its body with a kind of dull golden scale pattern on its torso and its forearms and hind legs, which all sported wicked looking claws. It walked on all fours mostly, or at least when it popped up out of the river. I didn't start filming until it was *there*, or we wouldn't be having these arguments over it today.

Even from where I was, about, what? A mile away? Maybe a little less, I could see its eyes and they were watery, like big eggs made out of water. And they had life in them and that life was pointed right at Monster Zero. Look at the film; when it raises its big old head, right before the camera shifts – I was so nervous I stopped cranking – and you can see that moment when it locks eyes with the Japanese monster. And then that big blackout that occurs right after that on the film? That was Monster Zero passing right next me.

The smell of it, the *stink* of it nearly knocked me off the tower. I wasn't worried about it brushing into me and collapsing the tower – I was worried the stench would do me in!

Back in the 80s I saw this Japanese cartoon that one of my grandkids was watching. In it they had what I knew to a certainty was supposed to be the fight between those two monsters in 1937. I don't know who made that goddamn thing but they had it all wrong who won. Japanese bias, that's what it was. It wasn't just a fight, it was a slaughter.

Monster Zero made a beeline right for – what do they call it now? The "Foo Dog"? Damn silly name. Anyway, the Japanese dog went after the Chinese dog and when they slammed up against each other I was sure it was the end of the world.

I felt the tower had had it, so I undid the camera and practically jumped right off the thing. If it did fall after I got down off it I have no idea; I was running away, trying to protect the camera. Don Witnes, Man on the Run!

[*Cough, then sounds of drinking*] Ran and ran for I don't know how many blocks; wanted to get some distance between me and that fight. Behind I could hear them pounding away at each other, the crashes and booms of each hit, and that lion-thing howling and roaring. Of course, Zero didn't make a sound. I found a relatively-intact building and got up on the roof of it somehow. I didn't bother to set up my camera – I had had enough of that. I was tired of looking at the world through a lens. Wouldn't have mattered much anyways, 'cause the fight was throwing up so much debris and dust that you couldn't see anything at all through it. Not at first.

About a minute or two into those two giants battling, the guns started up again. I could imagine commanders on both sides wondering what the hell was going on and then remembering they had a war to conduct. Keeping my head down, I sat and listened to it all, monster fight and human fight. The monsters were louder.

I got the sense that it wasn't going well for the Chinese lion. Its roars were laced with *pain*, and getting to be pretty pathetic. I...felt for it. A wind whipped up and suddenly a good portion of the city was clear for me to get a good look at it, such as it was.

So [*long pause*], here's the part, the important part, that I've never told another living soul.

I spotted something pretty strange. Strange in the sense of humans and war and how they think and move around, I mean. I could see that the Japanese forces were *protecting* a certain clutch of vehicles. Armored vehicles. Tanks, a few of them, and a truck or two. I watched, squinted through the dust and it started to dawn on me that there was one truck that they were all clustered around. No markings on the truck, but it looked armored. And if it moved it moved slowly. And it moved with Monster Zero.

I'm ... I'm not a hero. Sometimes...sometimes you see that in a book, or on the TV. If they bother to mention me at all. Hell, on the other hand sometimes people say it was all *my* fault, as if me filming those damn things is the reason for them being there in the first place. You know, if I had just minded my own business than the world need never have known about monsters...except of course for the, you know, destruction of Shanghai and all [*laughs humorlessly*].

Okay, so I got down there. On the ground. And I crawled through rubble. I climbed over burning wreckage. I hid behind shattered walls. I listened until my ears hurt and little by little I made my way to that truck.

They never saw me coming. Why? Well, they had a lot of other things on their minds, the Japanese. And I was so covered in dirt and dust and mud and blood I probably looked like just another piece of the goddamn scenery. I don't know how I did it; don't ask me for the details. I don't know. I don't even *want* to know. It was damn stupid. Stupidest thing I ever did, and I've done a few doozys.

So, I got right up to that truck, right around to the back of it, and just walked up to it and opened the back door.

And there he was.

[*Muffled speaking, possibly swearing*]

The goddamn son-of-a-bitch was sitting there with two, three other guys around him. And he turns and looks at me. Just looks at me. Slow and easy as can be. Completely deadpan.

He was wearing a big sash with several pounds of medals on it, and there was a sword sitting there next to him. His hair was *perfect*. Little round wire-rimmed glasses and some stupid little moustache – you know the kind, like it's just sort of *painted* on. A little smudge on the upper lip. If I had to sum him up in one word it would be "child-like." As if I found a little china doll sitting in the back of the truck, playing dress up. But he was Japanese through and through, not made of china.

There was no concern in him, just a blasé look that I wanted to slap right off his face. I'd heard he was smart, wrote for scientific publications, but that he had replaced his father because the old man had some kind of mental illness. Maybe that's what I was seeing then: the family crazy.

Took me a moment to recognize that he had a set of headphones on his head and a little microphone in his hand. The whole gang was sitting in front of a console with a bunch of dials and levers and buttons. Maybe the creepiest thing of all, even beyond all that, was the priest that stood up far in the back. Shinto? Is that right? The Japanese religion? Not sure of what they call it, but that guy was a priest, and he had headphones on, too.

Camera? I had left my camera up on the roof, under a big mess of tarps I found there. Good thing too, 'cause I doubt if I would ever have seen it again after that.

The world stopped as I stared into the eyes of God's presence on Earth. Slowed right down and damn well nearly froze. Not exactly slow-motion, but a frigid freeze. Then, someone grabbed me and I started swinging. Someone threw some Japanese at me and there was yelling and shouting and I got clubbed down to the ground and again and again and again until I blacked out. Still can't do a few things with my body today because of that beating. They knew their stuff.

[*Tape machine shut off, then turned back on at a later, indeterminate time.*]

WITNES: [*sniffles*] I woke up some time later a prisoner of the

Japanese. They didn't call it that, but that's what it was. I was questioned through a translator and they accused me point-blank of being a spy. What could I really say? On the surface of it, sure; I could see their point. Especially after I told them I was a newsreel cameraman. Then they wanted to know where my camera was – I told 'em I lost it in the rubble.

Then I made the mistake of asking them about their monster, what had happened in the big fight. They weren't real happy about that. At first I thought it was simply because I had the balls to ask *them* a question. Then I realized it was because something had gone really, really wrong for them.

They, ahh...tortured me, I guess. Sure, that's what it was. Torture. The Japanese are good at it. *Were* good at. I dunno if they still are. They're our friends now, right? Good buddies.

I sat in a cell for who the hell knows how long. Not even sure where that cell was. I might have been anywhere. Kept demanding that they let me talk to my government, my bosses at the studio, but no soap. Their anger lasted for a good long time. You could feel it in the air.

In all, I was held for...about a year, then released. Back in China. I wanted to go straight to my camera, see if it was still there along with my film reels on top of that building, but I figured I was being watched. I just prayed they were still there, that the *building* was still there. Found my way to an American consulate then and turned myself in. They told me later that the first thing I asked for wasn't food or water or safety or a picture of the president or a flag to hold, but news of what happened between the Chinese and Japanese monsters.

Later, I was shown a photo of the remains of Monster Zero. Yep, that one. The only one.

[*Coughs lightly, pauses*] Said the Chinese thing just went away after it ripped its wrestling partner to shreds. They said something had changed in the middle of the fight, like someone flipped a switch or something. No one knew what it was that turned the tide, but in a way, it didn't make a huge difference. Shanghai still fell, eventually, then Nanking. The "Foo Dog" didn't return.

Then came Pearl Harbor, then came us to the rescue of Europe, then a monster of our own to beat the living tar out of Japan in '45. You know the rest.

[*Long* pause] Let's...let's wrap this thing up, shall we?

I went back and got my camera and film cans. I gave one reel to the US Army brass and I kept one for myself. Maybe that was unpatriotic but somebody owed me something. I owed *myself* something, okay?

Listen – I'm not a hero, not a big man. I'm not a raging egomaniac like some of the trades back in the day used to say. Yeah, I had a nice career after that, after the war. People began to like to hear my voice on the radio, on the newsreels and then my face on TV. I don't know why; it just was. Together we all watched the parade of monsters, a parade of moments, I guess you could say, one after another, just like my little trip to China.

The big stone lion-dragon-thing did eventually show up again, though why did it take so long, why didn't it stick around to protect China during the war? My thought is that after the bridge was gone and after the pummeling it took from Zero, it needed a lot of time to lick its wounds. But, it came back after a while and kind of weird for me when it did, because I almost felt like I should have been there, filming it for my old bosses, the studio. But that was a stupid notion.

Remember what I said at the beginning, though? I'm gonna tell my story and the world can do whatever the hell it wants to do with it. Or nothing at all. It doesn't impact me one way or another anymore. I'm *old* and-and I'm gonna *die*, okay?

[*Long series of heavy sighs, coughing*]

One day, in the 80s – don't remember when anymore – I got a package left on my doorstep. Mail didn't deliver it. None of the neighbors had seen anybody put it there. Little box, wrapped up neat in some kind of really light paper and held together with string. Who the hell wrapped anything with *string* by the 1980s? Absolutely not punk kids or whoever trying to play a joke.

I took it inside, hoped it wasn't a bomb and unwrapped it when I was alone, pretty late at night. Inside was a coin. A Japanese coin, dated 1937. And a note. In a fine, delicate hand someone had written out some Japanese characters. You know, writing, words. I had 'em translated by this one gal who works at the university. You know what they said? It was two words, that's all.

"Forgive" and "tell."

Couple of nights after that I saw on TV that he had died. He was still hanging around by the 80s, just like me, but I outlived him in the end. And he had sent me a note before he kicked off, a reminder of our time together. Now, don't that just beat all?

Never did forgive and I never did tell. Until now. The second one, at least.

Forgive? Not sure if I can. Would we be in the spot we're in today if it weren't for the Japanese in 1937? I suppose there's a lot of debate both ways, but...I just don't know anymore.

See...you see [*coughs violently*], it's not *our* planet anymore, dammit. It's just *not*.

It's *theirs*. It's a *Monster Earth*.

[*Tape machine shuts off. End of recording*]

*Note: Donald Allan Witnes died on or about July 31st, 2001, from conditions resulting from pneumonia, at the age of eighty-five. Body was found by a neighbor of Witnes' on August 1st.*

*Unable to verify delivery of any package from Japanese government to subject, either in the 1980s or anytime after. Unable to verify veracity of all statements in recording. Awaiting further direction on disposal of tapes and other related artifacts.*

## 2

# THE MONSTERS OF WORLD WAR II, OR HAPPY BIRTHDAY, BOBBY FETCH

I.A. WATSON

*After the Japanese's loss in China, the lust for monstrous assistance in their empire-building knew no sating. By the dawn of the 1940s, they had made new alliances, not only with fellow human beings who shared their conquering spirit, but with that which would aid them in ways that no earthly army ever could.*

*In late 1941, the Japanese then turned their attention to the United States, a country they saw as complacent, insular, and undefended.*

IT WAS Robert Fetch's fourteenth birthday. It was a day that would live in infamy.

A bright shaft of sunlight through too-thin curtains woke the boy from strange and complicated dreams. He untwisted the sheets that had tried to strangle him in the night and tossed them onto the floor. He blinked as he sat up, and he looked around the unfamiliar bedroom.

"O'ahu," he told himself out loud, as he always did first thing in whatever new place his parents dragged him to. "O'ahu, Hawaiian Islands, 7 December 1941. Happy birthday, Bobby."

He checked the bandage on his left hand. The burn still hurt.

Yellow pus from his blisters had stained the linen wrapping. He suspected that when it was unrolled it was going to hurt.

Even from the upper floor bedroom he could hear his parents rowing. They did that a lot, and it was getting worse. Now they hardly exchanged a civil word. Bobby's memories of Dr. Thomas Fetch and his wife Lana working together on the various surveys the scientist did for the U.S. Government were old and blurry now.

Bobby checked the clock. 5:17. He decided to skip breakfast and his parents' inevitable pretense at harmony and unity because it was 'his special day'. He hauled on his pants and a white vest and lifted the sash to slip out over the shingles. From there, he dropped down into the compound yard, where the big truck and the two Auburn Cabriolets were parked. Lizards skittered for cover as he approached.

Nobody else was up yet. Yesterday had been a busy day at the mission site.

He took a moment to admire the view. The cabins of the new compound had been hastily erected on a shelf of the Koolau Mountains, with spectacular vistas over the bay below and the glittering azure Pacific beyond. Steep tree-lined slopes descended to the military installation of Pearl Harbor. The base was sleepy and peaceful early on a Sunday morning. The natural basin was crammed with military ships.

It didn't hold Bobby's interest as much as it had two months before when he'd first arrived on the island. By now he could name each of the big fleet vessels down there. A couple of times he'd even trailed into the base with his father and admired the fighter-planes arrayed wingtip-to-wingtip on their white runways. Perhaps at fourteen he was outgrowing planes and ships?

He rounded the side of the house. The angry voices in the kitchen were clearer and harsher from out here.

"Couldn't you put the bottle away for just one day? It's the boy's birthday, for God's sake!"

"If you were more bearable then I wouldn't need the bottle, would I, Thomas?"

"Or Linden Baxter?"

"You *always* throw Linden at me! Always! If you hadn't thrown him at me in the first place while you were off hunting monsters..."

"You're right! I should have looked for 'em closer to home!"

Bobby moved on. He didn't want to hear this. He slipped round the porch and skirted the back of his house. The sound of the projector clicking paused him at the open French windows of his father's study.

He peered into the deserted room. In front of the corkboard with the maps and pins of Moanalua and the Kailhi Valley was a canvas movie screen. The Keystone 16mm projector whirred away. While his parents played out their regular domestic drama in the kitchen, the grainy film rolled on unheeded.

It was *the* film.

It had been shot in 1937, and it had changed the world. It showed the advance of that black-shelled Japanese war-creature past the Marco Polo Bridge, the first time the world at large had irrefutable proof of the existence of giant monsters.

Even now, watching the footage five years on, it was hard to believe this wasn't some hoax done up in some movie-maker's studio. But the damage that Monster Zero had done had been real enough when it had been loosed against the Chinese. How many thousands had died before the second such monster of the modern age had arisen to kill the first and bring an uneasy pause to the Sino-Japanese conflict?

That was when Dr Fetch's work had suddenly jumped in priority up the U.S. War Department's budget list. The previous grudging academic grants became full-scale expedition funding with troops and materiel to back it up. The USA had an immediate and strategic need to develop a monster of their own, before some other nation gained such a military asset and deployed it against them.

Bobby looked at the giant non-reflective *thing* on the flickering screen as it tore through buildings, tanks, and men alike. He wondered how anything so terrible could even exist in a sane, rational world.

Except the world wasn't sane now, was it? The war in Europe had spread its madness over the world. The US had kept out of it so far, in part because of the strong isolationist lobby, in part because there were rumors of another Axis creature that might yet be unleashed against the Allies that opposed them.

The grainy footage had no sound. Somewhere in Dr Fetch's collection was a tape of Monster Zero's call, and of the roar of the Chinese Foo Dog challenging it. Sometimes when Bobby slept he heard them in his dreams; he remembered now that last night had been one of those times. The giant creatures had battled in his nightmares.

He heard a door slam. Angry footsteps headed towards the study. So his parents' fight had progressed to the walking-out stage.

He slipped away, hopping the picket fence and heading past the other temporary cabins towards the edge of the compound.

His hand twinged again. The girl had warned him not to touch the strange stone eggs but he'd done it anyhow. They hadn't looked hot, nor radiated any heat when his fingers were near them. It was only once his palm had pressed into that odd silicone surface that the black shell *had heated up!* Dr Fetch had been more excited about "the thermal event" than he had been about his son's burns.

As if thought had brought her to life, the girl rounded the corner from the water tower and waved at him. "Morning, Bobby."

"Hey, Lei," he greeted her, trying not to fumble simple English. At fourteen he was young enough to have problems talking to girls, old enough to know that this one was well worth talking to.

Leinani Keaunui was Hawaiian – she said Polynesian – and she had that exotic complexion, that dark-eyed dark-haired look that seemed to make her a natural part of these islands. She was no older than him and made no attempts to look beautiful in her cut-off jeans and check shirt knotted off at her midriff, but Bobby knew that some of the G.I.s attached to his father's expedition had noticed her. Dr Fetch had told them to stay well clear.

Bobby mooched over to the girl. "You're up early." It was the best he could do.

"I was swimming," she replied. He saw now that her long

unbound hair was wet.

He glanced down the slope to the distant blue sea.

"Not there!" Leinani told him scornfully. "There are pools in some of the caves. The water's very cool and refreshing." She looked at Bobby's bandage. "How's your hand?"

"Stings. How *did* those egg-things heat up like that? Mom speculated that because they're lodged in the rock – geological phenomena, she said – that maybe they're in contact with fumaroles." The boy hesitated. "Er, fumaroles are where lava streams poke up and..."

"I know what fumaroles are," Lei told him sharply. "I went to school. Which is more than you do."

"I get educated," Bobby argued. "My parents teach me. They've dragged me across half the planet on their work for the government, so it's not practical to put me in school." *Although perhaps if they split up I might end up grounded with one of them*, he didn't say out loud.

The Polynesian girl read the shadow that crossed his face. "Come on," she decided. "I'll show you my pool. You can bathe that palm and maybe it'll hurt less. This way."

She gave him no time to argue. She just sprang up and scampered off through the compound and out up the side of the hill.

The little boy inside Bobby told him that when a girl challenges you to chase her you have to run after her. The growing man inside him told him that when a girl wants you to chase her... you *have* to run after her! He hared off behind Leinani, away from his quarrelling parents' birthday preparations, into the tree-covered slope of the Moanalua.

Away from the Kailhi Valley that offered one of the few road connections between the two sides of the island the terrain changed quickly. Gentle inclines became steep shelves. The trees became denser in some places, completely absent in others where there was no topsoil to disguise the wind-shaped mountainside. Ten minutes' mad scramble after Leinani took him to a different world.

Bobby ignored the stinging of his hand and struggled to keep up with the local girl. He hoisted himself over a wide shelf and found her crouched beside a low wide opening in the rock wall.

"Mind your head here," she advised him. "Slither on your belly for about four yards. The roof opens up then."

She shimmied through the crack. Bobby had to follow her.

He emerged in a carved chamber. Higher gaps in the cavern cast shafts of light over ancient wall-sculptures. The boy's jaw dropped open. He was so distracted that he failed to arrest his belly-slide and slipped on the shale right down into the natural pool that flooded the bottom of the cavern.

Lei laughed.

Billy dragged himself out of the shallows. "What *is* this place? It's fantastic!"

"It's very old," the girl said. "And secret. Please."

"This is just the sort of thing my dad's looking for! There were all kinds of rumors about the Caverns of Kalamainu'u, enough to drag him here when the Italian trip crapped out. This would help him so much in his investigation!"

"*My* dad says not to show him this," Lei replied. Her father was the Elder who maintained the Caverns where Dr Fetch was examining the strange fossil eggs. "Your people are already talking about cutting open the rocks in the other caves. He doesn't trust them with these secrets."

Bobby nodded. "I guess," he conceded. "Then why show me?"

"I felt sorry about your hand."

That burned palm was in the crystal waters right now, and the cool soaking did make it feel better. Bobby fumbled to unwind the bandage.

"Let me," said Lei. She knelt down beside him at the pool's edge and unpicked the knots on his linens with delicate fingernails. When she eased the pus-sticky bandage away under the water it hardly hurt at all.

Bobby looked up at the ancient carvings. They showed something large, if the bipedal creature was in scale to the trees and mountains it strode over. It wasn't Monster Zero or the Foo Creature, but it was like them. "What is that meant to be?" he asked Leinani.

The girl pulled off her sneakers and dangled her toes in the pool.

Bobby suspected from her lack of bathing suit or towel that when she usually came up here she wore nothing at all. “My father calls that Kalamainu’u,” she answered. “You know the legends?”

“My mother collects them,” Bobby admitted. “According to the old stories, there was a woman – or a monster – of that name. But she was beautiful. She seduced a chief called... Puna... somebody.”

Puna’aikoa,” Lei supplied. Her tongue made the name sound like liquid velvet.

“Right. So he goes off with Kalamainu’u to her cave, and they’re happy, I guess. At first. But Puna’s wife’s not so pleased with the arrangement. She goes and complains to her big sister, who just happens to be Pele the fire goddess.”

Lei smiled at him. He carried on.

“So next time Puna’s let out of Kala’s cave to go surfing he gets approached by his friends, who he’s promised his new sweetie not to speak to. But he does talk to them, and they warn him that his new girlfriend is really a monster, a... a...”

“A kupua,” Lei prompted him. “See the engraving there? That huge lizard-thing is Kalamainu’u as monster. That tiny woman below is Kalamainu’u as person. Puna’aikoa’s friends made him see her as the monster not the girl.”

“Yeah. So in one version of the story he goes back, sees her in her real form, and doesn’t care. He loves her and stays with her anyway. In the others he flees back to his wife and his family hides him. Kalamainu’u becomes the monster, raises her kin, and they all go rampaging to find him. When Pele objects they spit their poison phlegm into her volcano and damn near extinguish her.”

“But they forgot one vent,” Lei took up the story. “The fire gods rallied, there was terrible war, and the lizard gods were defeated or destroyed.”

“That’s the way I heard it,” Bobby acknowledged. “But see, my dad thinks that old legend is a kind of half-remembering of something that really happened. Ever since Monster Zero, all the old myths are being re-evaluated. He thinks there really were giant-sized lizard entities on O’ahu that were killed or sent to sleep, maybe in the very volcanic caves that your father looks after. And maybe those old stone eggs are just that – the monsters' eggs!"

Lei smiled. "Sometimes the old stories are just stories. Lucky for you, Bobby. After all, you let a girl drag you into her cave. What if I'm a monster?"

Bobby thought his dad would shout that all women turned into them eventually. He sighed. "I guess I *should* be getting back. Mom and Dad don't argue as much when I'm around, and they'll be on best behavior today for my birthday."

"It's your birthday? Why didn't you tell me?"

"I guess I didn't want to make a fuss."

"How old are you?"

"Fourteen."

Lei's eyebrows went up. "In the old ways that is when a boy becomes a man." She looked across at him for a moment, her face uplit by the ripple reflections from her pool.

Then she kissed him.

"Where were you, pal?" Dr Fetch asked his son as they boy finally appeared at the breakfast table. "There's a whole mess of scrambled eggs in the trash that were supposed to be your breakfast."

Bobby glanced at the kitchen clock. It was still only seven thirty. The days started early on O'ahu. "I took a walk with Lei," he answered.

His mother frowned. "You're not going to have time to open your cards and presents now," she scolded him. "We're due down at the General's office for eight-fifteen sharp and we can't be late for this."

His father eyed him speculatively. "You need to keep your distance from Elder Keaunui's daughter," he warned. "We need that old man's goodwill if we're to get what we need out of this site without trouble or delay."

"Thomas, he's just a boy!" his mother argued.

"He's fourteen today, Lana, and that's old enough for him to watch out. I won't have this mission complicated by trouble with the natives."

Bobby grabbed some toast off the table and swallowed it along with any retort.

"Get your good jacket," Lana Fetch told him. "The General's got someone from the Governor's office down to meet us today, for permission to start cutting and drilling in that formation cave. Maybe that'll placate Elder Keaunui and his people."

"I don't think they want you chopping their site up for any reason," Bobby ventured. He was glad now that he'd promised silence to Leinani about the pool cavern and its reliefs.

"We'll do the least damage possible," Dr Fetch promised, "but we have to understand what those nodes are. This could be a major step forward in my researches."

Bobby found his coat and didn't protest too much as his mother scraped a comb through his hair. "There'll be time for your birthday later," she promised. He could smell the first gin of the morning on her breath. "You do see how important this meeting is, don't you?"

The boy was hurried out to one of the big black cars. The driver was a uniformed soldier assigned to the project. As soon as the Fetchs were in, the vehicle swept out of the compound down the twisting spectacular rode toward Pearl Harbor.

"So what were you doing with Lei Keaunui?" his father asked as they descended the mountain.

"She told me about kupua. People who look like humans but who have a monster-form as well."

"That's a common myth in these islands," Lana Fetch commented. "Westervelt lists many different kinds. The ka-poe-kina-mano, who were shark monsters, the ka-poe-kino-manu who were giant birds, ka-poe-kino-laau which became monstrous trees and so on. Even the ka-poe-kina-pokaku, the monsters of peculiar stones."

"The boy doesn't need a lecture, Lana," Thomas Fetch chided his wife.

"He asked a question," she snapped back.

"Lei said that Kalamainu'u, who the caves were named for, was a kupua," Bobby went on, to try and offset the quarrel.

"In a lot of the stories, yes," agreed his mother.

Dr Fetch snorted. "So that Hawaiian prince somehow doesn't spot that his new squeeze is a hundred-foot-tall dragon-creature? Give me some of what he was drinking."

"Kalamainu'u may have been a shape-shifter," Lana objected. "A more likely reading of the original language is that she was a woman who could project her mind in a second body. She left her mortal flesh and woke the monster."

"Like... getting off your bike and driving a car?" Bobby suggested. "Or a tank?"

"Perhaps a *little* more spiritual than that," his mother advised. "But that's one gloss of the source material anyhow. And an important one, whether your father might think so or not. It isn't enough that we locate a monster, you see. We also have to be able to direct it, as the Japs commanded Monster Zero."

"By plugging in minds to occupy it?" Thomas Fetch shook his head. "Monster Zero and the Foo Dog were natural, if enormous, biological entities. Not magic creatures from fairy tales. Creatures of science, not bogeymen of magic. If they're controlled, it's through training and conditioning, just the way an elephant can be tamed, or trained to fight in war."

"You don't know that! In fact after how-many-years of dragging Bobby and me from country to country you still don't know anything, do you?"

"I know that I'm on the verge of a big breakthrough when we can split open some of those egg-nodules and maybe get a look at what might be inside of them. And it won't have anything to do with shapechangers and mind-swappers."

"And I know..."

"Hey, we're nearly there," Bobby interrupted. The car was running past the naval yard. "There's the *Missouri* and the *Arizona*."

Dr Fetch glanced over at the big battleships. "Maybe I can get you a tour one time," he offered. "Maybe even today, for your birthday. Would you like that, son?"

"Sure. Why not?" Anything to stop his parents tearing at each other.

Thomas glanced at his watch. "Just turned ten to eight. Plenty of time to get the room set up, check the slide projector, and be ready for the governor's aide. You want to work the slides, son?"

The Cabriolet turned onto Main Street, past the softball field and the Community Building.

A bizarre disturbing noise echoed across the base.

"What was that?" Dr Fetch frowned. "That's not a siren."

Bobby tried to place the sound, a long screeching wail that seemed stretched out and angry. He'd never heard anything like it before, but it put him in mind of...

Lana's nose wrinkled. "Lord, what is that stench?" she complained. An acrid choking odor of rotting fish and sculpture made everyone cough. Bobby's eyes watered.

The car came to a halt outside the Admin Building. The slightly-worried driver turned for instruction. "Sir?"

Before Dr Fetch could answer him, Bobby spotted the *Arizona*. "Look!" he gasped. "Dad, mom! Just *look!*"

The 608 foot long ship was rocking wildly like a child's toy in a bathtub. As the Fetchs watched, a huge suckered tentacle snaked round if from the other side, wrapping over the top of the ship beside its central stack.

Another screech wailed across Pearl Harbor like the wrath of the sea.

"What *is* it?" Lana Fetch whispered. "What the *hell* is it?"

The creature beside the *Arizona* rose into view, taller than the conning tower. Other tentacles wrapped the vessel, spilling it sideways. Sailors fell off deck into the churning waters below.

"A kraken!" Thomas Fetch breathed. "That is a kraken."

The monster flexed its house-wide tentacles and snapped the *Arizona* in two.

Dr Fetch shook his head. "We have to get out of here!" he decided. "Corporal, get us back to the compound, pronto."

"Sir!" agreed the driver. He shifted the stick and sent the Cabriolet screeching off the parking lot.

The base was running mad. The creature's shriek had affected some of the personnel. They had lost all control and were fleeing for their lives, careless of their fellows, possessed only by a primal fear from an ancient ancestral horror passed down in their genes. Others scrambled to find guns, as if any firearm might stop the titan that now rampaged through the shipyard.

The monster dropped the wreckage of the *Arizona* and moved towards the *Missouri*.

"Why is it attacking them, not all the smaller targets?" Bobby wondered. He stared out of the rear window as the car swerved along Main Street, avoiding pedestrians and other traffic by the narrowest of gaps.

Another sound mingled with the cries of the marauder. The drone of many planes warned of an incoming flight.

"The air fleet!" Thomas Fetch cried out. "Now we'll see some action!"

Lana looked up at the formation of planes overhead. "Those aren't US planes!" she gasped.

Bobby saw it too. The underside of the Japanese Type 00 Carrier Fighter bore the insignia of the rising sun.

The monster rose high above the dock, smashing through concrete and steel like matchwood. The fighter planes dove on the harbor front, shooting down anyone who moved. Across the way at Ford Island's landing strips, the Japanese bomber wave began the systematic destruction of grounded US planes.

A huge section of conning tower ripped from a battleship smashed down in the roadway. The Cabriolet driver jinked to avoid it, almost losing control and careening into Furlong Field.

Lana held on to the side of the vehicle. "Tom! That monster is being controlled by the Japs!"

Dr Fetch nodded grimly. "We need to get back to the camp. We need to get on the radio and see if we can find any kind of command frequency. It's all we can do!"

Bobby watched as a hundred-foot tentacle smashed through the Laundry Building. It turned the brick structure into mere rubble then swept it out as shrapnel at the approaching army trucks. Someone managed to get off a mortar from the anti-aircraft emplacement. The monster crushed the whole area into the sea.

The USS *Oklahoma* tried to resist. She turned at anchor to try and bring her guns to bear.

The monster opened a beak-rimmed maw and vomited some kind of acid across the ship. Sailors on the decks screamed and melted. Steel bubbled and deformed. When those coiling tentacles snapped the warship apart there was nobody alive on board to perish.

Plumes of black smoke rose from the airfields. Another wave of Japanese planes passed overhead. A pair of them strafed the road, clearing it of vehicles.

The corporal behind the wheel of the Fetch's car gasped and leaned forward. The vehicle lurched and swerved, spinning to a halt at the side of the road.

Thomas Fetch leaned forward and inspected the soldier. "He's shot," he called. "Help me with him, Lana!"

*So this is what it takes to make them cooperate*, Bobby thought absurdly. He noticed the neat circles in the cracked windshield. He traced the other two bullets to the leather cushion between his mother and himself.

Dr Fetch felt the pulse on the corporal's neck. "He's a goner," the scientist realized. "Help me haul him out."

Lana joined him in struggling the corpse from the driver's seat. "We can't just leave him on the roadside," she protested.

"Getting out of here's our priority right now. We need a radio and we need to think. If Japan's got another *kaiju* then we need to warn our nation."

Bobby had never seen a dead man before. Now, as he stared back along Main Street, he saw plenty of them.

Thomas Fetch slipped behind the wheel. He scraped the gears

but he got the Cabriolet moving.

The kraken picked up the USS *California* and slammed it down on the *Nevada*.

"Such power," marveled Lana Fetch. "Such rage."

The car picked up speed and raced out of Pearl Harbor. Behind it the new monster destroyed a fleet and announced a fresh phase in the Empire of Japan's war of aggression to rule the Pacific.

Ten minutes of frantic driving saw the Fetches seven miles up the Kailhi Valley, back at their research compound.

"We need to warn Lt. Ferry what's happening down there," Thomas announced as he swung the big vehicle back into the yard, "If he can't see from up here already."

It was ten past eight. Dr and Mrs. Fetch weren't even late yet for their appointment with the General and the Governor's aide.

There were more vehicles beside the compound buildings than usual. "I guess aid has arrived," Lana said.

Japanese soldiers with machine guns emerged from the admin cabin and the Fetch's house.

"Get out of the car!" an officer barked.

Thomas Fetch glanced behind him to see if he could reverse away in time. A rattle of gunfire warned him not to try.

"Out! Out now!" the Japanese commander demanded.

Bobby counted nine solders, plus one man in civilian gear who carried a pistol instead of a rifle or machinegun. The troopers bundled the Fetches out of the Cabriolet and patted them down for weapons they didn't have.

The officer turned to the Japanese man in civvies. "This is Dr. Fetch?"

"*Hai.* This is he."

"Dr. Fetch, I am Lt. Commander Takashiga Butei. You are my prisoner. If you do not cooperate, your family will be shot. Do you understand me?"

Thomas Fetch swallowed. "Yes," he replied.

Bobby was bundled first into the Admin Cabin. Lieutenant Ferry was there, leaning against one wall with a compression bandage on a gory arm-wound. Lei Keaunui was there too, trying to staunch the blood that still seeped from the wounded U.S. soldier.

Bobby broke from the invaders that escorted him and rushed over to the girl. "Liu! You okay?"

She managed a brave fake smile. "This man is very hurt," she warned.

"What happened?"

"They came soon after you left for town. They were looking for your father. There was shooting." The Polynesian girl winced. "I think everyone else is dead."

"Why were you here?"

She snorted a half-sob half-laugh. "I was bringing you a birthday present."

"I thought you already gave me my birthday present?" Bobby leaned in to her. "I kind of liked it."

"A different birthday present," she clarified. "But these men came."

Fetch and his wife were bustled into the cabin. Commander Takashiga pointed to the boxes of notes his men had begun to take from the filing cabinets of the research station. "You will assist with the packing of your research," he ordered the scientist.

"What for?" Thomas demanded. "You already have another goddamned monster working for you!"

"And we do not want any other to have his like!" snapped the commander. He turned to Bobby and Liu. "You know where the Caves of Kalamainu'u are?"

"I do," Bobby answered. He was surprised how much angrier he was than frightened. "Leave her out of it. She's got this guy you shot to look after."

Takashiga pulled his sidearm and fired a bullet through Lt. Ferry's head. Flecks of blood spattered Lei's check shirt.

"Now she does not have to attend him," the Japanese officer said.

"Come."

Soldiers dragged Bobby and Liu towards the exit. "No!" screamed Lana Fetch. "He's just a boy! He's only a boy! *It's his birthday!*"

Takashiga called a sergeant forward. "Make these two take you to the Caves. Set the charges well. Nothing must remain."

"Robert!" Lana wailed as they took her son away. "Bobby!"

Leinani was trembling. Bobby took her hand.

Five of Takashiga's men led them along the mountain track to the opening of the main cave. They were made to stand with their hands on their heads as three of the soldiers went in and searched.

"What can we do?" Lei whispered to Bobby. "They must not be allowed to destroy the Caves."

"I dunno," Bobby admitted. "Everything's going crazy. Did you see that thing in the harbor?"

"Saw it and heard it. Its cry shreds men's souls, I think."

"It tore apart ships and buildings like they were nothing. I don't know what can stop it."

Lei risked a fearful glance at the soldiers guarding them. "What are these men doing on O'ahu?" she fretted. "America is not at war with them."

"I kind of think we are now. If they can take Pearl then they've wiped out damn near all of our Pacific fleet, although I didn't see any of our carriers in port."

"The man in the suit, I think he lives here on the island."

"Yeah. They've been planning this for a while, I think. Makes sense they'd put spies in." Another thought came to the boy. "But if they were watching my dad's work, if they sent soldiers to blow this cave up as soon as their attack starts, then that means that *Dad must be onto something!*"

The guards shouted something sharp in Japanese, which combined with their gestures and pointed guns definitely meant *silence.*

Bobby stood beside Lei, wondering what he as supposed to do. When the bad guys had you and the girl at gunpoint, you were definitely meant to protect her and save the day. He just hadn't got any idea how. These Japanese soldiers didn't look like they'd be easy wins for a 14-year-old to fight. He didn't like the way they looked at the Polynesian girl.

In the movies he'd jump one, grab the soldier's gun, the shoot down the other before the Jap could react. Bobby knew that would be suicide here.

The sergeant returned, dragging Elder Keaunui with him. Lei's father was pulled along between two soldiers, bleeding where they'd hit him in the face with a rifle-butt. The girl gasped and would have run to him, except the guards turned their barrels at her as she made to move.

Bobby grabbed her and held her back. "Stay cool," he warned her. "These guys probably don't know you're his daughter. If they did they could force him to do what they want, like they're doing to my dad."

Lei's head was buried in his shoulder but he felt her nod.

Elder Keaunui barely looked at them. He stood staring straight forward, ignoring the trickle of blood from his forehead, proud and serene despite his circumstance.

More time passed. The soldiers hauled satchels into the cavern; Bobby assumed they contained explosives. He kept holding Lei and glanced over to her father. The old man ignored him.

From the lip of the cave Bobby could see the smoke rising from Pearl Harbor. The occasional chilling creel of the monster that was loosed there echoed even to the Cave of Kalamainu'u. He wondered what was happening down at the base – or at nearby Pearl City or Aifa. Even Honolulu wasn't far away from the kraken's range.

He could see smudges of smoke out at sea as well. With a chill he realized that the Japanese fleet was closing in. The invasion of Hawaii had begun!

Bobby judged that he and Lei were kept standing under watch for more than an hour. He stroked her long hair and tried to comfort her. If she'd not been there, been so scared, he'd have panicked instead. Now he had to be strong for her. "We'll get out of this," he whispered in her ear. Her fingers tightened on his shoulder.

The troopers snapped to attention. Lieutenant Takashiga strode up the track, flanked by a pair of his men and the civilian spy. He barked an enquiry at the sentries watching the prisoners and received a reply. From the soldier's hand motion it was probably that the sergeant was still inside the cave.

Takashiga moved over to Elder Keaunui. "Does a monster sleep in these caves?" he asked the old man in English. "Did some ancient creature leave its eggs to hatch at some future time?"

Lei's father turned slowly to give the officer a look of withering contempt. He said nothing.

"We are very well informed, Elder Keaunui," Takashiga warned. He gestured to his spy. "We know your family is ancient guardians of these caves. Their secrets are known to you. We will make you speak."

The old man said nothing.

"We know you have a daughter, too," the Japanese officer went on. His gaze flicked over to Leinani.

Elder Keaunui closed his eyes and remained silent.

Lei looked up from Bobby's shoulder. "He will tell you nothing," she assured Takashiga. "He loves me, but he will never speak. He will die or watch me die and he will keep silent."

"That remains to be seen," the officer noted. "You are very young and very beautiful, and my men can be... imaginative."

"You keep your hands off her, creep!" Bobby spoke before he even thought about it.

Takashiga sneered. "The little American boy thinks he can play the man!" The invader strutted over to him. "Your whole race is soft and timid. You have never known hardship. You have never known pain. When it comes upon you, you will crumble and yield."

"Says the guy who needs a whole bunch of soldiers and a huge rampaging monster to launch a sneak attack on a country you made peace treaties with!" answered Bobby angrily. "Well it's not going to be like you think, buster. You caught America with our pants down. Fine, good for you. But soon as we pull 'em up we'll be tightening our belt for a fight. We don't back down from bullies no matter how big they are, even if they're bigger than a battleship! Even if some of us are only boys. So chew on that, Tojo, and see how you like it!"

He never even saw the blow coming. He was on the ground, bleeding where the officer's crop had sliced open his face, before he realized that Takashiga had responded.

The officer said something disdainful in his native tongue.

Bobby struggled to rise. The soldiers pointed their guns at him. Lei knelt down beside him and held him back. "Don't die," she told him. Her eyes were wet with tears – and defiant.

Takashiga gave another order. The troopers dragged the youngsters out of the dirt and chivvied them with the Elder through the mouth of the first cave. They were pushed after the officer as he descended by torchlight through the network of lava-formed caverns to the deepest one where the stone eggs were embedded in volcanic shale.

Bobby felt his gashed cheek. His bandaged hand came away bloody.

"You were very brave, Robert Fetch," murmured Leinani.

Bobby felt taller than the kraken.

As they passed the upper galleries he noticed the support columns where the explosives had been packed. When he got to the lowest cave, where his father had installed a generator to power spotlights to aid in surveying, he was surprised to see no explosives at all. Instead a trestle had been cleared to make room for a heavy radio transmitter.

Takashiga caught him looking at the device. "You will find out soon enough," the soldier threatened.

The Japanese officer examined the egg-like black nodules that half-emerged from the larva shale. He called out a word and held out his hand. A subordinate hurried forward with a hammer. Takashiga smashed it down on the rock.

Nothing happened.

Elder Keaunui watched without expression.

Takashiga lodged a hand-grenade behind the furthest of the eggs. The detonation sent pumice shrapnel far across the rear of the cave. The black stone was unharmed.

"What are those things made out of?" Bobby murmured to Lei.

"Something older and tougher than that soldier," the girl whispered back.

Takashiga must have been drawing the same conclusions. He approached the Elder again. "Speak! What are these things?"

Keaunui said nothing.

"Old man, we do not have much time. The main invasion force will land within the hour and by then my orders demand that either this place's secrets are conquered or else it is destroyed. You have cared for these caverns all your life, and your fathers before you. Do you really want to see them destroyed?"

"He will," Lei answered for her father. "It is his duty." She stood up straighter. "And mine too."

Takashiga grabbed the Elder's head and forced it round to look at Leinani. "See her? Do you really want to watch her be tortured, humiliated, and killed? Only your confession can save her now."

"Boys, teenage girls, and now an old man," Bobby scorned. "Wow, you really are a brave warrior, aren't you?" He was deliberately diverting Takashiga's attention from Lei, playing for time. He suspected it was going to hurt.

The Japanese commander glared at the youngster. "When your father has told me all he knows about monsters, it will give me great pleasure to shoot you in front of him."

The radio apparatus on the trestle crackled to life. An operator hurried over to answer it.

Bobby held Lei again. "Is there any place we can run for it down here?" he asked her. "Some side tunnel, maybe? Some way we can make a break then go get help for your pa?"

"Not this deep. There's only one way out of this chamber, except for the deep crack that goes down to the volcano itself."

"Then how about I make a fuss and you get out the main way as fast as you can?"

"I don't think that's possible. There are guards at the cave mouth as well."

"We have to do something!"

"I know." Lei bit her lip. "But what?"

Takashiga was called to the radio. He held an earphone to his head and stiffened to attention as he was given orders. He replied with an affirmative and a salute.

He set the microphone aside and turned to his prisoners. "Time has run out, Elder Keaunui," he warned Lei's father. "You must choose between silence and your daughter."

Keaunui cast one regretful, haunted glance at Lei before he turned aside.

"I understand, father," the girl called to him. "It is the proper choice. I know that."

"He's sacrificing you?" Bobby objected.

Lei smiled bravely at him. "We're Polynesian. We do that sometimes."

"We're American. We don't bow to tyrants."

Lei smoothed the wound on Bobby's cheek. He would keep that scar for the rest of his life. "You don't understand sacrifice. We didn't give the gods a victim. We sent the gods a messenger. If it's so important that somebody gives up her life to ask something of the gods, then they *have* to pay attention."

"Old man," Takashiga warned, "Do you see the radio device we have brought to this place? Do you know what it is for?"

Suddenly, Bobby did. "Your monster!" he cried. "That giant thing with the tentacles went for the big ships first, the ones with the strongest radio transmitters! You've trained it to chase radio signals, maybe even got it to respond to certain frequencies!" He caught his breath. "The explosives above are just to seal off the exit. You're not sure even your bombs can shatter these nodules. You're bringing that acid-breathing horror here to destroy the cave and the eggs!"

"Very clever," scorned the commander. "Of course, we will not be here by the time Kuraak arrives." He pointed to Lei. "She will."

"What? What do you mean?" demanded Bobby.

Soldiers dragged the youngsters apart. The girl was manhandled over to one of the metal maniples that the researchers had installed for their spotlights. Takashiga locked a handcuff around her wrist and fastened her to the wall.

"Last chance, old man!" he called.

The Elder remained silent. Only Bobby saw the expression on his turned-away face.

Takashiga flicked a red switch on the radio and twisted a dial to its maximum. The valves burned brighter as its transmitter amped up its signal a hundredfold.

The soldiers pushed Keaunui and Bobby out of the cave. "Don't give up, Lei!" the boy shouted to her. "I'll be back for you! I will!"

The commander sneered. "If we had a little more time I would have worked on the girl and made her father talk. It would have been my pleasure. Terrible as that end would have been for her it is nothing compared to what will happen when Kuraak comes."

"You filthy murderers!" Bobby shouted, struggling until one of the soldiers slammed a fist into his belly. He rolled to the ground at the lip of the outer cave, vomiting up the toast he'd eaten for breakfast.

"Kuraak brings madness in his scream," Takashiga crowed. "Before she dies, the girl's mind will be destroyed, clawed into nightmare." He turned to his sergeant and gave an order. The charges were detonated, closing off the upper caves. Rock tumbled down, sealing the route to the chambers below. Only something as huge as the kraken could hope to break through to the egg-cavern now.

As the cave blew, a cloud of dust billowed over the soldiers. Bobby was already on the ground. He saw his only chance. He rolled toward the edge of the high path and hurled himself down the steep rocky slope beyond.

There was a shout from the nearest trooper. The soldier leaned over and aimed his rifle at the rolling and tumbling escapee.

Elder Keaunui barreled into the Japanese invader, sending him over the edge too, to fall headlong with a skull-shattering smash thirty feet below.

Lei's father turned and faced the incoming machine-gun fire with calm pride. His bullet-riddled body was blown off the path to drop after Bobby and the soldier.

Bobby landed in a gulley, bruised and winded. He barely had time to understand what had happened with the Elder before the troopers started shooting at him again. He scrambled for cover behind the nearest rock ledge and kept moving.

His heart pounded. He was running for his life.

The path up to Kalamainu'u's cave was thin and winding. The banks to the south were steep but not all sheer. Bobby found handholds and toeholds where he could shin along the side of what was not quite a cliff. He heard the soldiers scrabbling behind him. Once he heard a scream that ended abruptly.

When he had the opportunity to climb upward, he did. Some instinct told him to seize the upper ground. Only later did he realize that he'd also unconsciously been circling to return to Lei.

A rattle of shots sprayed the rock three feet to his left. He kicked out with one foot and displaced some of the loose shale to rattle down in return and deter his pursuers. He wriggled off to the right, squirming between a pair of tall outcrops, and half-slid half-fell into the gully beyond.

And he recognized it! Lei's secret pool lay just along the shelf.

He moved with new purpose, forcing his aching limbs to a last effort. He found the shallow mouth of the cavern and bellied through it. He dropped through into the cool waters, splashing full into the pool before he could stop himself.

It must be about mid-day. The sun shined perfectly on the twin images of monster and girl. Or were they both sides of the same creature?

Bobby heard noises outside, the harsh rattle of Japanese. The soldiers had followed him – but had they spotted the cave-mouth?

The youngster trod water and hardly breathed while the searchers called to each other outside. They didn't enter the unseen pool-cave, but neither did they go away.

The wailing cry of Kuraak reverberated over the mountain.

It was coming! Bobby pictured a huge, slithering thing heaving itself out of the water by its trunk-thick tentacles, dragging itself over the shattered remains of the military base, clawing a path towards the transmission that tormented it. Then he thought of Leinani Keaunui, shackled in the claustrophobic darkness with no escape and no comfort as the madness-bringing horror closed on her.

"I've got to get her out. I promised."

Bobby had never properly looked around the pool cave. He'd been very distracted the last time he was here, and the mid-day sun lit it better than before. He noticed a thin crevice leading off to one side, different from the impassable vent where the waters drained. The rent was almost too narrow to use, but it seemed to call to him.

He paddled over and inspected it. The bottom of the crack was only inches above the water. The air there had an odd smell, like hot stones in a hearth or...

"Volcano," Bobby said out loud.

*There's only one way out of this chamber*, Lei had said, *except for the deep crack that goes down to the volcano itself.*

Did this rift lead there, too?

Bobby forced his body into the narrow groove. He had no light to guide him. Twenty paces in, he was groping forward by touch. Twice he slammed his head on low rocks he could not see. He pressed on.

A part of him told him this was folly, futile, the way to certain death. If he turned back now he might be able to retrace his steps, get out, find his father, escape to the safety of...

Where? If Hawaii fell to the Japs then the mainland's west coast was wide open. California was no island fortress like Britain, where every beach was defended with wire and mines. With no Navy on the Pacific shore and the unstoppable Kuraak rampaging through Los Angeles or San Francisco what hope did the US have against the Nippon war machine?

And then there was Leinani. Her father had died to save Bobby. Now Bobby was responsible for her.

Let this vent go somewhere. Let it get me to her. Let that be my birthday present.

Bobby's wide-open eyes detected a glimmer in the distance.

He scrambled forward, heedless of the blisters on his rag-covered hand, the scratches and contusions of his fall, the new scrapes of his blind passage. He managed just to stop himself from tumbling down as the floor ended in a natural chimney that descended far into the bowels of the mountain.

The light came from above, and so did the singing.

The voice was Leinani's. Bobby didn't understand the words; something sad and beautiful in the old tongue of her people. The light came from the flickering generator in the cave of eggs.

"Lei!" Bobby shouted. "Leinani!"

The singing stopped. "Bobby? Bobby!"

The chimney was a smooth-sided tube over a yard in diameter. Bobby realized that the only way up would be to press his back against the far wall and shuffle up with his legs on the opposite side of the shaft. An unfathomable depth loomed below him if he slipped.

"Lei, I'm coming!"

Bobby forced himself up the side of the pit, heedless when his shirt-back tore out, then the skin beneath it. When his aching fingers finally found the edge of the cavern floor he used his very last strength to haul himself over the lip.

"Bobby!" Lei called to him. "How...?"

"From your secret pool," he gasped. He crawled over to her. "Lei, I'm sorry. Your father's dead."

Her tear-stained face crumpled with grief, then calmed again. "Later," she promised. "For now I must tend to you."

Bobby realized what he must look like, ragged and bloody and covered with volcano smut. "Maybe I need your pool again," he joked desperately.

The handcuff rattled as Lei helped him over to her. She pulled him close and kissed him urgently. "Thank you for coming," she told him at last. "Foolish and wonderful."

Bobby filed the kiss and the description away for later. This was not a birthday he'd forget. He looked around the cavern till he found the hammer that Takashiga had discarded. It had a claw end that served well to break the links of Lei's shackle.

Their jubilation at her release was cut short by a deafening screech of sickening noise. The creel seemed to scratch at their souls, raking up ancient fears that reduced them to mere animals, trembling in the dark for fear of monsters.

"Kuraak's here!" Bobby cried. "We have to get out."

Lei covered her ears and nodded. They clenched their teeth and scrabbled back over to the larval rift.

"Hold on!" called Bobby over the kraken's rising shriek. He grabbed a reel of cable left over from stringing up the cavern lighting and knotted it round the same bolt that had held Leinani. He paid it out as a rope, sending the spool over the edge of the crack to vanish as far as it could unravel. "Can you climb down that?" he asked the girl.

"Better than you," she answered, sticking her tongue out and beginning her descent.

"There's a crevice about thirty feet down," Bobby called to her. "That's where we turn off."

Another noise filled the caverns. This was the rending of rock as massive tentacles broke through the ancient mountain. The enraged kraken was digging through.

"If I'd been smart I'd have turned off that radio," Bobby chided himself for his dumb lapse.

"You are doing just fine, Robert Fetch," Lei assured him. She squirmed into the horizontal channel and vanished in darkness.

The mountain shuddered. Pebble fragments showered the youngsters. They groped forwards.

The kraken's rotting fish smell was strong now. The noise of splitting rock was more deafening than its creel. Bobby and Lei held down their panic and moved forward by touch.

Then came the choking acid stench that overpowered everything. Kuraak had unleashed its vomit to sear the Cave of Kalamainu'u to nothing.

It became hard to breathe. Lei stumbled. Bobby fell on top of her. "Keep going," he croaked. It was do or die.

Lei slithered round the next corner and saw light. Another thirty paces and fresh air greeted them. The pool cave waited, with its crystal cool waters to sooth and refresh them.

Lei plunged in first. Bobby followed her. They both surfaced, cleansed and triumphant.

"We did it! We got out!" the boy exclaimed.

"We did! I don't believe it! When I was trapped there, waiting for that monster to come, I thought..." Leinani's joyous testimony was silenced as she looked towards the cave's exit.

The passage was collapsed. There was no way out.

Bobby followed her dismayed stare. He glanced up at the other openings that admitted light onto the carved walls. He knew at once that he could never reach them. They were as sealed in here as Lei had been in the egg-cave.

Lei dragged herself out of the water and sat with her knees drawn up to her chest. Her dark hair covered her face so it was hard to tell if she was laughing or crying. Maybe both.

Bobby joined her. "Lei?"

She looked up at him and brushed her mane aside. "I never gave you your other present, did I?"

Bobby shook his head. "Things got kind of busy."

She reached into her cut-offs and pulled out a small chip of black rock. She laid it in the boy's palm. "Recognize that?"

Bobby inspected it. "Is this the same stuff those eggs are made of?"

"Were made of. They're gone now, melted by that kraken-thing. This is all that's left."

"I'm sorry."

Leinani shook her head. "None of this is your doing, Bobby Fetch. But the next part has to be. You own the very last piece of Kalamain-u'u, and I'm the last person alive who knows her secret."

"I don't understand."

"You will later. But that's your property now. Will you let me borrow it?"

"Sure. But why?"

"Be very sure, Bobby, because lending this to me will have a cost. It's a sacrifice, and they have to be made willingly or they don't count."

"Anything for you. Have it."

Leinani nodded. "So, then," she said, and kissed him again.

"Um..." Bobby said nervously as she began to peel her clothes off.

"Hush. It's not what you think. Sorry." The girl took the stone in her hand and plunged deep into the pool.

She looked just like the girl on the carving.

She drifted to the surface, unmoving, unconscious, her body floating like a star.

And under the mountain, she awoke as Kalamainu'u.

THE BLOCKED entrance to the pool cave shattered. Vast talons tore it open and hurled the stones aside.

Bobby looked up at suddenly open sky above the hidden lake where Liu floated. A huge bipedal dragon stared back at him. Her scales shimmered with lurid rainbow sheen. Her talons and spine-ridges were silver.

Her eyes were familiar.

"Lei?" Bobby stammered, looking at those haunting pupils. *Kupua*, he remembered. The Keaunui were an ancient family. An ancient family of guardians.

A hand the size of a car reached down for him, palm upward. He climbed onto it and was lifted to the dragon's shoulder.

"This is way better than a tour of the *Arizona*," Bobby told her.

The dragon shifted attitude. The boy had to clutch onto one of the ridges round her neck to avoid falling. The dragon's hide was warm and soft, like old leather.

"Mom is never going to let Dad forget about this," Bobby told Lei.

The monster was moving now. At first Bobby thought it was going to follow the trail of destruction left by Kuraak. The tentacled horror was already making its way back down to the sea to meet the incoming invasion fleet. Instead Kalamainu'u trod a lateral path along the mountain ridge; towards the research compound.

Lei was hunting the men who'd killed her father.

Bobby didn't have a problem with that.

The soldiers were at work in the compound yard, loading crates of Bobby's dad's notes onto the project's own truck. When they saw the vast lizard looming over them they screamed and scattered, scrambling to unshoulder guns that could never penetrate the creature's shimmering scale armor.

Liu's barbed tail came round with razor-slices and cut them down.

Other soldiers emerged from the Fetch house, firing machine guns. Kalamainu'u spat a five-foot wad of caustic slime at them. It detonated like a mortar, searing them apart and leaving their body parts burning.

Lt. Takashiga and the plain-clothes spy raced from the far side of the admin cabin. They reached one of the open-topped cars and tried to start it.

Lei picked up the vehicle and hoisted it seventy feet into the air to bring it level with her eye. Takashiga cringed before the maw of the dragon.

"Not such a tough guy now, huh?" Bobby called from Kalamainu'u's neck ridge. "How's it feel to get picked on by someone bigger than you?"

The spy pulled his pistol and fired off shots at the dragon's eye. She tipped the car, spilling him to his death. Takashiga hung on, dangling from the door of the inverted transport.

He screamed something in Japanese. Bobby found it hard to care that much what it was.

Lei hurled the convertible high over the valley ridge. It must have traveled half a mile before it crashed down in the forest, taking the commander with it.

"That was spectacular," Bobby admitted. "Can you set me down now? I need to check on my folks."

The dragon set him down by his house as if he were the most precious thing in the world.

Bobby rushed inside the house, stepping over the still-bubbling remains of the Japanese soldiers that Kalamainu'u had spat upon. It was only as he pushed open the kitchen door with his bandaged hand that he realized the blistering on it was completely gone.

"Mom! Dad!" Lana Fetch was handcuffed to a chair in her husband's study. Dr. Fetch lay stunned where the soldiers had struck him down before they'd rushed outside to meet the dragon.

"Bobby!" shrieked Lana. "*Bobby!*"

The boy made sure his father wasn't too hurt then broke his mother loose by the simple expedient of demolishing the chair that held her.

"Bobby, what *happened?*" Lana Fetch demanded. "That horrid Jap said..."

"It's not over yet, mom," Bobby interrupted. "Look after Dad. I've gotta go." In the first variant of the legend, Kalamainu'u's lover had seen her as the monster and had still loved her. Bobby liked that story better.

He rushed outside. The dragon was gone.

He could see her, though. She was winging and gliding her way down the mountain towards the incoming Japanese fleet.

"Go get 'em, Liu!" Bobby called, knowing that she couldn't hear him, cheering for her all the same.

The dragon winged over the shattered devastation of the Pearl Harbor base, past the wreckage of an entire fleet, powering hard over South Channel and Ford Island, ignoring the kraken's challenge from Hickham Field. Kalamainu'u was guided by a keen intelligence that could calculate and plan. The kraken was supreme in water. It could not compete in air and fire.

Lei went straight for the incoming fleet. The first planes that rose to stop her died in wads of spewed caustic goo. Others were reduced to scrap as the dragon simply flew through them. When she reached the first ship, Kalamainu'u grabbed its tower in her claws and capsized it as she passed. The next was seared by her sputum; its magazine exploded.

It had taken Kuraak less than three hours to destroy the American fleet. It took Leinani Keaunui less than fifteen minutes to do the same to the Japanese invasion. She was protecting her shores once more. Human, monster, and goddess acted as one.

Bobby remembered the field glasses in the admin cabin. The whole place was a ransacked mess, but only a minute's frantic searching found the binoculars. He raced back outside to watch what came next.

His parents had staggered out, too. They'd reacted to the broken soldiers scattered round the yard, to the burned and alkaline-dissolved men and buildings, and now they were watching the dragon in the bay.

Bobby ignored them. Maybe their mutual ordeal would spur them to overcome their differences and try again. Maybe what they learned today would give them the insight they needed to complete their government work. Right now all he cared about was the flying reptile tearing up the most powerful warships of Emperor Hirohito's navy.

Kuraak was closing on her. Even at this distance his screeching was audible, like the malice of the deep.

Kalamainu'u turned on him, her own fury rising as she recognized the destroyer of her cave. A second sound came over the miles between the monsters and the research camp.

Kalamainu'u was singing; and Bobby recognized the voice and the song.

More, the song broke the evil spell of the kraken's shriek. Men who had been raving and quivering, tearing at themselves and others since Kuraak's attack began, fell silent and instead began to weep.

Kuraak did not like the song. It opened its beaked maw and breathed out its acidic spray. A tentacle lashed into the dragon, slapping her from the air. Kalamainu'u dropped into the water. Kuraak fell upon her.

Bobby took a step forward as if he could somehow intervene. The sea was a churning froth. The kraken, slightly larger and far more muscled, lashed down with room-thick tentacles at the downed reptile.

The dragon made the surface and unleashed her own breath. The nearest of Kuraak's appendages was seared through; it dropped away, twitching. Several of the creature's eyes bubbled and boiled.

The rest of its tentacles thrashed down, pinning Kalamainu'u, leaving her vulnerable to that gaping maw. Kuraak's beak closed at her throat, scraping over her scales, seeking any weakness that would allow it to tear into her innards. Her own claws shredded at the writhing flailing appendages that beset her.

Between the wreckage of two mighty fleets, two mightier monsters decided the future of nations.

"Come on, Lei," Bobby whispered. "Come on!" Her kiss still tingled across his lips like the promise of paradise.

Kuraak pushed the dragon under the water again, climbing atop her to gain the advantage of its larger bulk. Kalamainu'u's barbed tail curled round and speared deep into the sea-beast, skewering deep and dragging it back.

For a moment both creatures reared to their full heights, dragon with wings outspread and kraken with tentacles coiling. They came together again with a crash that sent high waves breaking over the piers at Pearl Harbor. Kuraak pushed Kalamainu'u back and opened its beak to tear down on the reptile's snout.

Kalamainu'u pushed forward and plunged her entire head neck-deep inside the kraken's maw – and breathed caustic death.

The kraken twitched and struggled. It bit down, shattering the reflective amour that protected Kalamainu'u's throat. The dragon lifted the sea monster right out of the waves, hoisting it flailing and struggling out of its element. Kalamainu'u's own jaws were at work in the kraken's soft interior, tearing and shredding through to the vital organs at its core.

Blood and ichor stained the churning waters.

And Bobby remembered Lei's other words: *You don't understand sacrifice. We didn't give the gods a victim. We sent the gods a messenger.*

Everything was at stake. The whole future. Leinani had known that.

*If it's so important that somebody gives up her life to ask something of the gods then they have to pay attention.*

She'd feared even then that the long secret vigil of her ancient family might end with her. Bobby understood now.

*Lending this to me will have a cost. It's a sacrifice, and they have to be made willingly or they don't count.*

The cost to Lei was her life. The ancient forces did not like being woken, and they always demanded a price in blood. The cost to Bobby was Lei.

The kraken's jaws closed with a sickening crunch on the dragon's neck. Kalamainu'u flexed one last time. The kraken exploded around her, spraying the sea with gobbets of monster-meat for a mile.

Kalamainu'u staggered three steps then tottered. She fell sideways into the waves, dropping with a huge splash to vanish in the depths. A moment later, her carcass washed to the surface for one last salute to her island home. Then she sank under the waves a final time.

Bobby began to run, pelting up the track where Lei had led him just this morning, a lifetime ago. He ran till his lungs burned and his limbs numbed, but he did not stop. He had to scramble over new-*broken* boulders to find the roofless pool-cave.

He jumped from a broken rock right down into the crystal waters. They were lower now, slowly draining through new fissures in the shattered mountain. Lei still floated there like an exotic flower.

Bobby hauled her to the shore. She was not breathing. She would not breathe again.

Her hand fell open and released the black pebble at his knees. It was just a memento now, but Bobby Fetch would carry it to his grave.

It was the seventh of December, 1941. America had entered the Second World War. The vital strategic value of monsters had been proven again. A brave and lovely girl died to send a message and to save a people.

It was Bobby Fetch's fourteenth birthday, the time when Lei's people once believed that a boy became a man. From that day he would fight, and love, and protect what mattered.

He picked up Lei's body and carried her home. He had seen the monster and he still loved her. He always would.

3

# THE BEAST'S HOME

JEFF MCGINNIS

*In 1943, the United States adopted its first official monster, and, in doing so, almost went to war with Canada over the creature. But America's dominance in the realm of monsters found its ultimate expression in its dramatic and controversial attack on the Japanese mainland in 1945. Conditioned by rigorous training and on edge from a pharmaceutical cocktail, the beast was dropped on first Hiroshima and then Nagasaki, completely obliterating both cities. The Japanese surrendered soon after.*

*The post-war years brought with them their own challenges, and while the rest of the world sought to enter the monster race, the United States learned that the price of being a new world superpower was a high one.*

*Excerpted from The New York Times, September 3, 1945:*

PEACE!

*HIROHITO OFFICIALLY SURRENDERS*

*GIANT MONSTER ATTACK ON JAP MAINLAND ENDS FIGHTING*

ON THE DECK of the USS Missouri in Tokyo Bay, Sunday Sept. 2, Japan surrendered formally and unconditionally to Allied Forces in a brief ceremony which finally ended years of bloody conflict.

Coming mere days after the devastating attack on the Japanese mainland by the monstrous beast nicknamed "Johnson" by scientists, the end of hostilities brought cheers to the assembled crowds on the deck of the Missouri and to peace-loving individuals the world over...

...the monster, located by American scientists near the Canadian border late last year, was specifically credited by MacArthur in bringing about the surrender.

"It is not an exaggeration to say that the use of monstrous force saved hundreds if not thousands of American lives," MacArthur stated. "That beast is a true hero."

IN THE YEARS following World War II, Johnson -- the hairy, faceless giant which had finally caved Japan's stalemate -- became a new symbol of national pride. Where Uncle Sam and Washington had once stood, now a towering beast of indeterminate origin became a focal point of the American imagination. Johnson was on lapel pins and cola bottles coast to coast. Political candidates were quick to stress how supportive they had been of the Johnson project and, in fact, they were sure that if Johnson could speak, he would support their platform.

IN THE DAYS following the war, Johnson had been relocated to a hastily-assembled military base on Marina Del Ray in Los Angeles. The official reason was that since the last threat against America had come from across the Pacific, it was best to keep the monster on the coast. The real reasons had less to do with tactics than with atmosphere: It was felt a more consistent climate might keep the creature more docile and under control.

. . .

THIS THEORY HIT its first snag in the days following his arrival at the Marina in 1946. His containment unit was barely half assembled when Johnson first escaped, tearing into the mainland with a rampage that was described as both "horrific" (by eyewitnesses) and "minor" (by officials in its aftermath). Twelve died before he was subdued, but Johnson's popularity and notoriety were so widespread that press coverage of the event was practically non-existent. No need to dilute a great American legend with a pesky thing like the truth.

A FEW YEARS passed without incident, and Los Angeles had begun to return to something close to normal. Then came Johnson's second breakout in 1949. His handlers couldn't even blame a slow construction pace this time. Thirty-five perished in the three hours Johnson was on the loose. This attack managed to get a little more play in the papers, but since television was becoming the national obsession, who was paying attention to the papers anymore?

FOR THE PEOPLE of Los Angeles, though, the writing was on every collapsed wall. A mass exodus began. The entertainment industry left, taking the local economic infrastructure with it. Apartments sat vacant. Empty storefronts lined once bustling streets. What just a few years prior had been one of the defining cities of the American dream was slowly dying.

ALL THANKS to America's savior.

---

It was an annoyingly beautiful April morning. Marty walked down the boulevard, squinting against the sun and cursing his lack of dark glasses. The streets were quiet as he lurched towards work. Most days, less people was a bad thing -- when you're a cabbie, fewer bodies means fewer passengers. Today, feeling as he did toward the world and toward the hangover-induced agonizing pain in his skull, Marty had no -- *no* -- problem with it.

HE FINALLY ARRIVED at the TnT Cab Company -- "Taxi 'n' Transport," the cheerful mascot on the door explained -- just a couple minutes later than normal. Given how he was feeling, Marty deserved a damn medal just for walking in the door, to say nothing of being on time. Almost.

Tom, the company's dispatcher, had barely looked up from his paperwork when he said, "Dammit, Marty, you look like hell."

He was right, of course. Marty offered no rebuttal. "I need a cab."

Tom looked with sad eyes. "Go home, rest up. You need it. It's not like we're gonna be swamped today."

"I need a cab," Marty repeated.

Tom sighed. There was no way to out-stubborn Marty when he got his head fixed on something. Tom had known that for years -- his nickname in their platoon had been "Marty the Mule." And even -- maybe especially -- now that Tom outranked him in civilian life, it was clear that his attitudes had not changed.

"7116," the dispatcher said, snapping into business mode. He tossed an envelope and a set of keys Marty's way, and that -- *thank God*, Marty thought -- ended the conversation. Marty wandered painfully through the garage until he found his car, sat slowly behind the wheel and sighed to himself. *This day*, he thought, *will be a damn chore.*

BETTY SWEPT into the door of Freedman National Bank at 9:01 -- just in the nick of late. Al, the kindly guard by the front door who looked to be pushing 70, shook his head at her with a smile. She shrugged back. They rarely spoke to each other, but Betty liked Al more than almost everyone she worked with. At least he was kind and didn't seem like a creepy letch -- which was far from what she could say for the gentleman who was storming up to her now.

"Miss Grint, are we to tolerate your eccentric schedule on a regular basis? We expect punctuality here, do you understand?" Mr. Cosgrove asked, an edge to his voice.

"Yes, absolutely, Mr. Cosgrove," Betty replied, sounding genuinely sorry. She wasn't, of course. She had never been late before in her employment life. Her manager just took every opportunity to chastise her that he could. Partially it was a power trip. Mostly it was because he wanted to get a look at her gams as she walked away.

"Well, then, let's not have this kind of talk again, honey," Cosgrove said.

"Absolutely not, Mr. Cosgrove," she responded. *Honey,* she thought, retching to herself.

She walked away, knowing that bastard was getting a good look at her every step. Betty had wanted to say something for a long time, but all that would probably accomplish was the loss of her job, something she, and most everyone in Los Angeles, could ill afford.

Betty took her place at the counter -- last in the row, closest to Cosgrove's office, of course -- and began counting up her cash drawer. God, she hated this. She hated her job. She hated her boss. She hated the way new bills stuck together when you tried to count them. She hated dealing with dumb customer questions. She hated that she was stuck here. She hated herself for getting stuck here. She just hated.

Of course, anyone coming up to her today wouldn't know any of this. To them, she would just be the pretty young teller with the long brown hair and the kind smile. She was an actress, after all. Betty sighed to herself, took down the "Next Window Please" sign in front of her and called, "Can I help whoever is next?"

MARTY HAD BEEN DRIVING with little luck for about a half hour. He sat alone with his own thoughts as he cruised the streets of the once-bustling city. He had all but forgotten about picking up passengers when he first noticed the man on the side of the road. He wore a dark suit with a red tie. Hair neatly groomed. He carried a single duffel bag that seemed to hold little. When he signaled Marty, it finally jolted the cabbie out of his reverie.

"Hiya, where to?" Marty asked, the required amount of TnT enthusiasm in his voice, as the man got into the back seat.

"Freedman National, off San Vicente," the man said.

And, with that, the man in the suit seemed to exhaust all conversation. He didn't say a word for ten minutes. As the taxi pulled through the lonely streets of the city, Marty followed the TnT Cab Company policy of initiating small talk about a variety of issues -- the weather, the city, the many fine, fine innovations of the TnT Cab Company. The more you kept their mind occupied, the manual stated, the less likely they were to glance at the outlandish prices on the dashboard, or ask questions about another of TnT's "innovations," the small switch just below the price list which automatically locked the rear doors in case a patron tried to stiff a driver on his fare.

Marty brought up all pre-designated topics, tried a few of his own, even talked about how he was the only one talking. No luck. Finally, Marty admitted defeat and they simply sat in silence for the duration of the ride. As much as Marty was uncomfortable with the company policies about constant chatter, silence bothered him more.

They finally pulled up in front of the bank about fifteen minutes after their trip began. Marty slid the cab into park and was about to announce the inflated fare to what was sure to be another thoroughly disgusted customer. To his surprise, the man in the suit spoke first.

"I'll have another fare for you if you'll wait. Sound good?"

"Sounds fine, sir," Marty said. But given TnT's strict idling fee, it probably wouldn't sound fine to the man in the suit once he got wherever he was going. *Damn my conscience*, Marty thought. He began to turn. "Look, sir, I should tell you..."

The gun, a revolver, was pointed straight at Marty's temple.

"Hands on the wheel, now." The man in the suit's voice was disturbingly calm.

Marty surprised himself by moving his hands dutifully to ten and two o'clock. "Look, buddy, you're my first fare all day. You can have whatever you want, but...."

"Stop talking, please," the man in the suit nonchalantly commanded. Marty fell silent.

"Now then. I would introduce myself, but my name is unimportant. The fact that I have the gun is *very* important, I think you'd agree. You don't have to introduce yourself. Your name is Martin Plume, as it says on your cabbie license there on the dash, right next to your photo and the ridiculously high rates list. Do folks call you Marty?"

Marty didn't respond.

"I'll call you Marty. More friendly. Anyway, Marty, I know who you are. You don't know me. That puts me at an information advantage. So, here's what's going to happen. I am going to rob this bank. I will walk in, show this gun to a teller, get as much money as possible and walk back out. I wasn't lying. I have another fare for you. Your fare is to stay right here with the engine idling until I come out. I will get into the car and you will drive away. If all goes well, no one will get hurt, and you will receive a very generous tip. You will never see me again. If you decide to flee, Marty, I will pay a visit to you very soon and put a bullet in your head. I'd hate to have to do that. You won't make me do that, will you, Marty?"

Again, Marty did not reply.

"Very good. Engine running, doors unlocked, and I will be back in just a few minutes. Thank you for your help, Marty."

The man in the suit opened the rear door, placed the gun under his jacket and swept out of the car in what seemed like one fluid motion. Marty, hands still on the wheel, watched as he moved past the car toward the front door. He walked smoothly, heel to toe. He swept into the bank like he owned the place. In a second, he would.

Marty didn't move. His hands stayed on the wheel. The man's voice. The calm, even voice. That rattled him more than anything. The man had believed every word he was saying. Marty believed it, too. If he drove away, Marty knew he was dead.

That scared him.

It truly scared him.

Martin Plume stayed put.

~

"BURGER WITH MUSTARD AND ONION, Frankie. Plenty of each," Officer John Schwartz said to the vendor as he got out of his car. A breakfast for champions, to be sure. Schwartz was en route to his station to end a long night's patrol when hunger began to hit him, hard. He usually ate after he checked in, but his last meal had been a quick bite at Moe's over five hours ago. He needed something before then. Thankfully, he spotted Frank's stand on San Vicente, just a few blocks from home.

"You got it, Johnny. How ya been?"

"Tired as hell. Just finishing up. Gonna go home and do nothing for about nineteen hours," Schwartz said.

"Ah, sounds nice! That enough?" Frank said, holding up a burger with mound of onion at least double the size of the patty. He knew what Schwartz liked.

"Perfect," Schwartz said. He took his first mouthful before Frank had even handed him his change.

"You're on nights now? Must be rough," Frankie said.

*Not at all*, Schwartz thought. In fact, he loved seeing the city after dark. Cruising around the empty streets on a late spring night, he could imagine that everyone was just home asleep, and the city was still as buzzing as it ever was. Damn, it hurt to see LA turn into such a ghost town.

"How are things with you and the wife?" Frank asked.

Schwartz wiped the mustard from his upper lip as he considered the best way to answer. "She's good, she's good. How about your mother?"

"Holding up. Having trouble getting around, you know."

"Sorry to hear that, Frankie. Listen, if there's anything I..."

"...can do, let you know," Frank finished. "I appreciate that, Johnny. But, actually, I'm closing up next week."

"Ah, visiting her in San Fran?"

"No. I'm...I'm closing up."

Schwartz tried to hide how stunned he was. Frankie tried to explain how he knew a guy who could get him started in San Francisco, his mom needed the help and so on. Schwartz listened and nodded when it seemed appropriate. Damn, this one hurt.

Schwartz smiled. A little. "Thanks again, Frankie," was all he could manage. "You have a good day, OK?"

"You too, Johnny."

Schwartz walked back to his car, leaned on the hood and ate in silence for a moment. He took another bite of his hamburger, chewed slowly. He glanced up at the clock outside Freedman Bank. He was gonna be late checking in. He didn't care. You didn't rush one of Frankie's masterpieces. And any small pleasure was worth savoring right now.

CAFFEINE. That was what Betty needed right now. As her eyes drooped in exhaustion, she was desperately in need of some chemical encouragement. After all, if she made it through today there were only three days left in the week. Sigh. Still, only one more customer probably stood between her and the break room. This customer. A man in a suit.

"Hello, can I help you?" Betty asked, smile on her face.

"Yes, you can," the man said in a pleasant tone of voice. He walked close to the counter and opened his coat slightly, just enough for Betty to see the revolver tucked away inside. The man put his right hand on the handle of the gun and kept it there.

The adrenaline now coursing through her veins worked better than any caffeine ever could. Betty looked at the man's face. He held a single finger to his lips. *Shhh.* She didn't make a sound. Wasn't sure she could.

"Hello, Betty," the man in the suit said quietly. "That's your name, Betty, right? My name isn't important. And yes, you can help me. The first thing you can do is place both hands on the counter and leave them there. Go on, do it. Now."

Betty slowly moved her hands to the countertop. She'd been told in any situation like this that the robber's demands were to be followed. The bank was insured, after all. She glanced around briefly at the half-empty lobby. Still plenty of people to be at risk.

"Good job, Betty. Now, is that your manager back there? The bald man in the ridiculous suit?"

Yeah, that was Cosgrove. She nodded.

“Good. Would you call him here, please?”

Betty turned slightly. “Mr. Cosgrove, may I see you at my counter? A customer would like to speak to you.”

Cosgrove, busy chatting up another young female employee, turned toward Betty, annoyed. "It'll be a second, honey."

*Dammit, now is not the time for your lazy ass.* "Mr. Cosgrove, this customer needs your help now," she said, a little louder, more urgency.

Cosgrove, flat-out ticked off by this point, excused himself from his current conversation and walked with strident purpose toward Betty's counter. He gave her a glower as he brushed up to her side, which quickly turned into his usual slimy charm as he addressed the man in the suit. "Hello, sir, can I help you?"

"Yes," the man said, opening his coat to reveal his weapon. Betty would be lying if she didn't admit that seeing Cosgrove struck speechless pleased her, just a little.

"Now then, Cosgrove, as you can tell, I am robbing this bank. If you say anything to alert anyone, set off any alarms or inhibit my actions in any way, I will put a bullet in your head. Understood?"

Cosgrove didn't nod, didn't even move, his eyes still focused on the weapon the man was concealing. The man closed his jacket slightly but did not take his hand away from the gun.

The man placed the empty duffel bag on the counter. "Now, you will go back to your vault, take this bag and fill it with as many loose bills as you can. If anyone asks, I am making a rather substantial withdrawal, and I am demanding cash. You will not be lying, that's what I'm doing. I just don't have an account to be doing it from. Then, you will bring the bag to me, and I will walk out the door. If all this happens, no one will get hurt. If it doesn't, I make no guarantees. Do you understand?"

Cosgrove nodded slightly, his eyes still wide as saucers.

"Then why are you still here?"

Cosgrove blinked, then turned hastily toward the bank vault.

THERE WAS a term around LA for people like Sid and Erma Reeve -- "MFers." The M stood for "Monster" and the F, well, it can probably be guessed. Tourists obsessed with the creature named Johnson had turned up frequently in the years following his first exploits. It seemed to matter little that the containment unit he had finally been sealed into offered no view of him, nor could anyone even get close thanks to the military guard. They just wanted to be near him. Eventually the large MFer fad died off, but a few still showed up now and then.

That was the Reeves to a T. Ever since the first news stories of his discovery up north had begun to reach them, they had collected every news clipping, read every book, found every piece of unofficial merchandise. Their son Brian was given a "Lil' Johnny" doll for Christmas every year, no matter what he really wanted. One year, Brian's birthday "present" was the news that he was being moved to a brand new room -- much smaller, of course -- so Sid and Erma could move their growing collection of Johnson memorabilia into his old one.

Despite their fanaticism toward the new symbol of American pride, the one thing Sid and Erma hadn't done was visit Johnson himself in Los Angeles. Part of it was financial: Traveling was a tad expensive for a little family out of Boise. But mostly it was understanding the realities of Johnson's storage. As he was housed in a giant steel structure with a double-reinforced roof, containment of the beast was still designed with virtually no consideration for tourists in mind, aside from making sure that Johnson didn't kill them, of course.

For years, the Reeves had pondered the problem. They were desperate to visit their icon, but didn't want to take a few pictures of a giant metal box from half a mile away and go home. They wanted – needed-- something very special, some kind of interaction with Johnson himself; something that would be theirs and theirs alone.

One day, Sid had a revelation while tinkering in his basement with some radio equipment. If they couldn't *see* Johnson, maybe they could *hear* him. If they bought some long-range audio equipment, worked at magnifying its distance and aimed it directly at Johnson's "pen," maybe they could record Johnson's sounds as he slept, walked around, played with Army trucks as toys (that was a guess on their part).

And so the plan was set in motion. After months of adjustment, they had a recording device and microphone that was extremely accurate over long range and compact enough to fit in a relatively small carrying space, a medium-size suitcase, to be precise. And the initial tests of the device were very promising. From a half-mile away, they were able to hear perfectly what little Brian was doing in their own house. (They had a conversation with Brian later that night about staying out of Daddy's closet.)

Now, here they were, less than a month later. The family savings were sunk into this trip, and even then could only cover two of the three Reeves. (They told themselves Brian would be fine for a few days, and made sure to leave some TV dinners for him in the freezer.) They were in LA. They were less than a mile away from him. He was Right. Over. There.

In the heat of the MFer craze, a few local businesses had installed rickety "observation towers" on the roofs of their buildings, each one boasting of having the most powerful binoculars for not seeing Johnson with. Now that the fervor had died down, the towers sat unused for months at a time. This was unknown to Sid and Erma, who proceeded to rent one of the vacant towers for the afternoon for an amount of cash that the shop owner had simply made up off the top of his head.

Once on the roof, the Reeves quickly proceeded to unpack their equipment. They needed to take advantage of every moment. They had brought enough tape to record Johnson's grunts, growls and possible snores for only seven hours or so. The grins on their faces were approaching ludicrous levels. They put on their headphones (one set, each cramming one ear into one side) and Sid pointed the microphone at the metal tower in the distance. They turned the equipment on.

At first, there was nothing. For a few heartbreaking seconds, the Reeves each wondered if the tower was blocking their signal, if they wouldn't get anything, if all this had been for nothing, if...wait! A sound! A minor grunt. It wasn't human. Oh my God! It's him! It's him! We're hearing him! Sid almost fainted, and Erma came as close to climax as she ever had in her life.

But then, a few seconds later, the grunt took on a different tone. It sounded less content and bored, and more irritated. Annoyed. Angry. Very angry. Very, very angry. Something was bothering Johnson! What was it? Could they do anything? Were those horrible military people hurting him? What?

What was bothering him, of course, were the Reeves themselves. A factor that had gone completely unaccounted for was the noise their makeshift audio equipment produced. To be fair, Sid and Erma couldn't have known, as it was far above the spectrum of normal human hearing. But Johnson could hear it. Oh, yes. And the high-pitched screech that now hit the monster in his pen seemed to reverberate off every wall. It was driving him into a frenzy.

The Reeves, oblivious, continued to record. The sounds they picked up got more and more interesting, and their concern for Johnson was tempered, because what they were getting on tape was so amazing. That's Johnson yelling! That sounds like people shouting! Hey, was that a chain snapping? That almost sounds like fists pounding on a large metal door!

~

Betty struggled to not make eye contact with the man in the suit while Cosgrove made his journey to the vault behind her. The man stood in front of her, casually leaned forward on the counter, a pleasant look on his face. He looked bizarrely at peace with the world, like a guy waiting for a bus in a Norman Rockwell painting. It was only if you looked in his eyes -- his grey, vacant eyes -- that you got a sense of his true nature, she felt. Betty really believed that he could kill her, or anyone else, at a moment's provocation. So she did everything possible to not give it to him.

It seemed like an eternity before Cosgrove returned carrying a the bag, so comically filled with bills Betty half expected to see money jutting out of the top like in a cartoon. Cosgrove put on his best No-I'm-Not-Scared-Out-of-My-Mind smile and said, a little too loudly, "Well, sir, I'm sorry you are closing that account, but here's your cash, sir, and thank you for stopping by, sir!"

The man in the suit put on a look of ever-so-slight exasperation, the first appreciable change in emotion Betty had seen out of him. He then took the bag off the counter, nodded with a smile and began to turn away.

"Hold on there, son," Al said from behind him.

*Oh, God, Al, why now?*

The old guard stood behind the man in the suit. He was as deaf as Beethoven and his eyes weren't much better, but even he had been able to tell something wasn't right. Al's hand was on his weapon, preparing to draw.

"This doesn't have to go any further, son," Al said slowly. "If you leave right now, you can walk away with a clear conscience."

The man in the suit looked up and finally caught Betty's eyes. She could see that a clear conscience was not going to be a problem for him.

Before Betty could even scream Al's name, the man in the suit whipped around, drew his weapon and fired one round, point blank, into the old guard's stomach.

Pandemonium broke out in the half-empty lobby. Screams of all pitch filled the air as Al slumped to the floor. Betty ran to him from around the counter, falling to her knees and trying to talk to him. Another teller rushed up and applied pressure to the wound. An appalling amount of blood oozed out from between her fingers. Cosgrove cowered behind her counter, and only from that vantage did he feel safe to sound the bank's alarm. People ran for the door, ducked behind desks, filled the air with shouts of panic.

Betty looked for the man in the suit -- he hadn't moved. He stood, an oasis of calm in the storm. He still clutched the bag of cash in one hand, his revolver in the other, but for the first time seemed unsure of a course of action. He looked to the door, looked at his bounty, looked for something, anything he could use to his advantage. The man finally settled on the young teller at his feet who was trying to tend to her friend.

"Get up." Betty glanced up to see the barrel of the man's revolver aimed at her skull.

"I am not leaving him," she said, calmly, resolutely.

The man in the suit changed his aim. "Get up now, or the next shot's in his head."

Betty didn't know enough about wounds to know if Al could survive, but she wasn't going to make things any worse. Slowly, she stood.

In a flash, the man in the suit was behind her. He slung the bag of cash over his shoulder, wrapped one arm around her throat, and pointed the revolver at her temple.

"Walk," he said.

MARTY HAD to admit he'd felt a dull sense of relief when the shot sounded from within the bank. With any luck, that meant his role in this melodrama was now finished. His hopes were dashed quickly as the man in the suit emerged from the bank, forcibly accompanied by a young woman. She was a beautiful girl, early 30s, Marty guessed.

The man held her from behind by the throat, his gun pointed at her head.

The two of them walked toward the cab, the woman putting up little resistance. Her eyes betrayed no fear, though. Marty thought he saw something else. Anger? Defiance? He wasn't sure. But she walked along, nonetheless. *She may be pissed off, but she ain't no fool either,* Marty thought. They were almost to the cab when a new voice shouted "Freeze!"

Schwartz stood about ten feet away from the cab, gun drawn. Marty wasn't sure whether to cheer or shudder. The officer held his gun squarely in the direction of the man in the suit. The man, still clutching the young woman, re-aimed his weapon at the cop.

"Let her go," Schwartz said. His voice was soft but powerful.

"We both know that's not happening," the man in the suit said, almost bemused. "You're going to let me get in this cab with my hostage and we're going to drive away." The man's tone was the same as it had been a few minutes before, with Marty, the tone that had convinced him to stay put.

The man in the suit began to shift his weight, ready to begin moving again. Schwartz spoke before he could. "Take another step and I'll give you a third eye socket. Stop."

The man in the suit -- really? really? -- paused. He seemed to be considering the threat. Analyzing it. His gun never wavered from the cop's chest. For a long, agonizing moment, there was dead silence in the air.

Then, a sound began to drift in. It slowly made itself known, as if apologizing for intruding on the drama. Schwartz lifted his eyes at the noise, slightly. The man in the suit took advantage of his shift in focus and pulled the trigger -- but a sudden struggle by the woman threw off his aim. Schwartz fell to the ground and instinctively returned fire. The man in the suit threw open the front passenger door of the cab for cover. Marty crouched down behind the steering wheel, praying to gods he didn't believe in anymore.

The man in the suit, still struggling with Betty in his grasp, pointed the gun at her head. "In the car," he said. She was in little position to argue. She climbed in the front seat as the man in the suit peeked over the door, then fired two shots toward Schwartz on the ground in front of them. They missed by a country mile as Schwartz rolled to avoid the bullets. This seemed to give the man in the suit an opening he needed. He slammed the front door on Betty and dove into the back seat of the cab, tossing the bag of cash on the seat next to him.

He aimed his gun through the cage at Marty. "Drive. Now."

Marty followed orders. Park to drive, petal to metal, zero to whatever-this-cab-in-disrepair-could-go.

As the taxi and its three occupants tore from the scene, the sound that had interrupted the stand-off continued, magnified in intensity. It had been a while since anyone in LA had heard that alarm. About six years, to be precise.

Johnson had escaped.

BETTY HADN'T TRAVELED in a car for years. It had been out of her pay grade even before Johnson had arrived in town, and she'd gotten very used to traveling on the limited forms of public transit still available. So a ride in a taxi would have felt foreign and unusual in most any circumstance, to say nothing of a wild ride through the streets with a psychotic armed robber in the back seat.

She glanced back at the man in the suit, who was too busy looking through the cab's back window to pay attention to her. In addition to the monster warning alarm which was now sounding from the top of some of the tallest buildings in the city, another siren could be heard, the higher pitched wail of a police car giving chase. The cop was on their tail.

The man in the suit fired out the back window, shattering it. He brushed the remaining glass out of the way and aimed more carefully the second time, trying to hit the cop behind the wheel, but missed wildly. Betty crouched down in her seat to avoid any return gunfire, but there was none. The cop seemed reluctant to shoot with her and the cabbie in harm's way.

She glanced to her left. The cabbie was mid-40s, she guessed. His name was Martin Plume, she knew from the license on the dash. He had kind eyes, Betty thought, eyes which were wide with terror as he tried to keep the car under control.

Then his eyes -- impossibly -- got even bigger.

She glanced in the direction he was looking.

It was him.

Though Betty had lived in town for a few years by now, she had never seen the monster known as Johnson with her own eyes. She had seen plenty of pictures in newsreels and propaganda posters, but never as a living, breathing thing in front of her. No one had for years.

Johnson was about a mile away from the cab, down the long expanse of road that was Venice, and yet there was no mistaking his presence. The tallest building that stood along either side of Venice was about 20 stories -- and the monster dwarfed that. Even at this distance, she could make out the long, dark, matted hair that covered most of his body. It obscured almost all his features aside from his feet and hands. Betty couldn't make out anything resembling a face -- but she could swear the thing was staring right at her. At the cab.

She glanced at the cab driver, who was clearly considering the same thing. The beast continued to rumble toward them, the distance growing shorter by the second. Then, the driver's attention briefly turned to the other monster -- the one who sat in the back seat. The man in the suit was reloading his weapon. He hadn't looked forward.

The driver -- Martin Plume of TnT Cab Company, the license said -- turned to her. She'd never met this guy. And yet, they were about to have the most important conversation of their lives. And they would do it without saying a word.

Marty gestured with his head toward the car door.

It took Betty a half second to realize what he was proposing. Her eyes grew wide as it sunk in. She shook her head, slightly.

Marty's eyes insisted. He gestured again to the door with a quick snap of his head.

Betty thought. She looked at him again. She'd been right, his eyes were kind. She nodded, slightly.

Marty nodded, more forcefully. He looked in the rear view mirror again, checking the man in the suit's gaze. He was still focused on the cop. Marty slowly began to unfasten his safety belt. Betty hadn't even thought to put hers on. She put her hand on her door handle.

Left hand still on the wheel, Marty put his right hand on the seat in between them. His index finger was extended, beginning a silent countdown. *One.*

*Oh God oh God oh God, what am I doing? I can't do this. I'll kill myself if I do this. Oh God, no.*

The second finger extended. *Two.*

*He'd kill us both anyway. We have to do this. Okay. Jump, tuck, roll. Jump, tuck roll. Jump tuck roll. Jumptuckroll...*

The third finger shot out from the fist. *Three!*

Betty and Marty threw open their doors. Betty was first to jump. She clumped to the pavement with a thud, back first, and rolled away from the car toward the sidewalk.

Marty jumped second only because he remembered to do one last thing before he left the car. He flipped a switch underneath the dashboard, just below his license photo.

THE MAN in the suit didn't notice he had lost his hostages -- future victims -- until he saw Betty rolling along the pavement to the left of his peripheral vision. He turned to see Marty that had joined her, then he yelled in disgust and frustration. Now the lone passenger of a driverless vehicle, the man in the suit went to open one of the rear doors only to find it locked tight. He made a mad scramble for the back window.

The cab, with no foot on the pedal, had been slowly decelerating ever since Marty had dove from inside. But it still was moving fast enough. It crashed, and the man in the suit was jolted forward, head first into the cage in front of him.

His vision blurry from the impact, the man was shaken but unbowed. After taking a second to hold his head while wincing in pain, the man grabbed the bag from the floor and slung it over his shoulder. He was determined to get out of this car. He had a promise to keep.

*If you decide to flee, Marty, I will pay a visit to you very soon and put a bullet in your head.*

Marty had fled. Very soon was now.

Then came the roar. It was impossible to hear any other sound. The roar echoed down Venice with the impact of a thousand train crashes all at once. Three buildings on either side of him had windows shatter. Despite the man's efforts to cover his ears, the noise deafened him.

The man in the suit finally turned to look out the front window, to see what he had hit.

It was a foot. A foot the size of a milk truck.

For the first and last time in his life, the man in the suit screamed in fear.

He made a final scramble for the rear window of the car. Too late. Johnson reached down and, like a man swatting away a bothersome ant, tossed the cab aside. It crashed, roof first, through the first floor of an office building.

MARTY WAS PRETTY SURE his ankle was broken. He'd felt the explosion of pain out of his left leg as soon as he hit the pavement, and now that he had finally come to a rest by the side of the road, he lay in agony, afraid to look. When he finally did and saw that his foot was facing the right direction, he was shocked. He expected it to be the wrong way around, or missing. That he seemed to have no other major injuries from his meeting with 40 mph concrete was little solace.

The woman from the bank ran up to him. *She can still run? Oh* that's *really fair*. She had a few abrasions on her arms and face, but seemed none the worse for wear. She kneeled down next to him. "Mister! Mister! Are you okay?"

"My ankle's busted up," he said. "Dunno if I broke it or what."

"We'll look at it later," she said quickly. "We gotta go. Here."

The woman got under his arm and pulled him up with all the force she had. She walked alongside him as a human crutch as they hobbled up the road.

"Where's the guy?" Marty croaked out.

"Still in your cab," Betty explained. "Last I saw the cab, it was in the lobby of the Stanton building."

"Gotcha."

"Hold it right there!" a new voice said.

*Aw, dammit to hell, what* now?

It was the cop. He'd stopped his car a ways up the street about the time he saw Marty and Betty pull their little Hollywood stunt show, and was now racing up to them on foot. He turned to Betty first.

"Ma'am? You alright?"

"Betty," she replied. "I'm fine. This guy here, though..."

The cop turned to Marty. "What the hell were you doing, driving that maniac around?"

"He told me I had to or he'd kill me," Marty tried to explain through his teeth, clenched in pain and a rising rage.

"I saw you waiting for him! Were you two in cahoots?"

"Are you *kidding* me, bud? I had no choice!"

"You coulda just drove away!"

"No, I couldn't."

The woman -- Betty, she'd said her name was -- reached out and slapped the cop across the face. Both he and Marty were stunned into silence. "Can we *please* do this when the giant monster isn't coming up the street?!" she yelled.

Johnson was now about 100 yards behind them. They saw her point.

The cop -- Schwartz, Marty read on his badge as he ran to his side -- got under Marty's other arm. The three walked as fast as three people with one gimp leg could, away from the beast. Their path at first seemed to be toward the cop's car, still parked on the side of the road. But it was too late. At the rate Johnson was moving, they never would make it there in time.

Suddenly, Schwartz changed direction. "This way! This way!" He directed the three of them onto the sidewalk and quickly into a side alley next to an old, abandoned building. Schwartz led them down a set of four steps. They were now in front of a large, padlocked door. Schwartz came out from under Marty's arm and withdrew his billy club. Two quick downward swipes on the lock and it fell free.

Schwartz opened the door and got back under Marty's arm. "Come on! Coffin! Get inside!"

Before anyone could argue, they piled through the door. Schwartz slammed it shut behind them.

AFTER JOHNSON'S first rampage through the city, signs of the eventual mass exodus from LA began to appear. Several big ticket homes began to pop up on the market. Higher priced apartments throughout the city began to see more vacancies. Realtors and landlords saw the warning lights well before anyone else did.

In an effort to survive, building owners struck out for a new idea, something that would appeal to both the luxury and safety instincts of their prized clients. The answer: Steel reinforced concrete lining the basements of their structures, built to withstand almost any force imaginable. Inside, the space would be turned into luxurious living quarters, transforming it into a penthouse bunker. LA's richest and most powerful could now live in the highest class environs, secure in the knowledge that even if the very building above them collapsed, they would remain safe in their apartment down below.

The gambit worked, for a while. A few high profile names took up residence in the lower-floor-luxury-homes, which were formally branded as "Monster Proof Living Spaces." Then, not long after he took up residence, a powerful studio exec named R. Jackson Lubbey became trapped in his new home, not because of Johnson, but a 6.5 earthquake which rocked southern California. The building above him crumbled on top of his apartment. Remarkably, the Living Space's structure held, and Lubbey was indeed safe and sound. Unfortunately, Lubbey had yet to stock his apartment with more than one day of groceries. By the time rescue workers reached him, he had been dead for a week.

Landlords who had spent thousands on the idea of Monster Proof Living Spaces tried to spin the tragedy as a positive sign, noting that the apartment had survived, even though its occupant hadn't. But the damage was done. The high rollers of Tinseltown wouldn't set foot in one of the Spaces now, and in a turn of morbid humor, they soon became known as "Lubbey's Coffins." Within a few years, Lubbey's name had disappeared, and the empty and padlocked structures sitting at the bottom of many buildings were simply dubbed "coffins."

The coffin Schwartz had steered the three into had only the barest amenities left inside. A table covered with a white cloth sat inside the door, which they quickly took advantage of by hiking Marty and his bad ankle up onto it. Betty took off Marty's shoe and sock to take a look.

"I don't think it's broken," she said. "Looks like a severe sprain. Probably hurts like hell."

"Amazing diagnosis," Marty replied sarcastically.

"Need to get something to give you some support. Officer? Can you look in the bathroom and see if some first aid supplies were left here?"

Schwartz took a quick look and returned. "There isn't even a toilet left in there."

Betty frowned. "We'll have to improvise." She picked up the corner of the sheet covering the table Marty was on and tore off a long strip of fabric. She began wrapping the makeshift bandage around Marty's foot. "This'll do until we get you to a hospital."

"What were you, a Girl Scout?" Schwartz asked.

"Eh, you have a younger brother, you learn a thing or two about ankle injuries," Betty said.

As she wrapped Marty's leg, Schwartz stood by the wall and put his ear to it. Coffins came equipped with windows, three inch thick ones toward the ceiling designed to let light in, but they were essentially useless for seeing what was going on outside. Instead, Schwartz tried to listen for details. He could hear the "thump" of Johnson's footsteps, but they sounded vague and distant. He wasn't sure if that was because the monster really had left the area, or if the walls of the coffin just muffled sound effectively.

"I think he's walking away from here," Schwartz said finally, with a little more volume. "I think we're safe for now."

Marty, pain in his voice, half chuckled. "If you think you're ever safe in this town, you haven't lived here long."

Schwartz turned to him, annoyed. "Only all my life, bud."

"Oh, a townie!" Marty responded. "I was wrong! That's a totally different kind of madness."

"Hey, leave the guy alone. He did kinda save our lives, here," Betty said as she prepared to tie a knot into Marty's makeshift bandage.

Marty snorted. "Well, what about you? Betty, right? You said your name was Betty? How long you been here?" Marty asked.

Betty looked up. "About ten years. Moved out in '45, right after the war."

"I'm gonna guess your line is you wanted to be an actress," Marty said.

Betty put on a sad smile. "You'd be right," she said. "Of course, right after I get here, Tinseltown bolts. Leaves me behind, no money, no career."

"So why didn't you just go home?" Marty asked.

Betty thought about her dad, who always laughed about her dreams of Hollywood, about how she'd never make it, about how she was wasting her life even to try. She thought of how damn smug she imagined he'd be, the day she finally set foot back home. And she thought of how she'd rather die than put herself through that. "Long story," she said.

She looked over at Schwartz, still standing next to the wall. "What about you, Officer?"

"Schwartz," he responded. "John. My name's John."

"Okay, John. What about you? Why didn't you leave when the big guy showed up?"

Schwartz turned toward them. "This is home," he said as though it was the most obvious thing in the world. "You don't abandon your home."

Marty laughed. "Yeah, but what if home abandons you?"

"What's that supposed to mean?"

Marty rolled his eyes. "Oh, come on. This isn't LA anymore. This is the beast's town. The city got yanked out from under everyone. Why stay loyal to that?"

"It's not that thing's city, it's mine," Schwartz responded. "It's mine, it's yours, it's everybody's. I love this city. I'm not letting some mountain of fur take it from me."

"Too little, too late," Marty said, voice rising. "The war for LA is over, Johnny. It won! Why not cut your losses, grab the wife and kids and head on?"

Schwartz turned away and stood against the wall.

Marty stopped. Betty got up from the table. One step toward him. Two. "They left, didn't they?" she said.

Schwartz didn't turn. Silence was his answer for a few seconds. "Alice said LA was no place for children. I said this city was my life. She said I was choosing LA over them. I didn't mean that. She could be that way sometimes. She was gone the next day. Took our son."

Betty moved forward, but Schwartz waved her away. Marty shifted slightly on the table. "Have you talked to her since?" he asked.

Schwartz turned. "I've had a couple of calls. They're in Reno. Begged her to come back."

"But not for you to go to her," Marty responded.

"Why should I?"

"Because *that's* home, buddy. Not this shell that used to be Los Angeles. If you're waiting for her to cave so you can win, too late. You lost. She left. The best you can do is to admit it."

"That's enough!" Betty said, walking back to the table and shoving

Marty lightly. "Seriously, leave him alone. I see *you* didn't go anywhere, either."

"Yeah, you horse's ass," Schwartz said. "You're so high and mighty about us. You're still here, too. Why the hell are you in LA, then?"

Marty paused for a second. Two.

No.

He wasn't telling these people about his pain. It was his pain, his alone.

He wasn't telling them about his wife. About what it's like to watch the person you love more than your own life waste away to nothing in just a few months.

He wasn't telling them about the nights spent alone, with only a bottle of whiskey and a gun for company. He wasn't telling them about what it feels like to not know if you want to live anymore.

He wasn't telling them about moving to LA three years ago, after she died, about growing tired of seeing everything in his life that reminded him of her. About family and friends whose love meant nothing anymore.

He wasn't saying the truth. He wasn't saying that he was living in LA because he didn't have the balls to kill himself. He wanted the city to do it for him.

At least, he thought he did.

Then, about an hour ago, a madman aimed a gun at his head. And for the first time in five years, he had been afraid.

He had been afraid of dying.

He didn't know what had changed. He didn't know if the change was for good. But right now, all he knew was, he wanted to stay alive. For himself. For her.

"None of your damn business," Marty finally said in summation.

"Fine. So you're trapped here like the rest of us," Betty said.

"Nobody's trapped," Schwartz said. "You can always leave."

"Says the obsessed townie," Marty responded.

Schwartz turned. "I'm here because I want to be. I'm not trapped. Neither are you. There's always a way out, if you want it. You just have to take it."

Marty looked at him. "Sometimes you say the thing you most need to hear, you know."

Schwartz put his ear to the wall again. He turned back. "Okay, I'm pretty sure Johnson is gone. Listen. I'm gonna run out to my car, get on the radio. See if I can raise anybody, find out where the military support is on all this. If I can, I'll call for an ambulance. If not, I'll come back, we'll head to my car and get you to a hospital. Okay?"

Marty nodded. "Be careful," Betty said.

Schwartz walked to the door and slipped out.

Betty leaned on the table next to Marty. "Why were you so hard on him?" she asked.

*Like I said*, Marty thought. *Sometimes you say what you need to hear.*

SCHWARTZ WALKED SLOWLY up the steps outside the coffin's door. He crept up to the corner of the building, peeking his head around for a look. The street, which had been sparsely populated even before Johnson's arrival, was barren now. He took this as a good sign. He saw no one, but he saw no bodies, either.

He glanced up the road a way. His car sat exactly where he'd left it, thank God. In his haste to tend to the woman and cabbie, he hadn't remembered to take the keys. Anyone running past could have easily stolen it -- and frankly, given the circumstances, he wouldn't have blamed them if they had.

He looked to either side for any signs of trouble. None. He ran across the street into the open door of the police car. He grabbed at the radio.

"This is Officer John Schwartz, car 217, anyone copy me?" Static. "This is car 217, anyone copy?" No luck. A cloud passed overhead, casting a shadow across the car. "This is car 217, someone please..."

Wait.

He glanced up. Not a cloud in the sky.

"CAN I, I don't know, get you something?" Betty asked.

Marty glanced around the mostly empty coffin and had to smile. "Like what?" he said.

She realized the absurdity of her question and chuckled. "Like, something to drink?"

Marty shook his head. "Listen, I appreciate the concern and the desire to help, I do. But I don't think there's anything left here. Even if I wanted water, I'm sure the pipes aren't on."

"Hey, worth a try," Betty responded with a grin. She got up to head toward the bathroom. She turned slightly before she got there. "By the way, I haven't thanked you. You know, for saving my life."

"I didn't. I told you to jump from a moving car. And it was a very, very stupid idea anyway. I don't think anyone should be thanking someone for that idiocy," Marty responded.

Betty's smile didn't fade. "I do. So, thank you." She walked in the bathroom. A quick check of the faucet confirmed Marty's diagnosis. She began to walk out. "Well, you're right, there's no..."

She looked up.

The gun, a revolver, was pointed at Marty's head.

The man in the suit, standing just inside the doorway, pulled the trigger.

SCHWARTZ HAD BEEN RIGHT. The walls of the coffin worked wonderfully well at softening any sound coming from outside -- it was a feature the makers of the Monster Proof Living Spaces had highly touted in their literature. "Johnson could be tromping right outside your door," the brochure had boasted, "And it wouldn't even disturb your family dinner or an intimate evening at home."

So when Schwartz was sure, so sure, that Johnson had retreated a few blocks or even miles away, he had just wandered around the corner onto McLaughlin. As Schwartz had made the dash for his car, the monster had caught the scent of raw meat from a nearby butcher's shop, and was in the process of kneeling down to devour it. Not just the meat. The whole shop.

The sound of Schwartz calling frantically on his radio had brought the towering behemoth out of his crouch to investigate. As he clumped around the corner, Schwartz fell silent and still. Though the responsibility of containing Johnson fell to the military -- *Where the hell were they?* Schwartz thought -- all LAPD officers had been given rudimentary training exercises in dealing with the beast. Number one, guns were useless. Well, maybe they coulda guessed that. Number two, Johnson has unusually sensitive hearing. Do not make any sudden noises or they will draw the monster's attention.

Schwartz slumped in his seat and slowly, carefully, turned off his radio. Out of the corner of his eye, he glanced to his left, out the open door of his car -- just in time to see a giant hand clump down along side of him. It was followed closely by a massive mound of fur that crept close to the ground. Then turned.

Johnson's face was so obscured by the matted hair which covered almost his entire body that no one, not even the handlers who dealt with him every day, knew for certain what it looked like. But for the briefest of moments, Schwartz was sure he saw the beast's eyes underneath.

Schwartz didn't move as Johnson stared at him. Didn't breathe. If he could have willed his heart to stop beating, he would have.

He could hear Johnson's breathing, though, slight grunts coming through with every exhale as he looked into the car. Their face-to-face, such as it was, lasted just a few seconds, but to Schwartz felt like years.

Then, a noise caught the monster's attention. It came through the open door of the coffin Betty and Marty were still in.

A gunshot.

AT THE MOMENT, the man in the suit's aim was terrible. Understandable, given that he had just survived a wreck where the car he was in had been tossed aside like a rag doll. After he had crawled from the wreckage through the cab's open back window, the bag of cash still slung across his back, he had staggered up the street in the same direction Johnson was moving. Common sense would have told anyone to go the opposite way, but for all the man's strengths, common sense was not one of them. Especially when he had a promise to keep.

Seeing the cop exit from an alley along the side of the road, the man in the suit smiled. They had to be there. *He* had to be there. Getting away was not the goal. Marty Plume was.

He had descended the staircase leading to the coffin as silently as he could, and opening the door found -- no. It can't be this easy. Marty was lying on a table, apparently injured, *with his back to the door*. Yes, Virginia, there is a Santa Claus.

But when Betty entered the room, her presence was distraction enough to throw off the man's aim from his position just inside the door. The bullet he fired merely grazed Marty's ear.

Marty, stunned, rolled off the table to the floor, followed by a cry of pain as his ankle, thudding on the floor, screamed in protest. The man in the suit lurched to his right, trying to clear the table and line up a better shot. Betty ran from the bathroom door toward the man, attempting to tackle him to the ground. The man growled in anger at the interference, but in his weakened state he toppled to his hands and knees. The gun fell from his hand and skidded across the floor.

Enraged, the man in the suit threw a wild slap at Betty's face, knocking her to her back. Still on his knees, he began to crawl toward Marty who was writhing on the ground in pain.

His progress was impeded by a now-too-familiar roar from outside. Even with the sound-proof qualities of the coffin's walls, the noise was overpowering. The floor violently shuddered beneath them, followed by the sound of debris raining down outside the open door.

Johnson was attacking the building.

THE MONSTER HAD HEARD that sound, the sharp crack of a gunshot, plenty of times during the attack on Japan. Even though bullets could not harm him, his handlers were pleased that he had apparently learned that anyone who made that sound was an attacker, and was to be destroyed. Hearing the sound coming from inside the coffin, Johnson reverted to instinct.

The mammoth beast stood, turned to the building beside it and brought his fist down on its roof. The top three floors cratered in, pieces of the walls falling to the ground. The rest of the structure remained intact, barely. Schwartz could guess that one more blow would bring the whole thing down. Hell, it was almost certainly coming down anyway.

*Coffins*, Schwartz thought, still inside his car. *There's a reason they call them coffins. And I led them right into one.*

Well, there was only one thing to do, wasn't there?

As Johnson raised his right arm for one more strike at the building, Schwartz reached for his dashboard and flipped a switch. The car's siren blared to life.

THE MAN in the suit was little more than a bundle of instinct now. Even with the bone-rattling commotion going on in the building above, all he could see was Marty, writhing in pain on the ground. The man got unsteadily to his feet and staggered toward him. Marty didn't even notice his presence until the man was on top of him. He kneeled over Marty's prone form and wrapped one hand around his throat. The other covered his mouth and nose.

Marty scrambled to find some way free, his hands grasping for eyes, ears, *anything* that could find purchase. But the man in the suit would not allow it. Marty thought he could feel his windpipe constricting. Jesus, this guy was strong. The man in the suit leaned over as he continued to steal Marty's oxygen. He stared Marty right in the eyes. *He wants to watch it happen. He wants to see me die. He wants me to know that he wants to watch.* Marty's last thoughts would be nothing but horror and helplessness. And the knowledge that -- yes -- he wanted to live.

"Let him go!"

The man in the suit looked up but did not release his grip.

The gun, a revolver, was pointed at his head.

Betty was in point blank range.

The man in the suit smiled. "Honey, you don't have it in..."

*BANG.*

JOHNSON'S second attack on the old building was halted by the sound streaming from Schwartz's car. The monster turned as the engine roared to life. Schwartz pulled his service revolver and fired twice toward the beast. *It'll do no good except to draw attention. Which is all I need.* The monster roared with anger at the sound and brought his fist down toward the car, which lurched forward just in time to avoid the impact.

Schwartz hit the accelerator as hard as he could and roared away from the scene, leading his prey on his second high speed pursuit of the hour. *It's different when you're the one being chased*, he thought as he scanned the rear view mirror.

Johnson let out a roar and began his pursuit of the car. Schwartz allowed himself one moment to glance back at the building.

It was beginning to collapse.

TO A DEGREE, the man in the suit had been correct. Betty didn't have it in her to shoot him in the head. But she certainly had it in her to shoot him somewhere else, somewhere less lethal but certainly vital -- a knee, perhaps. A knee such as the one closest to her. A quick readjustment of her aim was enough, right as the man had taunted her.

The man in the suit cried in pain and grabbed at what remained of his kneecap, releasing his grip from Marty. The cab driver took in as much air with one breath as possible, then coughed as if he was hacking up a lung. As the man in the suit writhed on the ground, Betty ran to Marty. Before she could even ask the obligatory question about if he was alright, the noise above them began to intensify.

The building wasn't going to last long.

*Coffins. There's a reason they...*

"Come on! Get up!" Betty screamed as she pulled Marty's left arm around her neck. The two stood and began to stagger toward the open door, toward daylight.

The man in the suit cried out in pain and rage behind them, a pool of his own blood beginning to coalesce underneath him. He began a pathetic crawl toward the door, in an attempt either at escape or pursuit.

Betty dragged Marty up the stairs outside the door. They ran out of the alley and up the street as fast as they could. As they turned the corner, she could see the monster running up Venice ahead of them, his footfalls trembling the earth with every step. After a few seconds, she could just barely make out the shape it was pursuing -- a cop car, siren and lights blaring -- as it made a hard turn onto Inglewood.

She began to cry out John's name when the building finally gave way behind them.

Betty and Marty dropped to the ground. Dust and debris filled the air as they covered their heads against the onslaught.

When the noise had finally subsided, the two slowly stirred to life. They were covered in a loose layer of filth and stones, but alive.

Marty glanced back to where the building had been. The vaguest shape of the rubble was visible through the cloud of dust surrounding them, a mountain of ruin covering the shelter below. *Coffins*, he thought.

Betty looked up toward where she had last seen Schwartz evading Johnson. She thought she could still hear his siren blaring in the distance.

If he was on an open road, Schwartz might have had a chance to outrun the monster chasing him. The police car cruised at a steady 65 on the highway, and despite his long strides, stamina was probably not Johnson's strong suit. But they were on city streets, and in between keeping an eye on the road for obstacles and the small possibility of remaining pedestrians, Schwartz was barely staying ahead of the beast.

It was impossible to tell how close the creature was, Schwartz noted with frustration. Every time he looked in his rear view, all he saw was a blur of fur and movement, and the monster's sheer size made it useless to judge distance. Rapid thoughts ran through his head of what he was doing, how he would lose the beast, what the goal was of this chase now that the monster was away from the building, hoping Betty and Marty made it out, wondering what that gunshot was, whether he would live to know the answers.

Then, in the distance, Schwartz saw his savior. Approaching from the horizon he could make out the faint outline of an airplane, a black silhouette against the clear April sky. No, not black, silver. Air Force. About damn time. The military was coming to take the bastard down.

Schwartz would lead Johnson right to them. The plane was approaching straight up Inglewood. All he had to do was stay away from the monster for a few seconds more, they would begin their attack, and he could just keep on driving. Dear God, there was a way out.

He jammed his foot on the gas even harder, as if he could get the pistons to exceed their operational limit by sheer force of will. His 1950 Ford may have had a few years on her, but she could go when necessary. Damn, was this necessary. He was seeing all things at once as he scanned the road ahead for any slight obstacle, praying that a pedestrian didn't suddenly jump in his way.

He glanced for the briefest of seconds in his rear view. He saw no monster.

Oh, God. Did he leave the street? Change course? Was he going back to where Betty and Marty were? Did he lose him?

These thoughts came within a half a second as Schwartz's mind raced. They were answered with an Earth-shattering crash in front of him.

Johnson hadn't given up the chase. He'd won it. The monster, in a feat of physical dexterity that his handlers would debate for years, had leaped over Schwartz's speeding car and landed in front of him. Many would argue that this couldn't have happened, that the very idea of a nearly 300-foot gargantuan making such a leap broke more than a few laws of physics. The generally accepted response would be that the very existence of the monster called Johnson broke enough laws as it was. Why fuss over a few more?

The creature's landing shattered the concrete beneath it, creating a crater in the ground nearly 40 feet in diameter. Schwartz suddenly jammed his foot on his brakes, trying to avoid the sudden hazardous drop which appeared in front of him. The screeching tires cried for mercy as the distance closed to the edge of the crater. 20 feet...ten...five...one....too late. His front tires fell just over the edge. Schwartz tried in vain to put the car into reverse, but it wasn't going anywhere. At least, it wasn't until Johnson kneeled down and picked it up.

In one hand, the giant creature held Schwartz's car to its face, or where it was presumed his face was. Schwartz could hear the creature's angry grunts as it examined this troublesome pest. Finally, a roar came which cracked every window in the old Ford. Schwartz covered his ears in pain as his head rattled from the sound. Johnson's hand began to crush the car in his grasp, Schwartz curling up in his seat as the monster's titanic fingers closed the space in around him.

Then, suddenly, the beast stopped. Johnson turned up the road. His apparent gaze fell upon the plane which was now, at best, a mile away. It appeared Schwartz's distraction had done its job after all. Even with hearing as acute as Johnson's, he hadn't even noticed the coming assault until it was almost right on top of him.

The fighters had Johnson's full attention now. He roared in anger and released Schwartz's car from his grasp. Schwartz braced for what he was sure would be a fatal fall, but was surprised to crash to the ground from a height of only a couple dozen feet to the street below. It was jarring and hurt like hell, but he was alive. Alive. For now.

Run, dammit.

Schwartz tried to open his door, but there was no budge. The sides were crushed in from the effect of the monster's grip. He leaned back and kicked out the driver's window. As he climbed out onto the barren street, he looked toward the beast as it stood, roaring its challenge to the approaching plane. Schwartz almost felt sorry for the creature as it prepared to face its doom.

Schwartz staggered around the corner of an alleyway for cover. The planes were almost on top of the monster now. Schwartz crouched down and covered his head, braced for impact.

There was none. No gunfire, no bombs dropping, no noises of attack at all. In spite of himself, Schwartz peeked his head around the corner.

Mist. A dense mist was trailing from behind the military plane like a crop duster as it flew overhead. Another plane, close behind, dropped a similar payload. Johnson roared with disapproval as the fog descended toward him. He lurched toward a nearby building and rammed his fist through its upper floors as he yowled in distress.

They weren't destroying the monster, Schwartz finally realized. What an idiot he was for even thinking otherwise. The creature was far too valuable for that. They were just knocking him out so they could once again capture him.

It was in the seconds following this revelation that Schwartz had another. His lungs were burning. As was his face. As was his skin. He looked down at his hands and saw them blistering with horrific speed.

He could feel himself boiling alive.

For the past six years, the military had worked on what would be the most fast-paced, fool-proof method of containment if (when) Johnson would ever escape again. After many, many hours of testing on the beast during its confinement, a special brand of mustard gas was found to be perfect for neutralizing its nervous system for the necessary time frame to return it safely to storage. It was also dense enough that it fell precisely on target. The affected area would be limited to a three block radius of the initial drop zone.

The pinpoint accuracy of the gas helped soothe bureaucratic nerves about its one drawback, the particular concentration needed was extraordinarily lethal toward any living organism which was outdoors and unprotected within that three block radius. Considering how sparsely occupied the city was nowadays, such loss of life was deemed more than an acceptable amount of collateral damage.

Schwartz gasped for air that wasn't there. He tried to crawl up the street, away from the chemical assault. He made it about ten feet through sheer force of will before he collapsed. He rolled over and lay on the streets of his city. He looked up, could swear he could see the sun through the cloud of poison that was stealing his life.

His last thoughts were three words.

*Alice.*

*Ben.*

*Home.*

In the days following Johnson's third escape from custody, the official reports that came out painted a confident and heroic picture of the official response to the event. After all, the monster was recaptured in less than a half hour by officials, and when compared to previous attacks the amount of property damage was small. Any loss of human life was tragic, of course, but in balance the fact that only six people perished in Johnson's latest attack was held up as a shining example of the ability of the military to contain the issue as soon as possible.

These reports were both understated and exaggerated in almost every possible way. Whatever was claimed to the public, the seventeen minute time span that Johnson was loose was considered worryingly long, in most every official memo dealing with the event. Military response to his escape was trained to be on site within five minutes, maximum. It was determined that key communication wires had been severed during his escape, meaning the call for an air strike came several minutes later than expected. "Research into more reliable forms of long distance communication must begin if any further incidents are to be handled more carefully," an internal report read.

As far as the number of casualties, that too was a blatant lie, though in another direction. Despite the thousands of dollars of damage done to buildings, city streets, miscellaneous telephone wires and street lights during his escape, Johnson's rampage had not killed anyone directly.

Al Busam, a security guard at a downtown bank, died of a gunshot wound when medics, busy scrambling due to the monster's breakout, did not reach the older gentleman until it was too late. Months after the attack, workers cleaning the rubble of an abandoned building were stunned to discover a body in the coffin at its base, a man wearing a suit who was too badly decomposed to make any form of ID. The bag he was carrying went unreported by the men who found him.

And four people on the street died in the cloud of gas dropped by the military in the final assault, all deaths later ascribed to Johnson to maintain plausible deniability on the effects of the poison. One of them, a police officer named John Schwartz, was so badly mangled that he could only be identified via his badge.

Schwartz's funeral a week later was attended mostly by his fellow officers. Only a few people in civilian clothes were there. His rabbi delivered a lovely eulogy. A stoic woman in black and a young toddler received the flag which draped his coffin.

Betty was the first to cry.

Later that night, she and Marty sat in a cafe not far from the cemetery. As they ate, Betty spoke. Spoke of life, of death, of hope, of fear, of everything. He remained silent for a long time. Then...

Then.

"Her name was Suzanne," Marty began.

~

MARTY WAS STILL on crutches when he entered the TnT Cab Company a few days later. Tom looked up.

"Marty, what the hell you doin' here? I told you to take a month, for God's sake."

"I need a cab," Marty said simply.

"Plume," the dispatcher said with genuine concern in his voice. "Go home. Rest up. You went through hell and I don't want..."

Marty rapped his crutch against Tom's desk. "I need a cab."

Tom sighed. He brought out a key and an envelope. "7785," he said, resigned.

"Thanks," Marty said as he shoved the key in his pocket and went back out the door. It wasn't until Marty was already out of the garage that Tom noticed he hadn't taken the envelope.

A few minutes later, Marty pulled up in front of an old apartment building on Dauphin and honked his horn twice. A young woman, early 30s with long brown hair, ran to the cab.

"That all you're taking?" Marty asked.

Betty nodded, holding up one small bag. "All I need."

They had no destination in mind. "East" was as far as their plans got. They might not even be going to the same place, they agreed. They weren't “together,” after all, they were just...together. For this. Marty could supply the wheels. The rest they trusted to what felt right as they went.

Maybe Marty would end up back home in Chicago. It felt like it'd be good to see friends again, now. Betty thought Chicago sounded like a wonderful option for a young actress, but some place might strike her fancy between now and then.

All that really mattered was finding something else, somewhere else. If L.A. wasn't their city, they'd find one that was.

*There's always a way out, if you want it. You just have to take it.*

Hell, yes.

Hell, yes, there was.

## 4

# AND A CHILD SHALL LEAD THEM

NANCY HANSEN

*As more countries gained their own monsters, the remainder of the 1950s saw skirmishes increase between creatures controlled by several South American nations. In 1958, one such spot of troubles escalated into a full-blown war, a destructive conflict the rest of the world observed with a heavy heart, setting a cautionary tone for the coming decade.*

*The 1960s arrived, and as skirts grew smaller, pop music louder, and young men and women's minds freer, the world's monster population continued to grow, unabated by the dangers it presented to humanity.*

EVERY DAY, Rahul the tea vendor squatted on the concrete edge of his booth, stirring the steaming pot and singing out his inventory as people hustled by. Most ignored him. The sweat of the midday sun, combined with the moist heat coming off the big kettle of water, made his cotton shirt and trousers stick to him. He would have loved an indoor booth in the nearby market building, but the rent cost too many rupees, and business had been far too slow lately.

He watched through envious, half-lidded dark eyes as Sudhir Rishi threaded his way through the bazaar. The Swami was back in Jaffna again! The frail, elderly man leaned heavily on his walking stick these days, but his deep bronze face shone with merriment, and he still had a spritely manner. He greeted everyone with a big, friendly, gap-toothed smile that split his curling white beard. His manner was modest and austere. Other than several long strings of wooden beads, he wore little ornamentation, though his pouch jingled with the sound of coins.

Rahul glared as the barefoot man was mobbed with people begging for his attention. The Swami always did well on market days, eating and drinking for free while graciously accepting his followers' generous gifts. All of it went to support the poor. For many decades the elderly sage had been ministering to the villagers, offering advice and medical attention via the laying on of hands and prayers. He was a beloved part of their lives, and never did anyone speak a harsh word against him.

"Now, my children. Gather round. One at a time please," the jolly gentleman said as he sat down stiffly. He pulled forth a brilliant, green carved gemstone on a thong of woven fibers and touched several people with it, offering a blessing chant. Rumor had it this was a Cintamani, a powerful artifact from antiquity that gave the old man the ability to heal minds and bodies. He would always take the most pressing cases first, for the gem had limits that were tied to his own physical well being. He was very old and there were many poor and sickly in their rundown part of the city. He seemed very tired afterward, and found a secluded spot in a hollow beneath a palm.

Rahul's mind whirled with envious greed. A cousin who had immigrated to America had written that gurus both true and false were wildly popular amongst the dispossessed youth and trendy wealthy there. One such as Sudhir Rishi would do very well for himself, but the old man seemed tied to the island of his birth. Rahul coveted a chance to go where everyone was a millionaire. While he doubted that was true, his cousin claimed she—just a woman—was happy and enjoyed many freedoms! What could a man, with a head for commerce and such a prized possession as a Cintamani, accomplish in that wealthy land where the people did not know a true teacher from a counterfeit?

It was growing dark and the old man had not moved. Rahul kept an eye on him as he closed up his stall, the crowds having moved on to their homes. Most of the outdoor bazaar was vacated. Curtains were drawn and shutters closed. The dampness began to soak in as he wandered over.

"O Wise One, you seem very weary, and the wind from the water has a chill this evening. Perhaps a cup of tea would warm you up?"

There was no answer. Rahul bent down, and put his hand underneath the old man's nostrils. No breath. Two fingers probed for a pulse, finding none, and the skin was ice cold. The elderly man had passed on!

The tea dealer looked around quickly, and then reached around the hoary head, removing the thong with the Cintamani gem attached. Holding it in his hands, Rahul began to tremble in anticipation. Such a thing should never have been left in the hands of a doddering old fool. It was worthy of a rajah's treasure hoard!

The translucent green and faintly glowing stone was carved in the shape of a snake with a woman's head, torso, and arms. It held power, for it faintly throbbed. Rahul wrapped it in a cloth and stuck it in the Swami's money pouch. Tying that securely to his belt, he stuffed it inside his trousers. He drew a dirty piece of canvas over the man before moving stealthily away. He would head back to his hovel of a room, gather what few things he needed, sell his supplies to the chemist in the city, and be on his way to a new life with the dawn tide.

The buzzing of flies pinpointed Sudhir Rishi the next morning. Though he looked as if he was simply asleep, he was dead. There was much mourning as they bore him off to prepare for his funeral. Three days later, a pyre was lit on the beach he had loved to roam, and many came to view him one last time. They brought offerings of flowers and chanted as flames licked up over him, before returning to their everyday lives.

No one knew what had happened to the Cintamani, for Sudhir Rishi had been found without it. Most assumed it disappeared upon his soul's passage to meet his ancestors.

DEEP BENEATH THE INDIAN OCEAN, something huge stirred within an enormous cavern. Immense inhuman orbs with a central pupil slit opened. The gargantuan body undulated this way and that, as if in an elaborate dance, stretching and swaying through various postures as life-force flowed within.

Something was wrong in the world above. There had been prayers and lamentations most heartfelt for a moon cycle, and that had awakened her. A piece of the sky jewel her people had entrusted to the ancestral human line of Enlightened Ones had left the land of its Chosen, which was strictly forbidden. Such treasure was not meant to be touched by unconsecrated hands. In the possession of an impure person, used for corrupt purposes, it could be sullied forever. It must be brought back, at any cost!

She surged out of the cavern and squeezed through the chasm above, forcing her huge serpentine body through the winding crevasse. Once free of the rocky constrictions, with wide sweeps of her arms and graceful curves of her massive tail, she rapidly ascended toward the surface.

As her head broke through the waves, the foaming water cascaded down over her shoulders and back. Tilting her face upwards, she opened her mouth and gave a long, echoing screech of defiant anger. As dawn spread overhead, she began making her way toward the island of the Blessed One.

Most of the local boats were out for the day when a gigantic figure surfaced in the bay. The few ships that were tied rocked in their moorings, scraping docks and pilings.

Cobra hood and tattooed shoulders above the water, the monster called out, "CINTAMANI!"

Her voice echoed throughout the area, so loud and distorted that few could understand what she said. Seabirds left their nests and animals scurried for cover. People fell down in the streets, holding their hands over their ears as temple bells rang on their own.

"It's a Nagini!" someone shouted. All came running toward the beach to see one of the godlike, benevolent creatures of myth emerging from the depths. While monsters were known around the world, and the Angrez beast known as Humgum had passed through long ago, none of the giant creatures had been connected to their island nation before.

Standing up on her massive tail coils, she towered over everyone. Swaying slightly, she glared down at the humans gathered below, their upturned faces showing eyes wide with awe and fear. She was taller than any of the city buildings, her skin a pale shade of blue above the heavy lower length of darkly patterned scales. She wore an ornamented breastplate of beaten gold, and long ropes of gems and bells adorned her ebony braid. They rattled and pealed as she sidled in closer, slithering up out of the water and onto the rocky beach spit that fronted the outskirt village. Her colossal head had an impassive, narrow, high cheek-boned woman's face, and her tongue was purple and forked like a snake.

"Where Wiseman?" The Naga's voice boomed in a lowered tone, spoken in the old Tamil language with a peculiar accent.

The woman who had tended to Sudhir Rishi bowed before the Naga. "He passed from this world a month ago. His pyre was over there." She pointed to a dark spot on the beach.

The Naga frowned, showing the tips of back curved fangs. She crossed her arms over her chest. "Bring Cintamani to me," she said with a snarl that sent every able bodied person scrambling backwards.

The woman was trembling. "He no longer had it! We don't know where it went."

"Lie to me, and I kill all!" the Naga warned with a hiss while waving them off. The people withdrew further as she leaned forward and a long fingered left hand shot out. Golden nails like knives arched over and around Sudhir Rishi's funeral pyre as the hand came down, the tips digging into the sand, creating sort of a cage. A slit in her palm opened to reveal a large protruding eye of brilliant aqua with a violet iris. An aura of radiant energy, coupled with a background hum, left the eye as it scanned back and forth over the ash darkened sand.

The Naga withdrew her arm and pulled herself upright. She turned toward the bay, her eyes glowing bright with amber fire and hands making loose fists at her side.

"Stolen. I go for Cintamani. Someone dies for this sacrilege!"

The Naga uncoiled her lower length and, turning around, sidled back into the water. Sinking beneath the waves, only a bubbling wake remained as she headed out to sea.

IT HAD NOT BEEN a pleasant journey. There were many cargo port stops, but Rahul had little coin to spare. He was seasick most of the time and so had not always been able to earn his way by helping on or below decks. The crew didn't speak his language or much in the way of the pidgin English he had learned from tourists, so they communicated mostly by signs. The food was not to his liking, but he ate what little he could, though with barely being able to keep it down, he grew even thinner and more ascetic looking by the day. He stopped shaving and let his hair and beard grow out. By the time they docked in East Boston Harbor, his wild eyes burned with excitement amidst a tangle of curling locks, and he very much looked the part of a mystic.

A few discrete inquiries led him to a quiet neighborhood with a small, but close-knit population of Indian expatriates centered on a modest temple. A wash and a donated change of clothing, some coaching about securing his immigrant status, a hot meal in a local home, and Rahul walked out into the street a new man.

He watched a group of disciples in orange robes chanting, "Hare Krishna, Hare Rama," and handing out leaflets to passersby. Rahul smiled, and fingered the gem on its string around his neck, tucked into the shirt he wore. America was going to be very good to him.

It took time, but he eventually inserted himself into the neighborhood as a visiting guru. They were a quiet community, much looked down upon by their American-born neighbors; so they kept to themselves, protecting one another. No one turned him in for not having papers, for he was far from the only illegal status person on the streets. There was little crime there, and no serious encounters with law enforcement, which was kept far too busy in the more volatile parts of the city to care much about a group of relatively peaceful immigrants.

He renamed himself Kanar Maneesh, using his father's and grandfather's given names. He smiled and bowed to all he met, and though his English language skills were rudimentary, he made himself understood. He politely asked where the unenlightened, disenfranchised American youth gathered.

"In the big park, of course," he was told time after time. Getting some directions, Rahul begged a ride from a couple that owned an old automobile. They drove him to Boston Common, where everything was happening these days.

"WHAT WAS THAT?" queried a fearful voice in a fishing boat that was slowly moving out through the Red Sea, well away from the potential war zone where Israel and Egypt were drawing lines in the Sinai sand. Something huge sped past them underwater, entering into the Suez Canal.

"I don't know. A lost whale? A Soviet spy submarine? Something we don't need to know about, no doubt," a strained voice replied as the small vessel heeled to port after being buffeted by a tremendous wake. The two-man crew had to concentrate on righting the boat before it swamped and capsized. By that time whatever massive presence had passed by was well on its way, heading west.

"WHY YOU NOT SLEEP IN park tonight? I teach you names of the stars," Rahul asked around a lung full of aromatic smoke. Ganja and hashish were known in his homeland, though he had never been able to afford either one. He found it quite pleasurable, mind opening, even; though he refused a second hit. He must keep his wits about him to protect his identity, so he exhaled and passed the pipe over to the blonde, bearded young man on his right in the faded bell bottom jeans and tie dyed shirt.

"The Man is going to come down on us hard if we stay, Guru," answered the dark haired girl with vacant brown eyes and a very short skirt that everyone called Blossom. "They send the heat here every day at sunset to clear us out, so we beat feet."

"Yeah, things have gotten pretty heavy. Last time we staged a sit-in, the pigs went ape with their sticks," the blonde bearded one they called Bear added. "My neck was, like, almost busted, you know? I mean, I had bruises for days. It was unreal!"

A chorus of voices joined in. Rahul shook his head in mock sympathy and raised both hands in symbolic peace gestures, waving them around so all would see. He had no use for protests; he preferred these youngsters focus on bringing him more converts bearing donations. The Common was a sea of potential followers and his flock was growing steadily, as were his coffers.

"We need to find somewhere safe from these police, Little Flower," he said, drawing a finger possessively across her bare arm. Sitting more upright, he continued in a louder voice, "Tonight I teach you how we become one in mind and heart, so we remain free. You bring friends, some food, maybe a little cash or some baubles you no longer need." There was a chorus of cheers and whistles, and fists pumping in the air, along with a few peace signs.

"It is good then. Brother Bear," he pointed at the bearded one, "Will find place for many to gather. I go prepare myself." He regained his feet and bowed with palms pressed together, and then meandered off through the throngs of young people who already respected him as a sage and healer. He smiled and nodded endlessly, accepting proffered flowers, strings of beads, spoon rings, painted rocks, and other small tokens of affection.

He would discard them later, in private, after anything of value was sorted out for pawning.

It was the easiest life Rahul had ever known. He had food, shelter, clothing, and all the turned on/tuned out young women he could entrance with promises of peace, love, and forever youthfulness. America truly was the land of opportunity!

He pulled out of his tunic a gold neck chain, now hung with the glowing green jewel, and kissed it before letting it slide back to lay against his chest.

Boston was an interesting city, a contrast of traditional staid New England values and the multicultural liberalism of the colleges. Rahul felt very much at home. No one ever questioned his background or lack of employment.

"Here is something for you both, my friends," the false Guru said as he passed by a couple of the local buskers on his way to his car. With a radiant smile he dropped a few coins first in a basket, and then a chipped blue enameled cup before he went on his way.

The finely woven pine needle basket belonged to a blind, elderly Ojibwa man everyone called Nimkee. He pulled it toward him and fished the coins out. The cup was snatched by a former street urchin from the slums of Bangalore. Ajeet reminded Rahul very much of himself as a lad. The boy played a gourd and reed pungi to an elaborately wired rope that was tied to his waist so that it danced like a snake, while the old man beat a skin covered hand drum and chanted in his native tongue. They had become close over the years they had been busking together.

The boy eyed Rahul with distaste. He called after him, "Why you got a Cintamani stone, eh? You are not enlightened!" Rahul smiled and pretended not to hear.

"Leave him alone," the old man grumbled.

"He is a fake, you know," the boy said to his companion as Nimkee tied the coins in a grubby leather sack. "He uses mind tricks and some pretty words, and now these Americans think he is a god. In my country we know it is unlucky to steal such a treasure. He will pay for it someday."

"Fine. For now, his money is still good," the old man said and spat on the ground.

"It's not really his money, Nimkee! He takes it from fools who are too stoned to understand. That's bad karma. He will come to a no good end," the boy insisted, lifting his instrument as people began to hustle past in the dusk.

"Everyone down here does," his partner said morosely, taking a sip from a flask in his pocket before lifting the drum again and starting another round.

SOMETHING MASSIVE MOVED VERY fast underwater through the crowded Mediterranean Sea, disrupting normal ocean traffic. Local navies hurried to clear civilian vessels from its path as they monitored its progress at a discrete distance. Suspicions were already running high, with tension in the Middle East, the war in Vietnam, and the Soviet government doing its share of saber rattling.

It breached briefly near the Rock of Gibraltar, scaring monkeys and tourists alike as a gigantic head and massive shoulders broke free of the water and bobbed around. Within moments, it dove again and passed out into the open Atlantic, and everyone gave a sigh of relief. Let America deal with this one; they had monsters and firepower enough in that vast and wealthy country.

The official decree, agreed upon in a series of high level conversations between geographical neighbors, was a pod of fin whales passing through. Few believed it, as there was no further evidence of the large cetaceans in the area, but life went back to normal.

~

"ENLIGHTENMENT WILL NOT COME EASY. Always confront oppression with a peaceful heart. Forgive your persecutors' imperfections. Give up all worldly illusions, and put these material goods that others so covet to a better purpose." Rahul gestured expansively around the candlelit room, his eyes flashing. "You will ascend in spirit and embrace your higher self. There you will understand all; and this flesh life will mean nothing. Greed is why people do so much hating and warmongering. By giving up your possessions, you defeat enemies from within." He tapped a temple. "With the power of your focused mind, you will always be in control."

He went on for a while longer, until there was a mesmerized look on everyone, even those who weren't stoned. There was a lot of chanting and rocking once he finished.

Rahul peered around the room, smiling beatifically. The majority in attendance were young people, either transients or college students. There were some older faces; radical professors or activists from the local neighborhoods. He was glad to see them all, because while the youths had the idealistic enthusiasm to give generously, the adults had far more money. The big basket before him was already filling up with coins, cash, jewelry, silverware, and other household goods as well as a couple of checks. It had been a prosperous night.

A few months had made a huge difference in his ability to charm his way into their hearts. He had learned to speak American English more clearly from watching television, and how to work a crowd by observing the various street preachers and buskers in his walks around town. Sunday mornings brought evangelical programs on both radio and TV. Rahul studied them carefully, picking up mannerisms as well as vocal tones.

Sometimes he dreamed about robbing the dead swami and woke in a sweat. It always passed; for the Cintamani had been a benefit in convincing his followers he had otherworldly powers. Rahul never expounded on its origin or virtues, letting people think it was all part of the mysterious holy man he pretended to be. He basked in the crowds' adulation and enjoyed the steadiest income ever. Eventually he would move on to a bigger city and start anew.

The smiling man known as Guru Kanar Maneesh sat cross-legged in silk robes atop a colorful needlepoint topped cushion, surrounded with vases of flowers and candles. The flickering light illuminated a large group of enraptured faces. Piles of fruit, slices of dense whole wheat bread, chunks of cheese, and bowls of tabouli were donations from his flock. The cloying scent of incense blending with marijuana permeated the converted storefront hung with tapestries that was now their ashram.

"Who needs my personal attention tonight?" Rahul asked, pulling forth the stone on the gold chain and kissing it in a mock blessing, as people lined up. Though he never openly asked, it was understood that at least a small contribution was customary as compensation for Guru Kanar to continue his good works. He was careful never to appear overly ostentatious, for he stressed charity and self-discipline in relinquishing worldly ties were direct routes to ascension. That encouraged people to give generously.

With his charismatic charm and some crafty planning, the former tea merchant led a far more leisurely life. He rented a small but comfortable studio apartment inside a Back Bay brownstone, where no one minded the quiet, smiling neighbor who came and went at odd hours. He was careful never to appear in his official capacity there; and never entertained or allowed any of his 'disciples' to follow him home.

His modest automobile and the well paid former taxi driver waited outside to whisk him away as soon as he had performed several healings with the Cintamani. He was nowhere near as skilled with it as the swami had been, but it didn't take much to impress these nonconformist people eager for an alternative to the society they had cut themselves off from. He was becoming a local legend, and had developed a cult-like following.

"That is all for tonight," he said, rising slowly to his feet and bowing with palms pressed together. "Go with blessings. I will see you in a few days. Now I must rest." He bounded from the room, disappearing into the darkness outside. Shedding the voluminous robes, he became just one more immigrant in a land of many.

As his taciturn driver took him home in a roundabout manner, they had a magnificent view of the nighttime harbor. Something large stirred far out in the water, and for some reason that commanded Rahul's attention. He strained to see it, but could make nothing out, for the night was dark, even with the local lights shining over the water. He suddenly felt uneasy, and it didn't help that the gem which lay on his chest began to vibrate and grow uncomfortably warm. It had never done that before and it left him even more unsettled. He sat back in the car and tried to relax.

*I am just tired. No women tonight. I will go straight home, eat, and watch television. There should be something interesting on the news.*

THE NORTH ATLANTIC was mostly open water. The challenge was to avoid collisions with ships and icebergs. Staying well below the surface, she made good time. Temporal existence is meaningless for the longer lived supernatural creatures, for they never think in terms of what has passed. What must be done motivates them, and for the Naga, the Cintamani could not remain in impure hands. She was driven by the desire to take it back and relentlessly traveled on, ignoring all discomforts of frigid water and fatigue. No predator was large enough to attack her, so she swam night and day, not even pausing to feed.

Within a few weeks, the coastline of the United States was nigh, with far more ships to be dodged. She surfaced briefly once more, bobbing head and shoulders above the waves; scanning with all senses, some which mankind never possessed.

The Cintamani pull felt stronger from a certain direction. Her face contorted into an angry hiss and claws involuntarily unsheathed. It would soon be back where it belonged.

The Naga rolled backward and dove deep, skimming the ocean floor to avoid the traffic of the humans above as she swam over and around underwater obstacles, heading unfailingly toward Boston Harbor.

THE TAKE that day had been poor, since many people now avoided the Common, because of the shocking behavior of the free-spirited flower children. Few of the well-to-do would stroll down to the waterfront even in the daytime, disgusted with the unruly crowds and the crime, filth, and depravity that followed in the wake of the hippie invasion.

Nimkee and Ajeet had secured food and a place to sleep at a shelter in the South End. The old man was already intoxicated when they got there, but other than grumbling that his cot smelled like piss, he drifted off to a troubled sleep rather quickly. The boy lay awake longer; his eyes squeezed shut so he didn't have to talk to anyone. His young mind wandered back over the last few years.

Ajeet was an adoption runaway. His always angry American father had regularly beaten his quiet voiced mother. Whenever the boy tried to stand up for the once enthusiastic Peace Corps volunteer who had plucked him out of the gutter to give him a better life, the man she had come back to Boston to marry took his fists to him as well. The two adults argued regularly, until one day the woman fell and did not rise again. Ajeet abandoned his unhappy new home and fled back to the streets.

The boy from the slums and the elderly blind man had been together for over three years. They had not spoken much of their past though Ajeet knew Nimkee had an American name, had been in a very big war, and had seen some horrific things. Nimkee often cried out in his sleep and cursed the ghosts of his past on days when the drink was in short supply. The both found solace in music and the company of another lost soul. The best days ended with a filling meal, an indoor bed and cheap whiskey for Nimkee.

Ajeet had a feeling of uneasiness that would not relent as he tossed and turned on his own cot, twisting the threadbare blanket, and knocking off the thin stained pillow. Living outdoors for so long, he had developed a sixth sense about things such as weather and impending hostilities. The sky had been clear and the sunset lovely, but for some reason, there was an ominous feeling to the day's end.

Something very bad and dangerous was going to happen! Even if it didn't affect Ajeet and Nimkee directly, it would keep the tipping customers away and that meant no extra food and no bottle for sleeping well. When Nimkee hadn't eaten enough and had no whiskey, he took to living in his own world, a place where the night demons visited during the day and he couldn't tell the difference between what was real, and what lived in his mind. The last time he had landed in jail for several days. He was not always a pleasant companion, but he was all the family Ajeet had now. He had to get Nimkee a bottle of whiskey somewhere.

Ajeet would see about it first thing in the morning, even if he had to steal it. The old man must not go without again.

TWO YOUNG PEOPLE found a quiet stretch of beach at dawn and then the age old frenetic rhythm of life took over. They rolled in the sand, changing positions often, lost in the blissful moments and totally oblivious to the waking world around them.

"Hey—where the hell'd the sun go?" the now thoroughly sated young man said, rolling off his partner and dropping to the sand beside her.

"Dunno," she answered vaguely. She was shivering in the sudden gloom, and lifted her head. "Something looks weird out there."

"As long as it's not bombers coming in, who gives a damn?" He ran a hand over her body, brushing sand off. "Man, I am sooooo wasted right now."

She pushed his hand aside. "No, something is moving out there—and it's big!" She sat upright and peered out under a raised hand, then gasped and pointed wordlessly down toward the water. Snatching up her clothing, she leaped to her feet, which made him look at her in consternation. "Hey, where are you going?"

Her scream trailed behind her in a benediction as a huge shadow loomed over her confused and rapidly sobering lover. He looked up and then collapsed in fright as his face blanched.

"Oh my God! OH MY GOD! Bad trip, bad trip!" he yelped in shock. He crab walked backwards in the sand to get away from the towering monstrosity that had risen from the water and was now rapidly slithering up the beach, bearing down on him. As tall as some of the buildings in the city and almost as heavy, the Naga left a gaping trench in the moist sand.

The girl screeched like a wounded animal as she took to her heels, nothing more than her discarded skirt clutched to her body. The naked young man was following her when one of those huge hands shot out and lifted him off his feet, kicking and screaming. The Naga drew him up to her face.

"Cintamani!" she demanded over and over, but he couldn't understand her and eventually fainted. She tossed him down on the sand in disgust as he had wet himself in fright. Locking the now protruding nails of her left hand over him like a cage, the eye in the palm opened as she scanned his mind for answers.

There was little enough to learn, but a random blurred memory of a recent encounter with a local mystic was enough to enrage her. The man in this human's muddled thoughts did appear to be Middle Eastern, and he must be found. She pulled back and stood up on her coils, swaying and glaring down at the puny human's limp form below her. If these foreigners were harboring the thief who stole the mystical stone of her ancestors, she would tear down their dwellings and kill as many of them as it took to get it back.

Contemptuous of the frail mortal that was just coming back to consciousness; her right hand shot out and grabbed him. She crushed the life from him and then threw his broken body far out into the harbor before heading up toward the city.

RAHUL FELL asleep with the cabinet style console television showing test patterns. He awoke in the early morning hours to the sounds of many distant sirens coupled with the Emergency Broadcast System trilling its warning tone as the picture tube crackled and the TV flickered back to life. A message flashed onto the screen with a recorded voice saying that this was NOT a test, but an actual emergency and to stay tuned for official information.

He sat up and rubbed the sleep from his eyes. There was a brief news conference from the president of America, and then the governor of Massachusetts came on with a short statement, right before the station shut down and he was instructed to tune into another one. Still unsure of what was happening; he twirled the VHF channel selector dial frantically, hoping it was just a drill. He watched in disbelief as evacuation information was updated for the areas involved.

IT WAS the harbor and surrounding neighborhoods that were under attack. But by what? The Russians, maybe?

They went to live feed. Once the shaky news camera footage started, what Rahul saw was far more terrifying than any foreign invasion. It was reported to be a rogue monster of unknown alliance, but he recognized it instantly as a Nagini, and it was shouting, "Where Cintamani?" in old Tamil as it tossed large boats aside like toys in a bathtub and smashed police and National Guard vehicles into buildings.

He jumped to his feet and began to pack. It was no coincidence that one of the ancient Devas had traveled to Boston's waterfront searching for a Cintamani. The carved stone lay heavy and hot, pulsing against his chest. He tore it from his neck and frantically wrapped it within a wadded up pair of socks before stuffing it well down inside a hastily packed suitcase. He looked around at his apartment and sighed, before hefting his bag and locking the door behind him.

Time to move on.

He went down to the street level and hailed a cab.

"Where to, pal?" the driver said in the usual nasal Boston drawl that sounded like he was talking out of one side of his mouth.

"Cross town please, away from the river," Rahul said quickly. The Naga should stick to waterways for a while.

"I'll try, Mac," the cabbie said with shrug as Rahul lifted his bag in and crawled into the back seat beside it. "It's gettin' tough to move on the highways, and the side roads are packed. The Staties are clinching the noose because there's some kinda monster making a mess of things downashore."

"Yes, I saw that on the television, how frightening," Rahul said quietly, suppressing a shudder. The cab was moving at a crawl, for the streets were crowded with people trying to get away.

The cabbie was feeling chatty, for Rahul was his first fare of the day. "The Guard will most likely take it out. Ya know, you got quite an accent. You ain't one of those off-the-boat A-rab princes, are you?" His bloodshot blue eyes met Rahul's dark and guarded ones in the rearview mirror. "No offense, but I don't take nothing but US dollahs, okay? But if ya got any of them Turkish Camel Killers on ya, I wouldn't turn down a smoke."

Rahul gave a frustrated sigh, but with effort kept his voice light and even. "I am not Arabic, and do not smoke. My money is American and I can pay my way. Please concentrate on your driving because I need to be somewhere else soon." He waved a twenty dollar bill, a lucrative fare.

"Sure, Mac, sure," the cabbie reassured Rahul as he aggressively swung out into traffic, eliciting a chorus of locked-up brakes squealing, horns blaring, frustrated gestures, and shouted obscenities.

Rahul sat back, trying to tune it out. He had to make it across town quickly, and then move farther inland, because the Naga would not be easily defeated. He would reestablish himself in New York or Washington DC, and make more money before working his way cross country. Any big city should have hippies and colleges, but he planned to settle well off the coast in some landlocked cosmopolitan area, where he could blend in easily and the sea loving Naga would be less likely to find him.

~

THE BOSTON PD AND METRO POLICE were the first responders. A blockade of MDC orange topped, blue-bodied cruisers kept the citizens out of the area, but they provided a meager impediment to the Naga, who scooped up vehicles and lobbed them down into the midst of the rapidly retreating figures with disastrous effect. She ignored the small arms fire, and the riot squad was ineffective against something that stood almost half as tall as the Custom House Tower. As the National Guard arrived, she was surging up from the beach, heading through South Boston towards the Charles River Basin.

With the Vietnam War eating up resources, national defenses were spread thin. Neighboring states had been notified and reserves were being called up; but it would take time to get them mustered, equipped, and in place. The local transit authority, in conjunction with the various law enforcement agencies and a few contingents of the National Guard, were evacuating people as quickly as possible. The highways and secondary roads were clogged, even though traffic was strictly one way and all toll gates had been ordered opened. Multiple lanes moved at a crawl.

The Guardsmen above the beach area had been busy setting up a perimeter, but the monster was just too large to contain. With wild swings of her arms, she cleared a path before her; those long, curving golden nails slicing through men like hot knives into butter. She shouted in a booming tone that made ears ring and road signs quiver, though the words were unintelligible.

When the shelling started, the Naga was initially staggered back, but quickly recovered her equilibrium. It hurt, but did not knock her down, and only made her angrier. Hood fully extended, she opened her mouth wide and shook her head back and forth, following the movements of the men on the ground while spraying a strong stream of potent venom that caused immediate blindness and skin breakdown. Many on the frontlines fell screaming and writhing under that unexpected assault as their flesh melted away. It was a horrifically painful way to die, and more than one man pulled his sidearm to end his own agony while he still had enough muscle control to do so.

The Coast Guard moved in cutters and other large vessels to secure the bay and keep pleasure cruisers and cargo ships out. Additional backup was called for in ground forces and air support before a regrouping was ordered. Some of the remaining Guard began collecting its dead and dying. Others tracked the monster's progress from the building tops, looking for an opportunity to get in a lucky shot. The Naga rippled past them, oblivious to their existence as long as they didn't try to stop her. The mobile equipment they had been able to bring in with them—mostly howitzers and a couple of mortars—had been tough to get into position fast enough to make any impact, and she was soon too far into the city to use any large weaponry without hazarding mass casualties.

Panicked and screaming people fleeing before the monster's advance filled every conceivable outlet, so anything that couldn't be carried was impossible to maneuver. Buildings leaned and upper floors crashed to the pavement below as she shoved them out of the way, opening a path that allowed her gigantic body to squeeze through. Entire neighborhoods were decimated, and blocks filled with dwellings and small businesses were reduced to rubble. The monster seemed determined to cross Route 1, so evacuation traffic had to be stopped while she surged forward unchecked.

With resources stretched to the max due to the Vietnam War, the federal government had no choice but to send in the one defensive entity they had in reserve. Project Skystorm was activated.

In an unnamed ancient volcanic cone somewhere in the Cascades, monitored by the United States Behemoth Corps, a hidden containment facility had been built. That morning, it was a hubbub of activity,

Klaxons echoed throughout the complex as strobing warning lights illuminated hallways where crew members rushed to their battle stations. Technicians sat at complex panels with dials, grids, buttons and levers, tweaking and refining the process. A huge elevator platform, with a sophisticated energy bar system, rose through a lead lined concrete shaft toward the gradually appearing daylight above. As it drew closer to the top of the tube, blast proof steel doors a yard thick retracted nosily into their channels. The platform with its caged enclosure came to rest where a waiting crew of handlers and officials in charge of the project stood by.

A collection of top tier military command staff observed events in a secured tower, with the base administrator explaining in a quiet tone how the system would be deployed. This was the first time Skystorm had been activated in five years, for it had previously proved uncontrollable. With the current system of checks and balances, it should be far easier to manage, though many had reservations about a cross-country flight. Skystorm's monster had the capability to move fast and strike hard, but would it be effective?

Someone gave the order to shut down the radiant pulse generator and open the cage. The crackling purple and white beams that spiraled each bar gradually dimmed and faded away. In the dawn's early light a huge, hunched, dark and hooded avian form could be viewed within. The top of the cage was unfastened remotely and a hovering CH 54 Skycrane dropped a grappling hook on a reinforced steel cable to yank the metal grid off to one side. Another chopper flew in, dangling the bloodied corpse of a cow while a speaker broadcasted a bugle solo of the military mess call. The creature within the cage lifted its head and, using its gigantic beak and talons, climbed the bars of cage to sit on the top perch and feast.

While it fed, dropping chunks of hide and gore all around, two Chinooks were brought in close while tall hydraulic platforms were quickly maneuvered into place by trucks. On top were men in protective suits being guarded by those with cattle prod-like devices on long poles. The ground crew scrambled to hook tether cables to breakaway connections on various parts of the body harness the creature wore. Others made sure the cables' far ends were securely fastened to the choppers.

With thumbs-up all around, the brass ordered that it was time to go airborne. The platforms withdrew and the Chinooks powered up again, getting into position to take up the slack. Someone gave the signal that they were ready to roll and the props whirled faster as the choppers went up and backed off sideways, out of range of the sweeps of massive dark wings.

"Are you positive the system will work this time?" one general asked the administrator curiously.

The younger man nodded gravely. "Absolutely, sir. Hooding the creature gave us the same kind of control a medieval falconer would have over his birds of prey, and it became quite docile. The training was fairly similar, just on a far grander scale. It wears a radio collar and we've worked hard to make sure it was conditioned to respond to certain auditory stimulus, similar in concept to a falconer's whistle, so that we can make maximum use of its, um, talents."

"Surely you're not expecting those helis to guide that thing all the way to Boston?" the general said with consternation. "They'll need to refuel and it'll never make it in time!"

"Absolutely not!" an Air Force Lieutenant General who worked onsite broke in quickly. "Once it's disconnected, this thing flies too high and fast for them anyway. The Hooks are just to get it safely airborne while hooded. We've scrambled some 101s from Beale to take charge once the blinders come off, and we have Air Guard units standing by to take over escort duty as it passes through their jurisdiction. Civilian and commercial air traffic has already been grounded or diverted all along the projected route. We planned this out carefully in advance, gentlemen," he added, sounding miffed that anyone would question Air Force tactics.

"Is that hood over its eyes why it hasn't flown off yet?" an admiral asked.

The administrator turned an ingratiating smile his way. "That's one reason, yes; but it also has been trained to wait for a particular sequence of music before leaving base. You see, this monstrous avian is what certain American Indian groups used to refer to as a Thunderbird. We've taken on a few local tribal consultants, because they have developed ways of communicating with it, and we've found it quite responsive to drumming. Once we understood that, we took full advantage of the knowledge to exploit it in initiating our own version of a call to arms."

When the music started, almost everyone shook their heads in disbelief and there was a smattering of applause. The creature, blinded by the great hood with eyecups still closed, unfurled and flapped massive wings the span of a city block as it took to the air, guided by the copters whose impromptu sound systems were blaring the drum solo from Iron Butterfly's "*In-A-Gada-Da-Vida*."

IT WAS NEARLY noon and the cab bearing a very angry and frustrated Rahul was stuck in heavy traffic on the Massachusetts Turnpike. They had been creeping along for several hours, trying desperately to get out of Boston, and were now at a virtual standstill. National Guard planes and choppers had been roaring over regularly, making low altitude sweeps of the entire area that rattled the glass. They kept the cab windows rolled up, even though it was stuffy, because it was better than dealing with the full force of the choking fumes and continuous noise outside. Even without the Guard buzzing them, horns were honking and shouted obscenities filled the air. Many people had gotten out of their vehicles to see what the holdup was.

"Was there no other road we could have taken?" Rahul leaned forward and snapped at the cabbie, who was equally irritated.

With the vehicle idling and threatening to boil over, the red-faced and cussing driver turned angrily, one hand still on the wheel. "Look, asshole! You said you wanted outta town by the quickest route, and the Pike is the best way–"

Catching sight of something out the rear windshield, he did a double take and his eyes went wide as twin moons. "Holy Mother of God—that thing's comin' straight up the ramp behind us!" Without another word, the driver threw open the door and bailed out, just missing being hit several times as he vaulted over car hoods and trunks, careening across multiple lanes of the highway.

Other people had seen it too, and were similarly abandoning their vehicles and running away in panic, many dragging wailing children or small pets with them. Rahul spun around and an involuntary gasp left his throat. Frantically, he struggled to evacuate the cab, but it was now jammed up very close against a car whose driver had hit the brakes hard to avoid an elderly couple skittering through the crowded lanes. He slid to the far side of the seat and got himself and his case extricated from the idling cab, but his time had run out.

The chorus of terrified screams reached a crescendo level when the mammoth figure of the serpent-bodied woman came winding up behind him, shoving vehicles aside and crushing people too slow to get out of her way. She bellowed, "CINTAMANI!" and a massive hand reached down for Rahul.

AJEET and a far too sober and sullen Nimkee gathered up their things and left early in the morning, when the evacuation was first announced. With one glance at the shelter's black and white portable TV that everyone gathered around, the boy's eyes lit up. He instantly knew why the monster had come.

He took the blind old man by the hand and led him unfailingly through back alleys and side streets, away from the noise and confusion of the major roads. There was no way they could afford to take the "T," and Ajeet had no idea how much of it was in service since the monster attack. It was likely crowded, anyway.

"Where're we going?" Nimkee asked in a shaky voice, his drum under his arm. He was trembling, the whiskey of the day before having long since worn off.

"Back to the big park," Ajeet answered.

"That doesn't make sense. Won't the monster see us there?"

"I hope so. I am not afraid of this one. It is a Nagini and they are good beings when you are respectful. Too many peoples are being hurt because these Angrez shoot before they speak. I know how to calm her down, and then we can tell her where the Cintamani is."

"We should stay out of this," Nimkee insisted as they hustled along. "I don't like monsters. We woke one up in the Argonne. I'll never forget that thing—it had tree bark for skin, and it was ugly and mean," he shuddered. "It went crazy with all the noise and starting tearing things up. We had to gas it. A lot of good men died that day."

He went on like that for a while. Monsters had not been tamed at the time, but they weren't unknown.

"My people worship the Nagas. They can be reasoned with, if you know how to speak to one. These Americans, they have no understanding of such things. If they can't make a pet of it, they want to kill it."

When they finally reached the Common, they found the monster had already passed and the area had been taken over as a command center and triage staging area. There were many wounded coming in from the path of destruction, and the Red Cross was busy. Canvas tarps covered the bodies of the dead until they could be identified. Police and guardsmen secured the area and directed refugees to food, water, and medical attention. Many of the hippies were helping out wherever they could, caring for the injured, shepherding lost children, and showing displaced people how to start fires and where to get clean water.

Power was out in much of that part of the city. Seeping gas from interrupted lines had started fires and fueled explosions. Many buildings had been severely damaged. A refugee tent camp was going up along the Park Street end. A public address system was being set up in the bandstand so that periodic announcements could be made.

"What do we do now?" Nimkee asked as they found themselves a spot in the shade away from the hustle and the milling, mourning crowds.

"We wait until it comes back this way," Ajeet said, looking around. "It will return to the sea by the end of the day." Guard planes and helicopters were crisscrossing the area, trying to herd the monster and take it out before it did more damage. Nimkee ducked and winced every time a low flying one passed overhead.

"I don't like this. They'll send something else after it. They always do," Nimkee said in a shaky voice.

"Play your drum and I will get us some food," the boy insisted, and ran off.

"Get me something to drink!" Nimkee called after him. He didn't mean water.

Once Thunderbird gained altitude, the eyecups of the hood blew off. Chinook leader radioed in that Phase One of Operation Minuteman had been accomplished and was given the go-ahead to initiate Phase Two. The locking systems on the cable ends of the harness released, and the fighter jet escorts took wing positions as the two choppers veered down and away, retracting the cables as they left.

High across the top tier states of the country flew Thunderbird, being periodically rejoined by a new pair of escorts, carefully guiding it so as not to encroach on Canadian airspace. Because it had fed, it did not stop to hunt and waste precious time. The thunderous roar of its wings filled the sky with the high and distant sounds of crashing cannonades.

At that altitude, no shadow was cast below, though anyone looking up into a clear sky might have gotten an impression of huge dark wings and body, and wondered what kind of plane flapped and had no contrail. It was not a well-known monster, as it had been hard to tame. The initial Skystorm mission had been disastrous, so the details were very quickly buried in classified files. Everyone involved was praying that with the intensive retraining and additional support, Thunderbird would be more of a help than a hindrance. It was the only aerial monster the US had trained for combat, and could move faster across the continent than any other gargantuan creature they had.

The reasoning behind deploying it was it takes a monster to effectively deal with a monster.

Just before noon Eastern Time, Thunderbird and its final escorts, a pair of F104 Starfighters, had rounded Lake Erie and were heading over New York state. On orders, they began to descend over Massachusetts. So far the flight had been flawless, and everyone was enthusiastic as the escort radioed in on a scrambled channel.

"Minuteman Base, this is Skystorm Leader. We're starting our approach and need a BSZ on that Monnie so we can send in the T-Bird."

The voice on the other end sounded relieved as the base radio crackled to life.

"Roger that, Skystorm Leader. We have you on radar. A visual of the target shows it is now moving northeast; check fifty degrees north and head for the river basin! Repeat: check five-oh north and head toward the river. Over."

"Copy that, Minuteman Base, hang in there. T-bird's already on the scent, so we're coming in hot!"

Possessed of faculties far more acute than those of any other creatures on earth, the monsters already sensed each other.

The Naga had quickly snatched up Rahul and was headed back toward the water with him gripped in one gigantic fist. Somehow Rahul had held onto his suitcase. She held him just tight enough that he couldn't slip free, not that he wanted to plunge 150 feet to the pavement and die. Terrified beyond belief, he could peep through her fingers and see where he was going. She was headed directly into the river. He was going to drown. Rahul didn't want to die, but was too stubborn to think of bargaining by offering her the Cintamani in exchange for his life.

The immense creature slithered down over the esplanade and was part way into the Charles River Basin, when there was a series of loud thunderclaps behind her.

MANY PEOPLE FELL to their knees in grateful prayers when the monstrous snake woman grabbed a single individual and then turned towards the river. Whatever it was she wanted with this unfortunate man, it was better than having her rampaging throughout the city.

The sky became overcast, right before there was a loud series of sonic booms. There were gasps and pointing fingers, as all eyes swiveled to several large flying objects emerging from what appeared to be large cones of clouds. Two of them were fighter jets, but the one in the middle was a colossal flying bird. It was wearing a harness with the red, white, and blue shield of the USBC on its breast.

Everyone cheered. At least this monster was one of ours.

Thunderbird was well in the lead with the accompanying fighter jets tailing to each side. The pilots had been ordered to hold their fire and let the monsters engage, not offering backup unless Skystorm's greatest hope got into trouble. The escorts initially veered off as they leveled out over the city.

While many people covered their ears and ducked instinctively, every gaze was riveted on the sky. The giant black and white feathered bird canted its massive wings at an angle and dove steeply past them, eyes glowing orange, hooked beak open, screeching in avian rage as it chased the blue skinned and mottle-scaled monster heading into the Charles River Basin.

The Naga swiveled and hissed as something huge and deafeningly loud came hurtling at her. The booming turbulence from its wings buffeted her backward before the massive talons struck hard enough to be staggering. She dropped Rahul and toppled over with a tremendous splash that sent wave-size ripples of the dirty, polluted water cresting in all directions. His suitcase floated off downstream as Rahul went under, coming up many yards distant, coughing and choking as he swam hard from where the two monsters were now locked in battle.

She came back up quick. Water flew all around the Naga as she swirled and resurfaced, ready to do battle. Jerking around in a semicircle with her hood fully erect, she extended long golden nails to rake at the creature passing overhead. A couple of minor body feathers with the resilience of spring steel was all she got as Thunderbird zoomed past, the roaring sound of its massive wings like the rumbling of violent storms coming in off the water.

Unable to bank sharply because of the tall buildings, the flying monstrosity had to gain some altitude before coming back down at her again. The sky was black and roiling now, clouds forking lightning between them. Drawing energy from the storm, the bird wheeled and stooped into another power dive.

The Naga was ready this time, as she tensed and stood her ground. She reached up to slice at Thunderbird as it dove at her, and when it kept coming anyway, released a spray of deadly venom at very close range.

The Winged Wonder of the United States was not to be taken so easily. Its titian orange eyes burned with radiant intensity until the dark pupils disappeared and each iris pulsed red hot. When the gaping maw of the enemy opened and the poison mist spewed forth; answering crackles of electricity streaked out from those crimson orbs and flashed into sheet lightning, vaporizing the spray before it could make contact. Talons the size and strength of logging grapples reached down for her.

The Naga hissed in defiance and lunged upwards awkwardly as Thunderbird grabbed hold. Sinking her razor-like nails deep into her adversary, she lashed her long tail up and around in an attempt to entrap the avian menace and bear it to earth.

Despite the pain, Thunderbird clamped its talons tighter to her shoulders and flapped mightily, trying to pull up and away. The two monsters remained airborne a short distance, moving toward the embankment before smashing heavily into the rocky shallows, spraying mud and debris for a couple hundred feet around, plowing a canal wide enough to navigate an ocean liner.

On its back in the muck and mire, Thunderbird was at a disadvantage. The Naga's body was far more flexible; adapted to terrestrial as well as aquatic life. She was able to roll sideways and squirm upright within seconds. Rearing back, with hood completely flared and long curving fangs exposed, her clawed hands came down to throttle the life from the other monster.

That was when the Starfighters came in for a strafing run, their rotating M61s belching smoke and flame. While a few minor flesh wounds opened up in the Naga's shoulders, shells bounced off her scales and didn't seem to do more than sting like birdshot.

To stay out of reach, the jets pulled up fast. Naga whirled and lunged, and a mighty fist crumpled metal. With his damaged aircraft yawing and hard to control, the pilot radioed in he was turning back. The attack was called off, as there was too big a chance of hitting Thunderbird while the monsters were engaged.

The distraction the fighter pilots provided was just enough to give the huge winged beast time to regroup. Random shells had gone through its outspread wings, but missed anything vital.

When the Naga turned her attention back to her adversary, its head was up, eyes glowing red. Before she could back away, bolts of energy at close range crackled out, hitting her square in the chest. The gold breastplate caught most of it, but it knocked the wind from her and she went down. Thunderbird was quick to regain its feet.

The Naga came up fast again. With flaps that boomed like rolling thunder and tore leaves from nearby trees and shrubs, Thunderbird hopped onto her shoulders and his curved beak came down to gouge her eyes. Raking nails unsheathed as long fingered hands shot straight up. Thunderbird could not build another charge that fast and was forced to take to the air.

It circled Naga, with head hanging low and talons at the ready as the energy beams recharged, but the Naga suddenly lost interest in fighting. She was surging back inland, ignoring the screaming people scattering below her, knocking over buildings and shoving aside vehicles in her haste to follow the one thing she came to Boston to retrieve.

GREEDY FOOL THAT HE WAS, even half-drowned and frightened out of his mind, Rahul was not about to let the Cintamani go. While the monsters were fighting, he retrieved the sodden suitcase before it sank, and dragged it up from the river. Ripping it open, he grabbed the glowing sock-wrapped gem and thrust it into a pocket before racing off.

More fearful of the monsters than of traffic, Rahul crossed the highway at a dead run. He was nearly hit several times before heading back into the city. As he fled through the mostly deserted streets, he already knew he was being pursued. He couldn't hear the relentless scraping of the Naga's sliding scales, but the gem was burning and throbbing in his pocket and there were the sounds of buildings tumbling behind him.

Rahul somehow stayed out of eyesight of his pursuer and she was soon left behind. The gem cooled down to dull warmth and no longer vibrated. He wanted to take the "T" but the lines were backed up with overloaded trains running late, and he was out of time.

He ran through the tent city into the park itself, grateful to see that a security perimeter was being set up. He headed directly for where he heard the most equipment moving around. If the Americans with all their military might couldn't protect him from the angry and vengeful creature, nothing and no one could. Losing himself in the crowd, he quickly threaded his way toward the medical and food dispensaries.

THE NAGA SURGED up onto Route C9, which ran along the river, causing serious crashes as the evacuation traffic screeched to a sudden halt. She brushed aside the pileup in front of her, jumbling vehicles into twisted, stacked messes as she sidled through. People who had gathered on the pedestrian overpass to watch the monsters battling panicked and ran screaming in the opposite direction, trampling each other in their haste to get away from the gigantic being. She ignored them and continued relentlessly, crumpling the old buildings and uprooting trees in her haste, heading straight for the inner city park.

Thunderbird was right behind her. It kept blasting away periodically, blowing the tops off of high rises and setting things afire, but it couldn't get between the buildings to snatch at the Naga. It circled the area at a higher altitude, waiting for a clearing to start another showdown. The avian creature had limited intelligence, but had been trained to fight in open areas to minimize collateral damage. The park was just ahead. As soon as the Naga was fully visible, the assault from the air would begin again.

RAHUL HAD BEEN SQUATTING in the shade of a tree, gobbling a Red Cross meal, when there was a sudden flurry of activity among the Guard encampment. A damaged fighter jet rocketed by low overhead, heading away from the river, and he lost his appetite. Dropping his food, he leaped to his feet, looking for a place to hide. The gem in his pocket was heating up and vibrating briskly against his leg. It was time to move on.

As he tried to worm his way quickly through the surging crowds of displaced civilians, aid workers, and patrols, there was screaming and shouting from across the park. Soldiers and equipment began to move into position and police lines formed, pressing everyone south, into the trees near Boylston Street.

She had found him again! The Naga was coming for him! And

there was no way to get free of the mass of humanity Rahul was walled in by.

He had never prayed so fervently in his life. Then he screwed up his resolve, and motioned to the nearest police officer.

"I am Guru Kanar Maneesh. I need to talk to the leader of the soldiers. This terrible monster was sent here to find me."

PANIC-STRICKEN people screamed and rushed to get out of the way as the gigantic undulating form of the Naga hurtled into sight. She was shoving herself between buildings that rocked and swayed; snapping big oak, maple, and elm trees and tall street lights like twigs, yanking out sparking utility wires and crushing vehicles in her haste to chase down the desperate man who had stolen the sacred gem. She surged across Beacon Street and into the open end of the park, bellowing for the Cintamani.

Right behind her roared Thunderbird, its eyes glowing red with pent-up energy. Its human handlers tried to prevent it from attacking, for if it fought the Naga in the park, many on the ground would die. Yet all attempts to ward it off with radio commands seemed to be in vain. The creature's bloodlust was up and it wanted to kill the other monster.

As the huge beast passed overhead, Nimkee cocked an ear and then stopped in his tracks, his wrinkled face alight with excitement. He smiled for the first time since Ajeet had known him, and he shook off the boy's tugging arm.

"Wait! I know that sound! It is animikii—a Thunderbird!" he said. "My people revere them, for they bring the rains and guard our lands. The lands we used to have before the government put us all on reservations." He looked morose and crestfallen again.

"Nimkee, it is going to attack the Nagini! "Ajeet shouted in alarm. "Can you speak to it? Make it stop?"

He shook his head, white hair flying. "No, we don't talk to Thunderbirds. But I can drum and sing, and I remember some of the ceremonial summoning verses. No matter, it would never notice me down here."

"I can make it hear you!" Ajeet insisted as he dragged the old man along. "Bring your drum, and hurry; we can stop this war right now!"

He led the old man up onto the abandoned bandstand, and parked him in front of a microphone set.

"Now play!"

It was a standoff.

Thunderbird made a couple of flybys and came in blasting both times, splitting trees in half, splintering boulders, and plowing furrows into the ground. People scattered in all directions, not knowing where it was safe to hide.

The Naga sidled along evasively, and though she was staggered a couple of times, she kept moving. Her attention was no longer on the other monster, but the humans who were harboring and protecting the thief who stole the Cintamani.

On the final pass, the faint sound of drumming filled the air. Thunderbird stooped lower than normal in its dive, skimming over the tree tops, trying to find the source. Foliage blew off ahead of it, like a tornado rushing through. When the chant started, its concentration was split between its adversary and the ritual sounds.

The Naga had been simply avoiding Thunderbird up until that point, but she was growing tired of the constant threat. Her amber eyes narrowed in rage as it flapped past her, close enough to reach with some effort. With amazing speed and agility, she lunged and snatched at the giant creature, digging long, golden claws into its steely feathers and thick hide. Whipping her body around, she spun, dizzying it, and then let go of Thunderbird, letting its weight provide momentum.

As it rocketed backwards in the air, a club-like swing of her long tail lashed out and batted it well over the trees lining Charles Street. It landed with a thundering crash in Boston Public Garden, smashing shrubs and digging a huge hole in the soil that would later become part of the lake.

Satisfied that she had defeated her foe, the Naga turned her attention back to the humans.

"Cintamani!" she insisted, her huge amber eyes narrowed and menacing, clawing fingernails that could cut men in half with a single swipe flexed and ready.

Grim-eyed Guardsmen, clad in chemical and biological gear and gas masks, formed up to meet her, weapons at the ready. A couple howitzers and one undamaged mortar were trained on the gigantic being. Several aging F-84s and the one remaining F-101 were doing flyovers, but had been ordered not to engage until there was no other hope of stopping the creature. Everyone knew there would be extensive collateral damage to take a creature that size down. The park was being quickly evacuated, as the orders were to kill the foreign monster. Backup was supposedly on the way, as the attack would be a coordinated effort from both air and land. Even after the disheartening defeat of Thunderbird, the military commanders were confident that they could handle it.

Most of the able bodied civilians, along with all the birds and wildlife, had fled the park ahead of the showdown. For the authorities, it was a matter of removing the wounded to protect those who might have a chance of recovery.

"Give Cintamani!" she screeched unintelligibly again, sidling forward. Her hood went up and head reared back, ready to spit her deadly venom all over those who refused to comply.

The command to fire was being hastily relayed, when over the abandoned and unguarded public address system, along with a few squawks and squeaks, came a strange concert of drumming and chanting, which was soon joined by the high pitched strains of a pungi.

The Naga stopped in her tracks, confused. She turned her head, trying to locate the sound, which was blasted from speakers all around. Her eyes closed, and with arms akimbo and claws retracted, she began to sway in a ritualistic manner.

"Stand down! I repeat, STAND DOWN!" The order crackled over radios and walkie-talkies throughout the park area.

"Did you find out where that blasted music is coming from?" a high ranking official bellowed loud enough to make the radio squelch break. It had been a difficult day, with mass casualties all over the ruined south end of the city, a botched evacuation, Project Skystorm deemed a huge failure, and both the governor and the President demanding answers. He had a babbling civilian of Indo-European descent in his tent, claiming to be a defected religious leader seeking asylum, insisting that the monster was sent after him.

Meanwhile a 200-foot snake woman no country claimed was now dancing in the park.

"It's coming from the Parkman Bandstand, sir!" someone said excitedly into a walkie-talkie. "I think some of the hippies are holding a concert or something,"

"They're doing what?" barked the incredulous reply.

It was confirmed by witnesses along the line. A crowd of flower children, promoting peace, love, and understanding taught by their beloved guru, had joined Ajeet and Nimkee on the stage, chanting and singing, while the boy and his mentor played on. A gathering mass of young people were rocking, clapping and swaying to "Blowin' In The Wind and "Eve of Destruction."

"Find out who's making that unholy racket, and bring them here. We need every advantage we can get!"

It was a scene of contrasts. Well-armed warriors, prepared to die to protect their land, knowing one blow from a fist or a drop of venom leaking in their gear would doom them, looked around in consternation. A bunch of free-spirited hippies, chanting and swaying, surrounded the monster. Some of them were braiding flower chains to offer it. Without weapons or any threatening actions, they had stopped the beast in its tracks.

The Naga took a defensive stance and glared down at the soldiers. Only two people in the crowd could understand what she said. Ajeet was the only one bothering to translate. Rahul stared at her with huge, frightened eyes. Nimkee stood with his drum and beater in hand, ear cocked, listening intently, wishing he had a bottle of whiskey to soothe his dry throat.

"I not come kill you, just him." She pointed at Rahul. "I take Cintamani and go home." Her arms crossed on her battered and scarred gold breastplate, she glared down at the humans like an elephant contemplating ants, which could be squashed en masse.

Ajeet left Nimkee and ran for the center of the action. Before anyone could catch the boy, he crawled through a makeshift perimeter bulwark. He dragged at the man in battle fatigues who was interrogating Rahul, begging the commanding officer to listen to him.

"Please, mister soldier, sir; don't shoot the Nagini! She is a blessed creature, and only came here to get her Cintamani back. It is a blessed gem, and this man stole it!"

MPs rushed in after Ajeet and grabbed the boy, but the officer waved them off. "What do you know about this?" he asked Ajeet.

The words tumbled out. "I am from India; the Nagas are sacred beings there. I do not know where this false guru is from, but he has a Cintamani, you can see it glowing through his clothing. He must have stolen it because those only belong to the holiest of holy men, something he is not! If you give it to the Naga, she will go home, and all your people will be saved."

The officer turned to Rahul, pulling his sidearm. "Is this true?"

"The boy is mad, I've nothing to give you—NO!" he squealed as Ajeet ripped his pocket off and the green glowing gem on the chain tumbled to the ground. "That's mine!"

"It was never yours! It belongs to the people it was meant to protect," Ajeet insisted.

"Take him away, and hold him for further questioning," the officer insisted and the MPs hauled off a sputtering and imploring Rahul.

"Tell me then, what do we do with that thing?" the officer said to Ajeet, as he held the chain of the gem gingerly.

"I am too low caste to touch this treasure, and I hope that false guru did not make it impure. We offer it to her," the boy added quietly. "If she accepts it, she will go home."

The man shook his head uneasily. "Seems too simple to me. Awfully risky. Well, I suppose we've tried everything else."

A few moments later, a contingent of guardsmen in chem gear led by a boy playing a pungi and wearing a green glowing gem around his neck walked through a parting circle of hippie youth until they came before the swaying monster. Ajeet stopped playing and handed his instrument off.

"Venerable Mother of Cobras, I have brought back your Cintamani," Ajeet said in his clear, high-pitched child's voice. "I hope I did not dishonor it with my dirty, low caste presence." He bowed his head as he held it out to her.

The Naga leaned down, and she smiled, showing the tips of enormous fangs. "You no dishonor Cintamani, boy," she said and extended one golden nail to take the thong. It disappeared into her hand.

"It is accepted. Play more for me, before I go."

"Bring me a personnel carrier with a loudspeaker system, and clear a path," an officer barked into his walkie-talkie. The Mutt that pulled up moments later was hauling a trailer with a generator and a makeshift sound system.

"I want Nimkee, too. He helped me calm the monsters," Ajeet insisted. The old man was brought forward while the boy played his instrument, bravely standing on the palm of the now becalmed gigantic creature, which was curled up, raptly listening to him.

Nimkee, his drum in his lap and face impassive, sat waiting in the vehicle while they hooked up the equipment. Satisfied all was ready, Ajeet crawled up into the trailer, and the radio base inside was flipped to loudspeaker. He played his pungi as they slowly bumped along, leading the swaying and now smiling Naga, her eyes half closed in ecstasy, safely down toward the beach by the most open route. A host of hippies and bemused citizens streamed behind, watching the gigantic creature following a small boy out of the city and back to the sea.

"I leave you," the Naga said in a far quieter voice, and began to sink into the water.

"Namaste," Ajeet said politely, and bowed over, palms clasped together.

Suddenly it grew dark. All eyes turned upwards as there was a roar like a storm coming in and lightning flashed down from on high.

A bedraggled but very much intact Thunderbird hurtled down past them with the idea of taking on the Naga again. She sank beneath the waves before it could get to her, but it continued to pursue her well out to sea until it was lost to sight. No amount of radio commands changed its course.

"Oh, no!" Ajeet said in anguish. "It will follow her home and try to kill her. We have to stop it or more people will die!"

The officer swore as he reached for his radio. "Damn it—that thing is worth millions of dollars, and we can't let it fall into enemy hands! I'll get clearance to send in a bomber and take it out."

Nimkee spoke up. "You are such fools! Have you learned nothing today? That creature is sacred to my people. You can't train it like a dog! It won't obey any white man, but it might come back if it hears my drum calling."

"Mike him up—loud and clear—and get me a flying sound system out there pronto!" the officer barked. "Open radio communications."

He turned to Nimkee. "Let her rip, old man. If you bring that thing back in, I guarantee you'll have the cushiest job in the civilian corps."

"Get me some whiskey," Nimkee said as he settled in to play. Radio open, a chopper zoomed overhead, blaring the drumming and chanting far out to sea.

THUNDERBIRD WAS BROUGHT BACK to land within the hour. After being fed, it began the long trip back to its mountain fastness. Operation Minuteman was deemed a success, even though eyewitnesses would testify from that day forward that the actions of the young boy, his elderly mentor, and the hippie crowd that bore them triumphantly on their shoulders back into town had more to do with resolving the conflict than the US Military did.

Project Skystorm's second deployment was viewed as having mixed results, but the research into handling Thunderbird more effectively went on, with Nimkee—officially known as George Thunderman—as a special consultant until the day he died.

After Ajeet was debriefed, he was turned over to a foster family in the Tamil area of the city. They were kind folk who treated him well, making sure he was educated without forgetting his Hindi roots. After learning to read and write, he often sent letters to his former companion across the country, and flew out as a guest of the USBC several times to see how Nimkee fared.

As an adult he attended the military funeral for the venerable old man, playing his pungi and placing a bottle of whiskey in the grave. He eventually returned to India, but with the US State Department, as an ambassador with ties to the USBC.

Rahul was detained in the United States where he was tried for causing an international incident. Even with his cousin and local people as well as the hippies he had befriended protesting his release, he found himself deported. He spent the rest of his days begging for a living, wandering footsore and penniless through the poorer streets of the city he had wanted so desperately to escape.

He died alone and no one ever saw his body. It is said a Nagini rose from the depths and took him away in chains to be her otherworld servant for all eternity, but that has never been substantiated.

Boston rebuilt the devastated South End, but most of the old neighborhood charm was gone, and new high rise buildings took its place. The 60s were over, the war dragged on, and the hippies moved to other places. Yet no one ever forgot the day that a child ended a monster's rampage.

## 5

# MIGHTY NANUQ

EDWARD M. ERDELAC

*As the 1960s came to a close, the decade still had a few more beats left in it. In the midst of a space race for the moon between the dominant countries, a horrific incident involving radioactive monsters transpired between the new Jewish state of Israel and a few of the Arab countries. Quickly thereafter, the Treaty of Monstrous Agreement was established worldwide, stating each signing nation must openly declare their monsters, and that each nation was ultimately and unequivocally responsible for all actions of their monsters.*

*In the United States, the lessons of the past would have direct impact on the events of the present.*

HAL ANAWAK SHOOK hands with Lt. Governor O'Dea and smiled for the cameras, the bulbs popping off like a chain of lightning among the gathered crowd on the lawn in front of Governor's House. Luckily his hooded eyes were naturally thinner than a white man's. Nobody would know he was closing them. George LeDuc would have thought that was hilarious.

But George was dead.

When the afterimages finally faded and he was thanked once

more for his timeless service and ushered down a chain of wringing hands, Hal's nephew Matthew's scowling face was the first he saw at the bottom of the stage steps.

The kid couldn't even be bothered to dress for the occasion. He wore his hair long and unbraided, his forehead covered by a broad red headband. His chin was weaselly and unshaven, with beaded plains-style moccasins under the cuffs of his ragged jeans. Somebody had convinced Matthew to trade in his dad's army jacket for a borrowed navy blue sport coat over the t-shirt he'd carefully selected, a plain white shirt with red letters that said RED POWER. He'd purposefully left it unbuttoned during most of the ceremony.

When Hal reached the bottom of the steps Matthew took the jacket off in full view of the popping cameras and tried to place it over Hal's shoulders, ostensibly to ward off the early morning Labrador air. Hal shrugged it off. He was Inuit. He could walk St. John's stark naked in January and call it brisk.

The jacket fell to the ground and the cameras followed it down.

Matthew let it lay for whichever member of the governor's staff had given it to him to pick up.

Hal took him by the elbow and forced a smile for the cameras, then marched to the waiting limousine as Matthew flashed a peace sign.

He practically threw the kid into the waiting car before he climbed in himself.

"What the hell's your problem, boy?" Hal snapped, loosening his constricting necktie when the chauffeur shut the door and walked around to the front.

"I got no problem, Uncle Hal," Matthew said. He reached out brazenly and held the Order of Merit hanging from the older man's lapel between two fingers. He snorted and let it fall contemptuously. "Pretty. So who's got a better handshake? O'Dea or the Queen?"

The chauffeur got behind the wheel and shut the door.

"Take us to the airport," Hal said.

The chauffeur glanced in the rearview mirror, then shrugged and nodded.

"Ain't we going to the big soiree?" Matthew said, watching as Governor's House swung away and the Lincoln headed down the long drive.

"Boy," Hal sighed. "I wouldn't let you eat in the kitchen dressed like that."

"I guess I'm an embarrassment to you and all your white friends."

"What the hell do you know about my friends? Or me? Or yourself, even?" Hal said. "Look at yourself. You got a goddamned pair of what, Cheyenne moccasins, and an Apache headband? And your hair. What nation's that? Haight-Ashbury Tribe? Yeah. With a handful of cigars you could make a nice livin' standing outside a dime store."

"Leave off, old man," Matthew said, scowling and turning to the window.

"Oh, what? Am I touchin' a nerve? That was disgraceful, what you did back there. To yourself and me, and to your people."

"What the hell do you know about our people? Right now nearly a hundred brothers and sisters are legally holed up on Alcatraz Island and the US government is shippin' Jolly Giant Johnson out to Frisco to kick down the walls and drag 'em out in a sack. *In a sack!* And you're off at Rideau Hall gettin' a medal from the Queen, and shakin' hands with the Man and goin' all over Canada on your grand tour, posin' for pictures. And what'd you even do?"

"You don't know what you're talkin' about, Matthew. I'm one of the reasons our people are better off than any other tribe in North America."

"Our people?"

"Yeah, Matthew. *Our* people. The Inuit. Maybe if your mama hadn't dragged your little ass down to the States, maybe if you spent more time up here learnin' about your own culture than soakin' up the sun and smokin' pot down at Berkeley, you'd know somethin' about your own people."

"Maybe if my daddy hadn't died for the white man six thousand miles from home, somebody would've been around to teach me."

Hal bit his lip. Matthew's father, Hal's only brother, had stopped a

Chinese bullet in Kapyong Valley back in '51 when Matthew was only a year old. His mother had moved them down to California for a teaching job and stayed. He'd only seen them maybe five times in the past eighteen years.

The kid was right. It had been his responsibility in the absence of his brother to teach Matthew. He'd been so caught up in his government work, he'd never seen to his familial duties. And now here they were, end of the line, and the kid was all he had, last in the chain. And he was angry, hotheaded. He could break generations of tradition and duty just by lighting up a joint, sticking his middle finger in Hal's face, and heading back to the States.

Hal had spent a lot of time on the phone with his sister-in-law to get Matthew up here. They were two of the same, mother and son, all for tearing down everything. Power to the people in nineteen sixty nine. Dubious that G-man Eskimo poster boy Uncle Hal had anything worthwhile to offer. But what did he expect? She had raised him alone, tough broad that she was. She had a right to raise him to be the man she wanted him to be. If Matthew's father had lived, who knows?

Eighteen years. A long time. Eighteen years ago Hal had only just begun to speak English. Now he was getting chauffeured back and forth from the governor's house.

They didn't say anything more to each other till they got to the airport.

Hal put his hands in his pockets and watched Matthew light up a cigarette as the chauffeur emptied the trunk of bags, the tinny voice of the announcer calling out arrivals and departures in French and English.

He couldn't get used to calling the place St. John's Airport. It was still Torbay to him.

"Guess this is it," said Matthew, slinging his father's old OD green rucksack over his shoulder after the limousine pulled away.

"The first thing you need to know," Hal said, "is that all things have *aniriit*."

"Huh?"

"Breath. Souls. Men, animals, hawks, seals, fish, bears. Even white men, believe it or not."

Matthew took a long drag on his cigarette.

"There's no corn on the tundra, no bread," he went on. "You hunt and you fish. There's an old saying that goes, 'the peril of our existence is that our diet consists entirely of souls.' Souls look to be avenged when they die. So to avoid the anger of the *aniriit*, the Inuit have to live by certain rules and customs. In this way, we atone. Like, when we kill a seal. A seal swims in salt water. He's always thirsty. So we spit clean water down the seal's throat, after a kill, so it will tell its brothers and sisters we were hospitable."

"Yeah so how do you know all this?" Matthew ventured, blowing smoke.

Hal grinned. Because of his short hair and his suit, the kid thought he was one of these Apple Indians, like they called 'em down in the States. Red on the outside, white on the inside.

"My father taught me. I'm an *angakkuq*."

"What's that?" the kid asked, dragging down to the filter.

"Whyn't you skip the plane back to California? Come on up with me to Kangiqsualujjuaq. I'll tell you all about it."

He blew the last of the smoke, threw down the butt and ground it beneath his heel.

"Mom'll be pissed," he said.

Hal shrugged.

"So let her be pissed."

~

THEY CHARTERED a twin engine to take them up to his place in Kangiqsualujjuaq.

The kid slept most of the way, and they didn't speak much till they were over the small airstrip, just a gray slash of gravel and some low buildings.

"Where are we?" Matthew mumbled, squinting out the window at the miles of snow covered granite hills.

"This is home, Matthew. You're looking at autonomous Inuit land, ceded to us by the government goin' on ten years ago now. You see, we Inuit don't have to park our dog sleds up on Parliament Hill to be heard. We mostly get what we ask for."

"Why? Why's it different here? 'Cause the white man don't want this land?"

"There've been attempts at removal and relocation. Oil companies, the fishing industry, NATO even wanted it for strategic purposes. But they get stopped at the highest level, before people even hear about 'em."

"You gonna tell me you stop 'em?" Matthew smirked.

Hal looked at his nephew meaningfully.

"C'mon," said Matthew. "Why would the Queen of England listen to you? What makes you so special? What do you even do? I mean, I read about you at all these rich parties, cuttin' ribbons on museums and breaking ground on cultural centers. But what do you really do?"

"I work for the government."

Matthew rolled his eyes and shook his head.

"But what kinda work do you do, and how do you reconcile your culture and working for the white man?"

"You gonna write a paper about it?"

"Seriously."

The pilot announced their descent then, and they were quiet as the plane was buffeted by the crosswinds and made an arm rest squeezer of a landing on the little field.

When they'd taxied to a stop near one of the blue green hangars that looked more like it was built to store snowmobiles than planes, Hal gathered his things and left the cabin without a word.

They tromped down the ladder onto the gravel and into the biting November wind. It was colder up here, and Matthew, a Californian from the time he was three years old, was underdressed.

"In a couple days we'll have to use snowmobiles or sleds," Hal said, as one of the mechanics brought a battered old Jeep around for them.

Matthew was staring down the runway at a pile of ten big black stones arranged to suggest a standing figure.

"What's that? An *inuksuk*?"

Hal smiled. The kid had done a little research anyway. But the cairn figure wasn't meant to be human.

"That's old Nanuq."

"What, like Mighty Nanuq?"

"You know him?" Hal asked.

"Sure," Matthew said drolly. "The Canadian government's big bad bear. Keeping the free world's breakfast tables safe for maple syrup and fighting the Soviet menace, plus the occasional rampaging giant walrus. All for Queen and country."

"Don't laugh at giant walruses," Hal muttered. "This is Nanuq, The Master Of All Polar Bears."

"So the white men named their monster after him, huh? Just another example of aboriginal culture being commercialized for anglo-Europeans."

"Looks good on a t-shirt," Hal said. "And we call 'em *kabloonak*."

"Huh?"

"The white man. *Kabloonak*."

"*Kabloonak*," Matthew said, trying it out and grinning slightly. "So do the Inuit believe in praying to bears or something?"

"Inuit don't believe," said Hal, tossing his stuff in the bed of the Jeep and slipping on his parka. "We fear."

As they bumped along the unpaved road and Matthew rubbed his hands in front of the heater, Hal continued.

"Inuit live in a changing world of storms and ice, migrating food sources. Hardship. We don't believe in praying for comfort, we honor and appease the spirits of *sila*, the sky, which is filled with the souls of men and animals, to keep the people going. These things I'm telling you aren't written down, Matthew. My grandfather used to tell me that paper can be ripped up and lost on the wind, or burned. These laws," he held up his three fingers and counted them off, "are eternal. There is *tirigusuusiit*, that which must be avoided, the *maligait*, that which must be followed, and the *piqujait*. That which must be done. That last one, that's an important one for you."

"How come?"

"Because you come from a tradition of *angakkuit*, dating all the way back to the *taimmani* time – the long ago."

"Was my father an *angakkuq*?" Matthew asked.

"He was too young when your grandfather initiated me. Then we drifted apart." Hal sighed. "But *you* might be."

"Yeah?" Matthew smirked.

"It's no little thing, Matthew. But it's the reason I brought you up here. I don't have any kids. And the tradition has to be passed on. It's *piqujait* for our family."

"We made a pact. Ages ago. This is back in the days when the *kavdlunait* threatened our lands. They were men from across the Atlantic. In dragon boats with yellow hair and weapons of steel."

"What, like Vikings?"

"Yeah," said Hal, waving to a broad woman bundled in a parka walking down the road with a child at her side. She waved back, smiling, and they went on. "They made their settlements up around the Tunulliarfik Fjord, and they started to push west across the strait, but somebody in our family, the first *angakkuq*, stopped 'em. He called on the power of Nanuq, the Master of All Polar Bears, and Nanuq froze their dragon boats in the water, and knocked them back across the sea."

The Jeep turned up an unmarked gravel road and groaned along to a simple brightly colored one room house set back in the hills.

"This is your place?"

"You thought it'd be bigger, huh?" Hal smiled.

"Well, you're like a national personality! You shouldn't be living in..."

"Hey. I live here because I choose to. I could build a big house somewhere away from my people, in Toronto or St. John's or something. But then I'd be exactly what you think I am, right?"

He killed the engine and went out into the cold without another word, greeting a pack of heavy coated dogs that seemed to come barking and leaping excitedly from everywhere at once, out from under the porch, from under a broken down and rusted-up pickup, from around back of the shabby little house.

He laughed and greeted each one in his own language, and Matthew wondered at him as he got the bags from the back and followed him inside.

The interior was dim and cluttered, the house of a man with no partner to tend to it. There were stacks of books and newspapers, and antlers and carved wooden masks covered the mantle. A pair of handmade snowshoes hung on the wall, and a harpoon. Hal took off his parka and draped his suit jacket over a chair, the red and gold medal dangling forgotten.

"I'll make some coffee," he said, and got busy doing it. "Get that fire going. You think it's cold now, it's gonna storm tonight."

Matthew lit the fire in the low stone hearth and fed it.

"How do you know? *Angakkuq* got some kind of weather sense?"

"*Angakkut* is the plural," Hal said from the kitchenette. "Nah, I heard it on the pilot's radio."

He returned with a mug of steaming coffee that had some kind of insignia on it: The Canadian Intelligence Corps.

Hal watched as Matthew turned the cup to read the insignia, and smiled.

"It's OK to drink out of it."

Matthew took the cup and sipped, feeling the hot brew warm his chilled insides. There was something else in there that had a bite of liquor.

"Now you asked me what I do for the government," Hal said, settling into a patched leather chair with a hiss and blowing into his mug. "It started for me, back in October of 1943. I was way up on Cape Chidley with my grandfather, undergoing the initiation rite to become an *angakkuq*. I had met my *tuurngaq*. That's the spirit helper, kind of a familiar that..."

Matthew had sat down on a foot rest, and as Hal began to speak, the kid's eyes slid along the mantle, over stone knives and arrow heads, and settling finally on a fearsomely carved mask that represented a bear's snarling face.

"Go on, take it down," said Hal, when he noticed Matthew's look.

Matthew blinked.

"Sorry."

"Nah, take it."

Matthew rose and touched the bear mask on the mantle, then took it in his hands. He grinned at the touch.

"Feel that?" Hal smiled. "The thrill of contact, the connection to ancient things?"

"Is this Nanuq?" Matthew asked.

"That's right. Try it on."

"Yeah?"

"Yeah."

Matthew turned the mask around and held it up to his face.

"It's better that I show you anyhow," said Hal.

And when the old wood mask touched Matthew's face, he wasn't Matthew anymore. He was young Hallauk Anawak, standing outside an igloo at the edge of a blizzard at the foot of the Torngat Mountains.

It was 1943 and his grandfather was dead.

HALLAUK WAS STARING down at the wooden mask, on the stony shore of the strait, deciding whether or not to fling the thing into the turgid sea, when a spluttering drone reached his ears above the howling of the polar wind. It quickly changed into a plummeting screech.

A silvery twin engine plane streaked at an alarming angle down from the impenetrable white sky, knocked off course by the storm. The pilot must have been crazy, trying to fly a hunk of metal like that through a cloud of blowing powder.

Hallauk could see no markings he recognized. She had flown up the coast from the south. Probably from Hopedale, or maybe Rigolet.

But she was no local. She was losing altitude fast, but the pilot was doing his best to keep her nose up.

Hallauk forgot about the mask for the moment and flinched as the plane's buzzing racket was cut violently short. He saw a plume of water and heard the tremendous noise as the belly of the plane met the churning water with a terrible impact and a spout of water, the wings shearing off and flopping into the waves.

Hallauk dropped the mask into his pack and pushed his whalebone and sealskin kayak out across the frozen surf to the edge of the roiling sea, then hopped inside and paddled as hard as he could for the sinking wreckage.

As he approached the swiftly disappearing machine, he heard a loud crack and saw the cockpit window burst open in a spray of glass.

A *kabloonak* appeared, blood pouring down his pink face. He cursed as he pulled himself through the broken window, then crouched precariously on the roof of the sinking plane and reached back into the cockpit to pull out a rucksack bulging with gear.

Hallauk called out to the man and made for him. The bloody *kabloonak* struggled with the rucksack and paused to wave frantically before falling to his hands and knees to scramble up the back of the tilting plane, grabbing for the tail section as the nose dipped under.

Hallauk pulled for all he was worth until the rising and falling bow of the kayak bumped alongside the hull of the plane.

He held out his paddle and the bloody man slung the rucksack over his back and steadied himself, slipping down the side of the plane until he laid sprawled over the bow, boots in the water, nearly upsetting the little craft.

Hallauk regained his balance and pushed off. He cut through the turbulent sea, away from the suck of the drowning plane. He aimed the bow for shore as the *kabloonak* wheezed and spluttered.

When they had reached the shore, the man flopped onto the ice, chilled from the spray of the icy sea, the blood freezing on his face.

Hallauk slipped from the kayak and pulled it onto the ice, then gripped the *kabloonak* by the strap of his rucksack and dragged him to the shore.

The man's eyes fluttered, and Hallauk used the back of one of his furred mittens to wipe away the blood from his eyes.

He was a strong looking man, clean shaven and blonde haired, with a long nose and bright eyes. The blood in his face had come from a gash in his scalp, nothing too serious.

The man was a Canadian soldier by his clothing, a heavy canvas jumpsuit with many pockets and a belt with an automatic pistol. He had wool gloves and a scarf against the cold, and heavy boots, but they were soaked and freezing, which worried Hallauk.

"My God, boy, where did you come from?" the man said in French. He almost laughed when he'd had a moment to study his savior.

"This man saw you crash from the shore," Hallauk answered haltingly. His French wasn't good.

"What's your name?"

"Hallauk."

"Hal, then. George LeDuc's the name. Major. Canadian Intelligence Corps." He sat up slowly, groaning, and looked back over his shoulder at the open sea. "Nobody else made it?"

"No," said Hallauk.

"Right," LeDuc breathed. He attempted to get to his feet and sat down hard. "Damn! I can't feel my feet."

"They are frozen. This man's igloo is only a little way up the shore. Let this man help."

Hallauk drew LeDuc's arm over his shoulder and stood up, supporting him. It was a chore dragging the larger man to the igloo, which he and his grandfather had built only yesterday, but soon they were out of the wind. The man fell on his back on the skins.

Hallauk took out his knife and began to saw away LeDuc's boots. It was tough work, and halfway through the first job LeDuc realized what he was doing and slapped his hands away.

"What the hell are you doing?"

"They will come off no other way," said Hallauk, and he pushed aside LeDuc's hands and continued to work.

"What are you going to do?" LeDuc mumbled after the first crackling ruin of a shoe was peeled away, revealing the icy sock beneath, which Hallauk also cut away until the pale shiny white skin and the rosy red toes were exposed.

Hallauk said nothing until the second frozen foot was exposed, then he turned and hunch-walked across the igloo to the carcass of the caribou he had shot only moments before his grandfather had walked off into the storm, leaving him alone.

He bit off his mitten and touched the trunk of the cooling animal. The igloo had protected it some. It was still a little warm, though not as much as he would've liked.

He dragged the carcass over and sliced the belly open. As the steaming guts bulged from the wound, he turned and grabbed the *kabloonak*'s ankles and thrust his frozen feet into the wound.

LeDuc screamed and cursed and hammered at Hallauk's arms and shoulders. That was good. If he felt pain it meant he would not lose the feet.

After a while, he released his hold on LeDuc and the man sat up. He did not remove his feet from the caribou.

"Where are we, son?"

"Ikkudliayuk."

LeDuc stared for a moment, blinked, and reached into his breast pocket. He pulled out a waterproof map and smoothed it on the floor of the igloo.

"Where?" he repeated, pointing to the coast.

Hallauk found the remote fjord and tapped it.

LeDuc nodded and traced a line to the northern end of the peninsula.

"I need to get here, Hal. Cape Chidley Islands. It's very important. Can you take me in your kayak?"

"No," Hallauk said. There was no room.

LeDuc put the heels of his hands to his eyes.

"Listen, boy. Maybe you don't know this, but there's a war going on. All over the rest of the world. Between us and the Germans. Bad people."

Hallauk nodded, but grew disinterested in the *kabloonak*'s banter.

His grandfather had told him all about the white man and his many wars.

"But it's going against us. In Japan and China, they've got these beasties. Big. Tremendous things."

He held out his arms to demonstrate, and let them fall with a sigh when Hallauk made no response.

"I don't expect you to understand. Look, they're monsters. Bigger than the biggest thing you can imagine. The SS, the Nazis… the Germans. They developed their own. And the Tracking Room in Ottawa, they picked up an Enigma code message. It was garbled. Something about Operation Fenris and Taskforce Jormungand. Look, don't worry about that. We think it's being escorted by a U-boat control. Gah!"

He pinched the bridge of his nose for a moment as Hallauk furrowed his brow. Then he continued.

"That's like a kayak that travels under the water. They're bringing their monster to shore at Cape Chidley. We don't know what it is, only that it's amphibious. They're going to march it south, right down to Ottawa, destroy the C.I.C. HQ and probably every settlement in between."

This made Hallauk pause. He knew of several Inuit communities between the cape and Ottawa. His parents and his young brother resided in one.

"God knows what it'll do after that, but it'll mean the Nazis will gain a hold in the North Atlantic, and a whole lot of innocent people will die. There's nobody up here equipped to deal with the thing and no time to divert any ships. My squad had anti-monster gear, but it's lost." He looked out across the crashing sea again and shook his head. "I'm gonna miss the landing, too. But I've still got to get to the cape. I've still got to *try*, dammit."

LeDuc turned back to Hallauk and shook his head.

"Is *any* of this getting through to you?"

Hallauk stared at the exasperated *kabloonak*. He understood that some of what LeDuc was talking about was very important to him. But he also understood what was important to him personally. His grandfather had said a test would come, just before he died. And his family lay in the path of this Nazi monster.

"This stupid man knows of monsters," Hallauk said quietly. "But you can't use his kayak."

LeDuc opened his mouth to protest.

"You can use his grandfather's, though, if it is so important. It is outside under the snow."

LeDuc pursed his lips. He smiled, and struck Hallauk an open handed blow on the shoulder that nearly bowled him over.

"Well, that's something," he said, and gathered his map and his rucksack. "Now, what about these feet? Am I going to have to stay in the kayak, or can I walk?"

"They are not too frozen. This unskilled man can make boots from this animal," he said, nodding to the carcass in which LeDuc's bare feet reposed.

"I've got a spare pair of dry socks in my pocket," said LeDuc. "So that's something else."

THEY CLEAVED to the shoreline out of necessity, for to drift to far out in the strait could mean getting turned around in the storm. They paddled without respite. Hallauk was impressed by LeDuc's resilience. He was not like the other white men he had known or heard of. Though battered from the crash, sore footed, and alone, he still kept pace with Hallauk, and argued that they should press on, even when the sun had sunk behind the Torngats and further progress was impossible.

The storm finally abated at sunset. LeDuc cursed Hallauk when the Inuit steered to shore and pulled his kayak out of the black water, but he begrudgingly followed, knowing well enough he couldn't go on in the blue dark.

They made a low fire in up in a cleft of rock in the foothills and huddled around it. Hallauk stared up at the ominous dark mountains.

"What the hell were you doing out here, Hal?" LeDuc asked. "And what happened to the man whose kayak I've been paddling?"

"The kayak belonged to this man's grandfather," said Hallauk. "He's dead now."

"Did you kill him?" LeDuc asked, twisting open a small can of rations and dipping a tiny fork into it.

Hallauk stared.

"I mean," said LeDuc around a mouthful of his noxious smelling food. "Don't you Eskimos abandon your elderly when they become a nuisance?"

"This man's grandfather was never a nuisance. When this man's grandfather lost his teeth, this man chewed his food for him, just as his grandfather did for his father when he was a baby," said Hallauk, looking into the fire. "Sometimes, if they can't care for themselves, in lean times, the old ask to be killed. Usually, they decide to die. Where did your grandfather die, Major LeDuc?"

LeDuc stopped chewing for a moment and swallowed, a reflective look in his eye.

"In an almshouse in Fredericton," he admitted.

"This man's grandfather walked into the mouth of a monster."

"You mean that storm?"

Hallauk lay his head on the ground and said no more that night.

In the morning, Hallauk woke to find the major already up and working excitedly.

There were a pair of binoculars dangling from around his neck, and the rucksack was open.

On the ground beside it was a pair of stubby, broken rifles (there were holes in the end of the barrel) with drums of ammunition, and a blocky canvas satchel.

Hallauk sat up as LeDuc picked up the satchel and one of the rifles and slammed a drum clip into the underside of it.

"My friend, this is where we part ways. Fortune's smiled on me this morning, somewhat." He took the binoculars from his neck and tossed them to Hallauk. "Here. As thanks. You can take that extra Lanchester if you like, as well, but I'm afraid I'll need the ammo."

"What are you going to do?"

"Looks like the Nazis ran into the same flavor of trouble from your grandfather's storm that we did. Take a look," he said, gesturing down the boulder strewn shore.

Hallauk put the field glasses to his eyes and peered to the north.

In an inlet in the rocky shoreline, an iron boat longer than a whale floated. A yellow bearded *kabloonak,* almost like the *kavdlunait* of which his grandfather had spoken, in a black reefer jacket stained with sea salt, and a high necked white sweater and cap, stood atop a tower in the center of the boat, shouting guttural orders to a gaggle of men in dark peacoats hustling to repair a gash rent in the starboard bow. A group of men armed with rifles stood watch. These had red armbands over their left elbows, with white circles and strange black symbols within.

A trio of men in drab grey coveralls were working to erect some kind of long, slim metal apparatus fixed to the side of the tower on which the captain stood.

"They probably ran aground during the storm. As we suspected, the Nazis are using some kind of radio antenna to control their monster. They've only just erected it," said LeDuc, sliding the action on his Lanchester. "Look there off that small island."

Hallauk swung the binoculars to the indicated area, and saw a huge swell in the sea. Something was circling nearby like an orca, but bigger even than the iron boat. Its huge wake rippled white in the icy waters.

LeDuc patted his shoulder then.

"Wish me luck, my friend."

"What do you hope to do?"

"Well, after I blow the control transceiver, there's forty more sailors down in the belly of that U-boat. I've got a hundred rounds of ammunition. Maybe I can take 'em by surprise, if they all line up, eh?"

A dark creature underwater, whatever it was, swam beneath the sheet of ice on their side of the strait, and with a flick of its head, thrust itself up through the frozen water.

What pulled itself from the hole and onto the shore a few yards north of the U-boat made both men shudder uncontrollably.

It was a thing of nightmares. A monstrous dripping black wolf head, the jaws lined with fangs each the size of a tall chest of drawers, between which a massive tongue lolled. Two sharp ears like the fins of airplanes protruded from its enormous black skull, and two unnatural, cloudy white eyes glistened in its horrible face. It looked about briefly, snuffling its black nose. Then a pair of long-clawed feet smashed through the ice and hooked into the shore, pulling the rest of its bulk out of the water.

The body that followed that terrible head was even more horrendous to behold. It was nearly twice as long as the U-boat, and about midway down its torso its furry canine shoulders gave way to a greenish, scaly fish body that tapered into a serpentine, finned tail. Its two rear legs were scaled and clawed, like that of a dragon in a fairy book.

The hideous monstrosity shook its immense head like a wet dog and arched back its neck, eliciting a bone-chilling howl loud enough to be felt beneath their feet and in their very bones. When the terrifying cry finally died off, they could hear the distant rumble of avalanches in the Torngats.

LeDuc snatched the binoculars from Hallauk and stared through them.

"It has a collar. That must be the radio receiver," he observed.

True enough, there was a metal collar around the creature's neck, marked with the same bent black crosses as the arms of the German soldiers down below.

"And there's our *monstrumfuhrer* on the conning tower," said LeDuc, pointing to the U-boat as a bespectacled man with a red armband in a green uniform and black jackboots emerged from the depths of the tower. He had a complicated looking metal helmet on, and was shouting at the men adjusting the antenna.

"Wish I had a proper rifle instead of this little typewriter," LeDuc said bitterly.

"This man thinks you will need help," said Hallauk.

LeDuc looked at Hallauk.

"It's good of this man to offer, but unless he's got a giant pussycat for that thing oversized mongrel down there to chase."

"This man has something better," said Hallauk, already digging through his pack for the mask.

Hallauk hesitated as he held the Nanuq mask in his hands. His grandfather had told him just what donning it to call the Master Bear meant.

But he saw the thing on the shore, saw that it was an abomination, and that the strange *kabloonak* with the metal hat on the iron boat (the one LeDuc had called the *monstrumfuhrer*) commanded this thing by unnatural means.

This was no monster of the depths or the mountains. It did not belong anywhere. And LeDuc had told him what these Nazis intended to do with it.

He thought of his mother and father and his young brother. His choice, after days of doubt, was as clear as the trackless fields of snow.

He placed the mask to his face and turned toward the mountains, raising his hands.

"Mighty Nanuq!" he roared. "Your people need you!"

LeDuc had watched him sideways with a cocked eyebrow until he stood up and began shouting into the waste.

Then he cursed and skidded down the hillside in a clatter of stones, diving for the cover of an ice capped boulder on the shore as the Nazis on the deck of the U-boat turned as one at the sound of Hallauk's voice echoing down the hills.

LeDuc heard the clicking of their Schmeissers and the harsh bark of orders.

But as the first rapid patter of machinegun fire ripped the length of the shore, a powerful wind kicked up, so icy and strong as to force LeDuc to grip the boulder or be blown out across the ice.

Hallauk stood with his arms spread on the hill, heedless of the

Nazi bullets that were too weak to reach his position anyway and struck only the stones at his feet. The fur of his parka flapped about him, a gust of wind flinging back his hood and throwing his black hair in his eyes.

From the center of the cluster of the Torngat Mountains a funnel cloud of snow gathered and rose, as if all the cold in the area were drawn towards that faraway spot.

And in the middle of that maelstrom of ice and snow, a huge shape reared, indistinguishable from the whirling powder but for a faint black spot in the center of its knobby peak, a hundred meters in the air.

There came a thunderous crashing noise, rhythmic and relentless, growing in power and sound, unimaginable footsteps that sent loose rocks tumbling down the mountainsides as if fleeing its dreadful approach.

The U-boat captain and the Nazi *monstrumfuhrer* raised field glasses to their faces and exclaimed.

But their shouts, already barely heard over the howl of the oncoming storm, were lost entirely by the cacophonous deep roar that resounded from the midst of the mountains, as if those prehistoric edifices themselves had found a voice.

And then Hallauk saw it for the second time, LeDuc and the Nazis for their first.

It would be the Nazis' last.

Mighty Nanuq. The Master of All Polar Bears. The White God Bear.

A pair of luminous blue circles over the black smudge of its long nose shined through the storm cloud like the beams of lighthouses.

Its head bobbed curiously on its thick sloping neck. It walked upright on its haunches, the gargantuan forepaws with their row of curling black claws pawing at the air.

Then, as its roar of challenge ended, it wavered and fell forward with a crash that churned the waters and broke the mountaintops. It began to run, an undulating lope over the spine of the Torngats, straight past Hallauk and for the U-boat and the Sea Wolf that snarled on the shore, kicking over boulders and smashing outcroppings to gravel as it came.

The Nazis on the slanting deck gripped the rails to keep from being shook off into the subzero waters. They screamed in abject terror at the approach of the monstrous polar bear.

Only the red armbands, the captain, and the *monstrumfuhrer* kept their heads.

The captain gestured at the large anti-aircraft gun mounted on a swivel mechanism midway down the deck, and two of the red armbands slung their machineguns and rushed to man it. Then the commander busied himself with rallying his panicked sailors, gesticulating for them to get below.

The *monstrumfuhrer* needed no such order. He snapped something at the captain, pointed to the Sea Wolf, and flicked a bulky visor on the helmet down over his eyes. In another minute he disappeared down the conning tower hatch.

The Sea Wolf snarled and slid like a seal off the shore, plunging beneath the water and coming up on the opposite side of the U-boat, interposing itself between the charging bear and its masters.

It pulled itself again on shore and half ran, half-slithered gamely out to meet its enemy.

Hallauk slid down the embankment and joined LeDuc behind the boulder as Nanuq reached the shore and skidded to a wary stop, kicking up an avalanche of stones, jaws popping like thunderclaps in anticipation of the clash.

"Great God, what is that thing?" LeDuc exclaimed.

"Mighty Nanuq," Hallauk said, his voice muffled by the mask. He took it off, but kept it by his side.

"God, man! Don't you need that to control it?"

"I do not control it," Hallauk said.

The Sea Wolf let out vicious warning barks, which Nanuq answered by raising once more up to its titanic height and opening its arms as if to welcome an attack.

The Sea Wolf spun suddenly, and its lashing tail swept the bear's haunches out from under it, sending it smashing on its back with such force that LeDuc and Hallauk both left the ground momentarily, along with every small stone on the shoreline.

Then the Sea Wolf pounced, its jaws seeking the bear's exposed throat.

Nanuq's paws clamped together, seizing it on either side of its head, and what followed was a savage clashing of teeth and claws. Clots of fur white and black flew into the air, along with gouts of blood that splashed all around like driving rain.

LeDuc peered around the rock past the battling monsters and saw the U-boat sailors regain their vaunted *Kreigsmarine* discipline. They were filing in an orderly line into the hatches, glancing over their shoulders, riveted by the spectacle of the two immense creatures.

He also saw the SS men climb behind the deck gun.

"Your big friend's about to take a pounding from that 105mm. And if that sub gets away from shore, we'll never catch it," LeDuc spat, fighting to keep the shakiness from his voice.

Hallauk's concerns were his own, or rather, Nanuq's. That tail lash. He'd never seen any creature fight like that.

"The *monstrumfuhrer* fights for the monster," he mused out loud.

LeDuc shook his head and primed his Lanchester.

"God save the Queen," he muttered, and broke from cover.

Hallauk watched the crazy *kabloonak* run past the wrestling monsters, splashing through the slick pools of blood, in full risk of being crushed or driven into the sea.

But the Nazis weren't looking for a lone soldier any more. Their attention was on retreat and covering that retreat with fire from the deck gun.

*Nanuq*, Hallauk thought, as he slipped the mask over his face. *You must break free from this creature.*

But Nanuq was totally engaged in the combat. Though his claws had torn rows of slashes in the Sea Wolf's black hide, his own shaggy white fur streamed with blood from his enemy's reciprocation.

Nanuq was a ferocious combatant, but the Sea Wolf shared its master's cunning. It ducked away from the bear's snapping jaws and nipped beneath its arms and chin, drawing out the stronger fighter's strength with bite after bleeding bite. Its claws raked and scrabbled at the bear's chest, and its coiling tail kept it from being dislodged.

On the U-boat, the big deck gun lowered and swung its muzzle in the monsters' direction.

*Nanuq, roll. Take the fight into the sea,* Hallauk thought.

The bear gave a colossal roar and did as Hallauk had suggested, feinting and rolling right in the wake of the scurrying LeDuc. It carried its snapping counterpart beneath is heavy bulk for a moment, and the deck gun opened fire, skimming Nanuq's shoulder with a whistling round that tore a shallow red furrow in its heaving shoulder.

But then the Sea Wolf was brought on top again, and both were on the ice, which gave beneath their combined weight and plunged them underneath the surface of the water.

Hallauk rushed to the other end of the boulder, and heard a chatter of machinegun fire that made him flinch back.

He looked toward the U-boat and saw the man who had fired the deck gun flip over the rail and bounce off the grey hull before splashing into the sea.

The second Nazi unlimbered his own machinegun and got off a burst of fire before LeDuc's Lanchester burped and flattened him.

Two lagging sailors reached the conning tower, but the captain had seen the lone commando and ducked below, the hatch slamming shut with a clang.

As the two stranded men fell to their knees cursing and banging on the hull, the U-boat's engines gurgled to life and it began to slide away from the shore.

LeDuc dropped his Lanchester and yanked the satchel from his shoulder, running to the outermost southern tip of inlet.

As the U-boat swung past, he fiddled with the satchel, cocked it back, and flung it high.

The bag arched up and the whipping strap looped over the tall, quivering antenna and went taut, sliding down it length to come to a stop directly on the apparatus, bouncing against the conning tower.

The two sailors stopped what they were doing and went to leap over the conning tower railing, but only one crashed clumsily to the deck before the satchel charge exploded, blowing the other man into the water along with fragments of the control apparatus.

Hallauk smiled and almost gave a cheer. Then a tidal wave of icy water suddenly crashed over the boulder and himself, drenching him and washing the mask from his grip. He collapsed, shivering, the water on his mittens quickly icing over. He felt the swift onset of permeating numbness, and knew he was dead.

Nanuq and the Sea Wolf breached, locked in each other's grip, biting and clawing with unfettered ferocity now, kicking up waves and overturning icebergs in their fury.

The Sea Wolf clamped its muzzle down on Nanuq's shoulder but the bear roared and took hold of it by the collar, wrenching it back and flinging it into the water.

The Sea Wolf rose again and swam at Nanuq like a hunting whale, closing the distance with a speed that seemed monumentally unfair given its size.

But the bear heaved its lungs and inhaled. All the snow ice seemed to be drawn into its gaping maw. Even the bobbing glaciers seemed to flake and crack asunder and flee into its yawning mouth.

Miraculously, Hallauk, close to the action, felt the bone chilling cold of death flee his body, and saw the white frost coating his mittens and arms fly off his parka, drawn into the bear's lungs.

Then, as the Sea Wolf reached Nanuq, the mighty bear exhaled for all it was worth, and a shockingly white hissing cloud of breath struck the monstrosity full in the face.

When Nanuq ceased its exhalation and the freezing cloud dispersed, the Sea Wolf, and the water surrounding it, was encased in rigid ice, flash frozen in mid-leap.

The bear lowered its thick brow and stood bloodied, glaring at its incapacitated opponent with its emotionless blue eyes. It huffed contentedly.

"Hey! Hey!"

Hallauk looked down the beach again and saw LeDuc waving his arms and jumping to get Hallauk's attention.

"The boat! The boat!"

The U-boat, smoke streaming from the destroyed control transceiver and dragging the broken antenna, was sinking beneath the water, diving for the open sea behind the triumphant bear.

Hallauk looked around and spied the mask lying a few feet away. He rushed over and snatched it up, slapping it to his face.

*Nanuq*, he thought. *The iron boat must not escape!*

Nanuq turned ponderously just as the U-boat's tower dipped beneath the surface.

But the bear went down to its forepaws and dipped its head into water.

When it came up, the U-boat was dripping between its jaws like a doomed salmon, and with a single shriek and groan of metal, Mighty Nanuq bit down and snapped the vessel in two.

There was an ear-shattering explosion and the bear let the broken halves of the submarine tumble into the water, to dive once more and forever to the floor of the strait.

"God almighty!" LeDuc exclaimed, limping up alongside Hallauk now.

The two of them were soaked to their skin and drenched in monster blood, but unharmed.

"Hal, you and your friend here just saved Ottawa and the C.I.C."

Hallauk grinned brightly.

"This humble man was only doing what he thought best."

"Humble? You're going to have to lose that trait if you're going to hang around me, my boy." He dug in his pocket and pulled out a crumpled package of broken cigars, and lit one.

He held out the other to Nanuq. "I've got work for you, if you want it, and we could desperately use your help. Uh, and *his*, of course," he said, glancing back at the towering bear wading around the frozen SS beast in the middle of the strait.

Nanuq took the offered cigar curiously, smelled the tobacco, and put it in between his lips.

LeDuc leaned in and lit it.

"Say, Hal. What happens now, with him?"

"Now Nanuq takes his reward," Hallauk said shrugging and drawing the smoke in.

He coughed.

And the bear gave a mighty snort and lunged toward the head of the frozen Sea Wolf. Its jaws closed around the wolfish skull and the ice began to crack with a noise that made them both clamp their hands on their ears.

HE WAS NO LONGER Hal Anawak, his uncle. He was Matthew Anawak again. But he knew everything. He had fought all the secret battles, in the forests and the ocean, against submarines and monsters. He had watched Nanuq bat Soviet spyplanes out of the sky. He felt the loss of George LeDuc to throat cancer four years ago.

And he knew the bear's price.

He took the mask from his face and looked at his uncle.

Hal was smoking a cigar and staring at him.

"George got me smoking these things," he said. "Should have never started. You'd do well to quit those cigarettes, too."

"You've got cancer."

"Yeah," Hal nodded, stubbing the butt out in a brass ashtray. "They'd have to cut my throat to dig it out. It's alright, Matthew. It's time for me to pay back Nanuq. The question is, what're you gonna do?"

Matthew watched the dying smoke curl up from the ashtray and dissipate somewhere near the low ceiling.

"In the Plains cultures, tobacco's used ceremonially," he said. "You present it as a gift to elders."

"Not among our people."

"Uncle Hal, they're all our people. Aboriginals everywhere."

"Kid, I've worked hard to keep the Inuit from getting the same raw deal."

"I know. I know all about it. This is how you've called in favors all these years."

"A giant bear's a pretty good bargaining chip," Hal said.

"You've single-handedly kept Canada in the Monster Race in exchange for autonomous rights for the Inuit."

"Yeah. George helped a lot with that. He taught me English, and the ins and outs of dealing with white men. I owe him a lot. I named the cultural center in Ottawa for him a few years back. After he died."

"I remember." Matthew put his head back on the chair and stared at the ceiling. "In this world, without a monster, a nation's got no voice."

"I know what you're gettin' at, kid. But I'm an Inuit first, Canadian second."

"But you've gone against the Canucks before," Matthew insisted, leaning forward.

"How do you know that? The mask?"

"Nobody even knew about Nanuq until two years ago, when that whole Israeli thing happened," Matthew said. "After that, the Treaty insured everybody had to put their monsters on the table. But if you brought Nanuq to the C.I.C. in '43, that means he was around for Hiroshima and Nagasaki, but he didn't participate."

"Sendin' Nanuq against a city. So many civilians," Hallauk muttered, shaking his head. "That's not what the bear is for."

"And Korea? I never heard of a giant polar bear fighting there."

"We didn't have any business there." Hallauk said. "I'm sorry, Matthew. We didn't. Your dad, he thought different."

"He was wrong. You were right. It wasn't our war."

"But if me and Nanuq had been there, maybe your dad…"

Matthew shook his head.

"And what about Vietnam?"

Hal opened his hands and shrugged.

"Canada ain't in Vietnam."

"Is it because of you?"

Hal stood up and paced.

"We got no business there, Matthew. Too many kids would've had to go over. You, if you ever came back. I couldn't take that chance of losing more family in some damn fool jungle fight."

He went to Matthew and took the mask from his hands, turned it over thoughtfully.

"They came to me with it," he said. "It was a big argument with the Americans, but I said no."

He set the mask on the mantle, straightened it.

"I wouldn't use the bear to invade the States, Uncle Hal. Just to give the Indians there a voice."

"You're talking about an international incident, Matthew. There are subtleties to this stuff. God, back in '43 we almost came to blows with the States over who had the right to that Johnson thing. If me and Nanuq hadn't come along..." he sighed and threw up his hands. "Hell, Matthew. What you do with the bear is your own business. I sure won't have anything to say about it. But before you pick that mask up again," he said, gesturing to the thing on the mantle, "you got to understand. Nanuq has his price."

MATTHEW ROSE EARLY, but not as early as Hal. He found the old man outside the igloo, feeding the dogs and ruffling their shaggy coats.

They were both dressed in traditional fur parkas, and Hal wore a pair of caribou bone *iglaak* slitted goggles. They were in sparse winter camp in the foothills, near the fiord where it had all begun.

"Thought you were never gonna get up," Hal said, his breath puffing in the cold air.

Matthew smiled. They'd driven the dogs all the way from Kangiqsualujjuaq, and Hal had used the time to answer his questions, teach him all that the mask hadn't already.

"Moment of truth, kid," Hal said.

He took the mask from the inside of his parka. Matthew hadn't seen it since the cabin, but he had known it was with them somehow, like a silent companion, or something tailing them through the cold wastes, just out of sight.

Hal kneeled down and set the mask in the snow, lingered on it with one hand, perhaps praying quietly, then stood up.

A gust of wind kicked up, stirring the snow into little shifting eddies and causing the dogs to howl and press close together.

"You follow the *piqujait* of our family, or you go back to sunny California. No shame in either. But I'm going out there," he said, pointing to the snowy mountains, shrouded in a descending curtain of pure white. "You can keep the mask or you can leave it here, but the next time you put it on, you know what it means."

He had said nothing about Alcatraz the whole trip. Neither of them had.

"So. This is goodbye?"

"Nah," said Hal. He stepped across the camp and grabbed the kid by his ears, pulled him close, and touched noses with him.

"*That's* goodbye."

He grinned, and took off his bone goggles. He slid them over Matthew's nose.

He walked past him then, and out of the camp, feet crunching in the snow.

"You know the way home, kid," he called over his shoulder. "So long."

Matthew did know the way home, just as he knew every inch of the coastline, every crook of mountain, and the foibles of each of the sled dogs.

He knew everything that Hal knew, and that was everything his grandfather had known, all the way back to the first *angakkuq* that called the bear to fight back the yellow haired *kavdlunait* (and as Hal himself did again, in a way, back in '43). The mask had told him most of it, and Hal had filled in the blank spots.

A tremendous roar shook the mountains, bouncing off stone and shifting snow and causing the hackles of dog and man to rise.

And deep in the midst of the whiteness into which Hal's fading footprints led, Matthew saw a smudge of black on high, and two burning blue eyes.

He looked down at the mask. The snow drifted swiftly across its carved face, burying it, swallowing it.

Matthew put his hands in his pockets and shivered.

*"We invite the United States to acknowledge the justice of our claim. The choice now lies with the leaders of the American government, to use violence upon us as before to remove us from our Great Spirit's land, or to institute a real change in its dealing with the American Indian. We do not fear your threat to charge us with crimes on our land. We and all other oppressed peoples would welcome spectacle of proof before the world of your title by genocide. Nevertheless, we seek peace."*

Richard Oakes, Mohican, IAT.

It was Thanksgiving Day, a little before noon.

Fisherman's Wharf was crowded with a boiling ocean of long-haired humanity, shouting slogans and waving signs, pressing against a navy blue wall of San Francisco's finest. The police faced the multi-colored mob with their riot shields set, a fence of scowling Spartans, batons at the ready.

The slogans and the shouting died out as Johnson rose to its feet in the middle of the police circle. The crowd reared back momentarily, a few shrieks breaking out, as the shadow of the enormous hairy biped fell across them.

Johnson was nearly a hundred meters tall, its features entirely hidden by ropes of long mossy hair. Some in the media had nicknamed it Cousin It for its passing resemblance to the hairy character on *The Addams Family*. The rising counterculture, often ridiculed for their own long hair, pointed to Johnson ironically as their representative in the federal government. Johnson was on t-shirts.

But Johnson was the least popular long hair on the Wharf today.

It had a massive canvas sack over its shoulder, olive green. Some had expressed disbelief at the audacity of the GSA's plan that been leaked to the news outlets, that Johnson was going to wade out to Alcatraz Island and gather up the insurgent Indians like wayward kittens and carry them back into police custody. But there it was, and at the sight of it the protesters forgot their fondness for and awe of the legendary creature and returned to the barricade line, hollering angrily up at the beast.

A few threw rotten produce up at it, but it would have taken Joe Namath to score a hit. But Johnson would not have noticed it anyway.

The hairy colossus turned its occult face from the excited crowd and walked to the water's edge, an event that caused windowpanes to rattle and residents blocks away to phone into emergency services and the police and demand to know if an earthquake were under way.

Johnson dipped its massive toe into the water, recoiled, then hopped into the bay, sinking to its thighs.

Heedless of the roar of the mob, it began to slowly wade out across the bay, causing the ships to bob in their moorings.

Seagulls circled the strange creature curiously, like a halo, as it left the shore behind.

In the center of the police, a few officers in military dress and men in expensive suits and sunglasses watched the creature's progress. Then the vegetables and furry fruit began to seek them out, and they retreated into a nearby limousine.

TV helicopters kept pace with the monster, pattering at a safe distance, zooming in on Johnson for the benefit of the home audience, record numbers of whom were tuning in to see those damn hippie Indians get what was coming to them.

A pair of Coast Guard boats escorted it.

On Alcatraz Island, the hundred members of the Indians of All Tribes watched the monster's slow advance across the bay. They were men, women and children of a dozen different nations. Apache, Arapaho, Eskimo, Cherokee, Sioux, Ho Chunk, Mohawk. Their ancestors would've had nothing in common with each other. But now they were uniform in two things; their mistreatment at the hands of the white government, and their purpose.

Richard Oakes was among them, their handsome Mohawk leader. He'd sent their demands to President Nixon and the besieging GSA and FBI officials.

They had legally reclaimed the unused penitentiary and The Rock on which it stood under the Treaty of Ft. Laramie.

They wanted an American Indian Cultural Center and Museum established on Alcatraz. A Native Spiritual Center, and a center for Native studies.

The feds' answer was making its way across the bay.

They lined the chipped and sea-scoured walls, now scrawled with INDIANS WELCOME and UNITED STATES INDIAN PROPERTY in big red letters, black hair, red armbands, the grandchildren of buckskinned warriors in denim and polyester. Some women and children watched the wading beast stoically, wrapped against the chilly sea air in colorful blankets. A few men sat in a circle, wailing and pounding out a soul soaring Lakota rhythm on a tom-tom, as a boy bristling with eagle feathers danced defiantly across the concrete.

Inside a makeshift booth within the prison, a young Santee Sioux named John Trudell keyed the mic to broadcast what he thought would be his last broadcast of Radio Free Alcatraz.

The Coast Guard cutters were the first to grind to a halt, a few of the men in orange life vests nearly pitching over the bows of their craft as the boats suddenly stopped dead in the water, as surely as if they'd hit a dock pylon. The engines groaned and smoked. Propellers chopped the water and then buzzed and chipped against solid ice, stopping altogether.

Men scurried on the decks to peer down at the thick ice spreading before their amazed eyes. It moved as quick as fire, and encompassed both boats, freezing them solidly in place before moving on across the bay, straight for the unsuspecting Johnson, up to his waist now in the bay.

The news choppers caught wind that something was wrong and circled in place, shutters clicking.

Then Johnson let out a confused, apelike huff and stopped its advance.

The ice encircled the creature, and crept up its belly.

The creature thrashed, and the ice cracked and gave way. Just as quickly, it renewed itself, and like quicksand, the harder the monster fought, the more entombed it became, until its powerful arms were pinned to its sides, and the glistening ice had frosted over its elbows, encasing Johnson in what looked like a glass column.

On the Wharf, every neck craned, every eye watered to see across the Bay. The limousine doors opened and the men who had gone inside to sit out the extraction stumbled out to see with their own eyes, shouting for subordinates to bring them binoculars.

Johnson moaned plaintively, pitifully, and shivered.

And at the foot of Alcatraz Island, something broke the surface of the water, something white as a mountain, and nearly as tall. It arose, water streaming from its sloping shoulders.

And at the sight of it, the Indians cheered.

The Master of All Polar Bears, Mighty Nanuq, shook the water from itself like a wet dog, and the cool bay water poured down on the Indians in a pelting rain. They laughed and cheered, and the drums thundered and the boy in the eagle feathers danced hard, though his costume wilted in the rain.

The bear roared out across the bay.

The mob on the Wharf went crazy.

The audience at home leaned forward in their La-Z-Boys or stood up, disbelieving, from their sofas.

John Trudell passed his microphone across the table to his guest speaker, who set his *iglook* glasses on the table, keyed in and said, across Radio Free Alcatraz into the ears of the stern men in suits who were listening and gripping the arms of their chairs two thousand eight hundred and fifteen miles away;

"This message is for the United States Government, and President Richard Nixon. My name is Matthew Anawak, *Anglakkuq* of the Inuit. Alcatraz Island is Indian land."

## 6

# PEACE WITH HONOR

FRASER SHERMAN

*High in orbit, Russia established the first space station, prompting both the US and China to begin to build their own stations. A Treaty of Cooperation was drafted between the three countries over shared use of the moon – and an agreement to keep it monster-free.*

*On Earth, the Vietnam Conflict gripped the entire world with its violent battles and ambiguous rallying points and tainted the newly-minted 1970s with its controversial progress.*

30 January, 1973: Vietnam, south of the demilitarized zone

Until the morning he died, 1st Lt. Jack Dane thought the worst thing about serving in South Vietnam was the temperature.

Alabama born and bred, Dane thought he knew from heat, but summer in Dothan was nothing compared to the heat and humidity he'd experienced in the four months since he got off the plane in Saigon. As he scanned the jungle below his tiny Army Cessna for North Vietnamese troops or mortar emplacements, the sun streaming into the cockpit made him feel like an ant under a burning glass. "Not seein' nothing, Eddie, you?"

"So much for military intelligence." Brooklyn-born Lt. Eddie Weaver replied with a grunt. "Tell the ARVN it's got nothing to worry about, then head back for beer."

"Let's be sure." Dane glanced back at where the ARVN—the South Vietnamese troops—were patrolling, in response to rumors of a major push by the north. "They got some Green Berets with them, you know what those guys are like when you—"

"What the hell is that?" Weaver's hand clamped down on Dane's arm. "Flying over the DMZ at us?"

"Flying?" Dane looked up with a snort, knowing MIGs couldn't get this far south without radar spotting them. "Buddy, that—"

For a second, Dane couldn't understand how a plane could have wings that flapped like a bird. Then he registered the monstrous bat-like face the size of a jeep, the fur, the leathery wings, and slammed the radio button. "Mayday, mayday, we got us a—"

The monster's mouth opened.

Sound washed over the plane, sound that drove knife-like into Dane's ears. Unimaginable pain swallowed up awareness of the plane, the controls, Weaver, everything but the sound.

Dane and Weaver screamed, but they couldn't hear their own voices. Out of control, the plane plummeted for the dense ground below, but never reached it. A single blow from the monster's wing shattered the plane like a balsa-wood model.

RIDING on the back of the Champion of the Viet, its long, silvery fur tied around her waist to prevent falls, Nu Ky gasped as she saw the American plane shatter. The sight of the two bodies falling amid the wreckage made the seventeen-year-old momentarily nauseous, then she reminded herself they were imperialists trying to conquer her country, just like the French.

The Champion circled around, looking for more planes, and then

Ky felt an explosion under the titan's belly. The Champion growled, twisting its neck to find the cause.

"There, Champion!" Down below, Ky could see South Vietnamese, reloading some sort of weapon. As if any weapon, even one built by Americans, could harm the reincarnation of the great Ho Chi Minh. Leaning forward, Ky pointed, though she knew all she needed to guide the Champion were her words. "Below, Champion. Kill!"

The Champion glanced down, gave what might have been a throat-clearing noise in a human, and opened its fanged jaws wide.

Ky knew the ARVN were imperialist lackeys who were as much the enemy as the Americans, and she shouldn't care about their lives. Even so, she looked away as the soldiers died in agony below her.

26 April, 1973: The White House

Three months into his presidency, Richard M. Nixon stared down at the photos on his desk. Wrecked tanks. Dead Vietnamese soldiers. Dead American soldiers. ARVN bases in ruins.

"Well?" Nixon looked up at the two men in his office, Defense Secretary Melvin Laird, and Admiral Thomas Moorer, chairman of the Joint Chiefs of Staff. "Can one of you explain to me how this is possible? You both told me sending in the Son of Johnson would win this war!"

"He hasn't lost," Laird said. "It's just that he hasn't had a chance to fight the Shrieker yet."

"As far as the public's concerned, trying and failing to catch the monster killing our boys is losing. And I'd say they're right." Nixon threw up his hands and began to pace. "Why the hell didn't Lyndon finish this war before North Vietnam found that thing?"

"The Joint Chiefs repeatedly advocated President Johnson employ our military in Vietnam," Moorer said. "We would have won by now even without sending in a monster, but you know his position."

All three men knew. President Lyndon B. Johnson's passion had been his "great society" programs and civil-rights legislation; he approached Vietnam mostly as a political problem Republicans could use against him. If communist North Vietnam conquered the South, he'd be pilloried for losing the country to the Reds. If he committed ground troops without sending in a monster, he'd be accused of wasting American lives. If he did send in either Johnson or the Son of Johnson, the Reds would paint America as a warmonger willing to turn a monster loose on ordinary humans—propaganda the US couldn't afford in the middle of the Cold War.

Instead, the president continued John F. Kennedy's approach: Financial support for South Vietnam, military aid and a limited number of Special Forces troops. It had kept South Vietnam independent for almost a decade, and neutralized the war as a political issue.

"So Lyndon gets two terms and his place in history and leaves me to clean up this stinking pile of crap!" Pacing back to his desk, Nixon scattered the photos with a wave of his hand. "I will not be the first American president to lose a war!"

"Everything we know about monster psychology says the Shrieker should have attacked," Laird said, lighting a cigarette and inhaling nervously. "Monsters are territorial, having Junior in South Vietnam should have drawn the Shrieker right to him."

"Only it didn't work!" Nixon scowled at the man. "Sonny Boy runs around Vietnam trying to catch this thing, and it just flies away from him and destroys more tanks. Or planes. Or soldiers. If the losses keep up, North Vietnam's going to win this damn war by Christmas."

"The thing's not invincible, Mr. President," Laird said. "It won't fly away from land for any reason, and it's vulnerable to napalm. They hit it with a shell when it attacked Da Nang and it retreated. We kill its rider, it flies back to its cave for a day or two until they find a new recruit."

"Which they always do," Moorer said. "Mr. President, the answer's simple. Now that General Giap has unleashed his own monster on the South, he can't accuse us of aggression if we send Junior against the North."

"How do we do that?" Laird jabbed out the cigarette in a crystal ashtray and lit another. "I asked General Abrams, he pointed out how many hundreds of miles of jungle Junior would have to cross to reach Hanoi. Nasmar could burn its way through, but—"

"Abrams is Army, of course he thinks of a ground assault," Moorer said. "And the Shrieker would knock air transport out before it crossed the DMZ. But if we send Junior north by ship, to Haiphong, if he attacks North Vietnam's major port, they'll have to send the Shrieker out to stop him."

"What about China?" Laird said. "It's close to their border, if Mao sends his own creature in to support Hanoi—"

"I'll deal with China." Nixon waved that aside. "Admiral, you guarantee this will work?"

"I guarantee it's the only thing that might work," Moorer replied. "Unless the Secretary has something better."

"He doesn't," Nixon said. "Tell Westmoreland what you need to make it happen, get it done. And the next time you're in this office, I hope you're bringing me 8 by 10 glossies of a dead Vietnamese monster."

2 May, 1973: The Cave of the Champion

HEART POUNDING LIKE A TRIPHAMMER, Li Anh emerged naked from the sacred underground pool, her eighteen-year-old body thick with the scent of flower blossoms that had been stirred into the waters. She stood alone in the small cave, illuminated only by one bare lightbulb.

It was chilly underground, but that wasn't what made her shiver. It was what lay ahead of her.

Anh knew her duty, though. She walked out of the cave and down the half-mile passage cut into the stone centuries before, now illuminated by a string of bulbs, powered by a generator. The Cambodians claimed the passage had been carved by the ancient Khmer, but Anh knew it had been the work of the ancient Vietnamese emperor, Dinh Bo Linh. No Cambodian could have mastered the Champion.

Near the end of the passage, Anh saw Le Tringh, her cadre, waiting. The cadre served as a combination big sister, Communist mentor, and trainer to riders and candidates. Although Tringh was graying and heavy in her olive green military uniform, Anh knew she was a patriot and a hero who once obtained vital military plans by seducing a French officer, then stabbing him with his own bayonet.

"I can smell the perfume coming off you, child," Tringh said, adjusting her glasses and studying the young woman. "Are you ready?"

"I am ready! Take me to the Champion." Unable to restrain herself, Anh jumped forward, and clasped the cadre's hands. "Let the great one judge my worthiness!"

"It's not a matter of worthiness," Tringh said patiently. "Uncle Ho's spirit did not enter into him, nor is he the god the Emperor Dinh thought, nor any of the other legends that you girls whisper among yourselves. The Champion is just a giant beast whom we have taught to serve the people."

"I am not superstitious like the other riders, cadre," Anh said, withdrawing her hands and standing at attention. "I know such beliefs are the opiate of the masses."

"Good." Tringh nodded and strode forward, beckoning Anh to follow. A few yards later, they emerged into the cave an army deserter had discovered almost four years earlier, with the Champion hibernating within it. Sleeping there, it was believed, since the temple overhead had fallen into ruin, centuries ago.

The Champion of the Viet sat in the center of the cave with its vast wings spread out across the floor, gulping down at least a hundredweight of fruit. Despite its fearsome fangs, it ate nothing but fruit, in vast quantities.

Anh had never seen the Champion so close, and he took her breath away. The wide, leathery wings with a faint pattern of scales. The thick white fur that shielded his riders from bullets and wind, glistening with iridescence in the light. The huge batlike face with the deep, dark eyes and high ears. Even the back legs, which seemed so small compared to the rest of him, had claws that could scar steel and strength enough to lift an American tank. Or kill a rider he rejected as unworthy.

Anh's heart beat even faster as she walked toward him across the hard stone floor, detouring around stalagmites. A part of her screamed in panic as she drew closer, smelled the overripe pile of fruit and the Champion's distinctive scent. Even following the flower bath prescribed in the ancient temple texts, there was no guarantee he would accept her.

It was a chance, Anh was willing to take. She thought of her grandfather and great-grandfather, who died fighting to free Vietnam from the French imperialists, her uncle who died fighting the Japanese, her father who lost his leg at Dienbienphu, the historic victory over the French. She thought of her brother, who died two years ago fighting the Americans and their South Vietnamese puppets.

Growing up, Anh never imagined that she could fight for her country, too. Now she had her chance if the Champion accepted her.

Nu Ky, his first rider, had insisted he was the reincarnation of the warrior woman Trieu Au. As a good communist, Anh knew that was nonsense: There was no life after death. Yet surely the Champion was no brute animal like the fat man-ape the Americans called the Son of Johnson. The Americans broke the Ape to their service; the Champion served willingly, under riders he chose.

The Champion's nostrils flared, sniffing the air. The scent of the flowers drew his attention away from the food and his eyes fell on Anh. Staring into the dark pools, she never felt so afraid. So awed. So hopeful.

Without a word, she knelt down before the Champion, and waited.

A tongue like a butterfly's, long and absurdly slender, reached out and touched her briefly on the forehead. Breath that smelt of fruit washed over her. Then the tongue stroked lightly down her back, checking for the flowery scent that marked a rider. The sensation of the tongue on her naked flesh almost made Anh flinch, but she kept herself still.

Deep in his throat, she heard a low, atonal humming, one that vibrated her very bones, though not painfully. A smile stretched over her face. The Champion had chosen.

She rose to her feet. The Champion resumed biting into the pile of fruit. Anh walked over, ran her hands through his strange, soft fur as Tringh joined her and slid the silken robe of a chosen rider over Anh's shoulders.

Stroking the fur, Anh barely registered her cadre's approving words. For the moment, she didn't need them. She was the rider now. It was her chance to prove herself a Vietnamese patriot like her kin, or die trying.

4 May, 1973: Base Titano

Even before opening the door to the airplane hangar, Dr. Alec Bannister could hear the Son of Johnson snoring. It made the hangar vibrate as if a freight train were rumbling through.

Chewing the spearmint gum that didn't really compensate for quitting smoking, Bannister cracked the door, so as not to wake the giant with the light from the setting sun behind him. Satisfied everything was OK with his charge, he closed the door. Then a firm hand fell on his shoulder, yanked him back and spun him around.

"Are you crazy, doc?" It was Captain Elijah Fox, the gaunt black officer assigned to mind Bannister, scowling and thrusting a flak jacket and an army helmet at the scientist. "I told you. Wear this when you're out. Any time, every time, you got me?"

"In this heat?" Bannister's gesture encompassed the moist air, the setting sun, the sweat trickling down his face and stepped around Fox. "I'll take my chances."

"No, you won't." Fox stepped into Bannister's path. "I could have you confined to quarters until we're ready to head north."

Bannister indicated the guards ringing Junior's sleeping quarters. "This is an American base, I'm surrounded by our troops."

"So was O'Halloran. Didn't save him when the janitor threw a grenade under his bunk. And Smith got it from a sniper." Fox didn't budge. With a sigh, Bannister donned the helmet and the specially reinforced, bulletproof jacket.

"And let's not forget the mess after Smith died," Fox went on, running a nervous hand over his five o'clock shadow, "when the big guy in there decided to take a walk around Da Nang with nobody holding his leash. That's why we built this base so far out in the boonies it makes my part of Georgia look like Atlanta."

"Junior's harmless," Bannister said, then laughed at the absurdity of his own words. "He's safe, if he's handled properly. And left somewhere secure like this hangar when he's alone."

"He plays with tanks like my nephew plays with his Hot Wheels set," Fox said. "You really think an electrified hangar is going to hold him?"

"Physically he could bust out, yes." Weighed down by the jacket, Bannister headed for the camp's small cluster of buildings. "But he's been conditioned with electroshock for years. Touching the walls reminds him that staying put gets him food, plus tanks and other toys to play with. It's the same way we controllers condition him to recognize and obey our voices. Having trained him from birth, so to speak, he's much more cooperative than his father."

"Cooperative," Fox said the word skeptically. "He's a lot fatter than his father, too."

"He's not fat, just round," Bannister replied, a touch indignantly, as they entered the office the camp had assigned him. Bannister slid off his jacket and turned on the better-than-nothing window air-conditioner with relief. "His shape doesn't change no matter what he eats."

"What counts is, can he fight like his father?" Fox said, pulling out a pack of Winstons. "He's never seen action in the field."

"I know he doesn't look as impressive as his pop, but he's got more muscle," Bannister replied, avoiding the question. Before Fox could say more, Bannister changed the subject to their families back in the States. Fox, 15 years younger than Bannister's 48, had his first son a few months back and happily pulled out the photos he'd received.

Bannister felt a little guilty about sitting indoors when other Americans were fighting and dying across Vietnam. He wanted to be out in the field with Junior, to have the confrontation with the Shrieker that would end the war. But he also knew there was no way to force that until they reached Haiphong.

Bannister tried not to worry about would happen then, when the Son of Johnson went into battle for the first time.

5 May, 1973: Khe Sanh

Buried in the Champion's protective fur, Anh felt only a slight pressure from the wind generated by his flight. Then she felt his speed slow, which meant fresh targets. Wriggling out from the fur and wiping off sweat, Anh saw the Hueys, the big American helicopters, a hundred yards away. "Strike, Champion! Strike for our country!"

The Champion had exhausted his voice killing a tank battalion a hundred miles away. Instead he charged into the flock of helicopters, knocking half of them from the sky with one sweep of his wings.

Fire from another Huey raked the Champion's back, forcing Anh to duck under his fur, then the Champion shifted, so the bullets bounced off his chest instead. Anh resurfaced in time to see him crush the Huey between his jaws.

A few seconds later, he had hurled the other copters from the sky. Then Anh saw a shell arc up from the jungle below, toward the Champion and tugged his fur, warning him to fly up.

The shell hit the jungle behind them a few seconds later and burst into fire. Napalm, she realized, the American liquid fire that had burned the Champion twice already.

The Champion remembered, too. He swooped down before she

could even command him, ignoring gunfire from below, snatching up the howitzer with his rear feet. He flew 50 yards up before he let go.

Anh saw men fall along with the American cannon, but felt no regrets. The soldiers had attacked the Champion cruelly, trying to burn him. Her hands knotted in his fur in rage.

The Champion craned his head back to look at her. She smiled and murmured endearments for how well he'd fought. Turning, the warrior winged his way back through the darkness, toward home.

6 May, 1973

"All right, gentlemen, you want a show?" Tall, blond, movie-star handsome, Alan Colt flashed a smile at the reporters and stepped back, bringing the megaphone to his lips. "Junior—smash tank!"

The Son of Johnson raised one hairy foot and brought it down on the tank. Fox, watching off to the side with Bannister, flinched at the angry squeal as metal rended and tore, the tank cracking like an egg carton under Junior's weight.

Fox still thought the monster was fat. With his plump, squat body and round head, Junior looked like the old comedian W.C. Fields, except, of course, Fields wasn't 100 feet tall, with thick brown fur covering his entire body except for two dark eyes.

"So how come he doesn't uh, stink?" one journalist asked Colt. "I mean, all that hair, this heat—"

"Junior has no sweat glands," Colt replied. "Like his pop, his body self-regulates its temperature without any need to sweat."

"Lucky for us," another man said.

Colt nodded. "It's the North Vietnamese who are going to sweat, let me tell you. Junior, smash again!"

Junior brought his heel down on another surplus tank, then picked up a boulder and dropped it on a third. In between the screams of mangled steel, Fox heard the camera shutters clicking.

A broken turret from one of the tanks clanked to the ground ten feet away. The cameras stopped clicking and the press backed up. Fox glanced back at Bannister to make a joke, saw the man's lips pressed close together. "You OK, Doc? Heat getting to you again?"

"Colt's not wearing his flak jacket, did you notice that?"

"Took it off at the last minute. Said it set the wrong tone for the photos," Fox said. "I couldn't lock him up with the press here, but he'll put it on when we're done, believe you me. And he's not the one supposed to be on the front lines when the bullets start flying so I don't need—"

Bannister made an odd, indeterminate grunt. Fox studied the scientist: Grey in his red hair, a lined face, a scar on his neck he had referred to as an old war wound. "Jealous, doc? He gets to stay safe, you're the one has to—"

"Controlling Junior is a serious responsibility." Bannister spoke slowly, as if weighing each word. "Handling America's greatest weapon, making sure nothing ever, well, goes wrong."

"Believe me, I know." Fox lit a cigarette from a crumpled pack. "All of y'all controllers but Colt have been plenty serious."

"Exactly," Bannister lowered his voice, although no could hear him over Junior crushing an army truck between his hands. "He's all ambition. That would be fine if it was tied to something, but it isn't. Working in Johnson City's just another rung to climb. He wants the glory of being associated with Junior's first battle, but that's all it means to him."

"I was in the army in the big one, you know? Just 18, but—." Bannister looked away, staring into memory. "If Johnson hadn't gone into Hiroshima, I might be dead by now, me and all my buddies. That's what led me back to the military and Johnson City after I got my doctorate." He looked at Fox, his gaze sharp, intense. "I volunteered to come here, Lieutenant. Safety's the last thing on my mind."

Bannister wondered what the hell he was doing, saying things that could seriously hurt his career. Colt had worked hard to make friends in the Pentagon; he'd seen what happened to people who bad-mouthed the man.

Almost as soon as he thought the question, he thought of the answer. He was scared as hell, getting more scared every minute, and talking about Colt made it easier to bottle up what really bugged him.

Junior, for all the war games they'd conducted, might not be a match for the Shrieker and its murderous, combat-hardened controller when the chips were down.

It bugged him that Bannister wouldn't be able to think fast enough to guide Junior in a real fight and keep him alive.

That he'd let Junior down.

Officially, of course, that was a meaningless thought: Junior was a weapon, not a soldier. Anthropomorphizing him, questioning the electroshock regimen that controlled him, had cost several men their jobs over the years. Complaining that an extra round of electroshock to get him to recognize Cole's voice was gratuitous; they already had a full complement of qualified men.

Bannister thought about his mortgage and reminded himself to keep his mouth shut for the rest of his tour.

### 7 May, 1973: The Temple of the Champion

"Are you a good Communist, Anh?" Standing in the small office the army had built among the temple ruins, Tringh folded her arms. "Your duty is to obey your superiors' orders, to carry out the policy determined by party leaders. Never to question."

"I am a good Communist and a loyal citizen," Anh protested. "I would never disobey our leaders. I only asked why the Champion should continue running from the Ape. If we destroy the monster, the Americans will leave and we can reunify our country at last."

"And you wish the glory of being the hero who saved the nation." Tringh's voice was a cold sneer.

"The honor of victory would fall to the Champion," Anh said. "All I want is to save the lives of our soldiers!"

"The first Ape, Johnson, ended the American war against Japan." Tringh, who spent time as a girl in a Japanese labor camp, hawked and spat out the window. "He then defeated the Koreans. Can you be certain the Champion will defeat his son?"

"He is the Champion!" Anh said, outraged. "The Ape has never fought against another monster."

"Neither has the Champion."

"And he has no experience of battle at all. The Champion will destroy him."

"Anh, the Ape is a distraction." Tringh's eyes bored into Anh, but her voice was calm. "By destroying the ARVN and their equipment, we make him irrelevant. Even the wealth of the Americans cannot continue to replace what he smashes."

"So we must continue to run like—" Anh stopped, remembered her duty and hung her head. "I am sorry, cadre. I am a soldier, and I will obey my orders without question. Forgive me for my incorrect thoughts."

Eating her rice dinner silently across from Tringh, Anh felt ashamed of questioning her path. She was not indispensable, no soldier was. If she died as other riders had, another would rise to take her place.

The idea pained her even more than Tringh's criticism. The thought of never again feeling the wind press the Champion's fur down over her, the power in the muscles beneath her, and of abandoning the Champion to someone else's care. Tringh called him a beast, but even a common pet was entitled to loyalty.

Then Anh thought about the Chinese envoy scheduled to visit the temple soon. What would the man say if confronted with Vietnam victorious? If the nation China had so often crushed and oppressed defeated the Americans? If the Champion could triumph over the Ape, would that not be a glorious feat to throw in the man's face?

But if that was to happen, General Giap, the leader of Vietnam, would give the order. Until then, Anh had no choice but to do her duty.

. . .

8 May, 1973: Base Titano

"So tell me, something, Dr. Bannister." Captain Hawke, a big, brawny Minnesota Swede, dipped his pipe into his tobacco pouch as he watched the huge truck rolling up to transport the Son of Johnson to the Coast. "If there's a dozen controllers—eight now, right?—shouldn't you all be here for this mission? Just in case you and Colt get killed like the others?"

"After the previous four deaths, the brass decided not to put more of us in the field. We have three more men holed up in Saigon for emergencies, but of course, they won't be onboard your boat." Bannister saw Hawke open his mouth, said quickly, "Ship, I mean." A former Army man, he enjoyed tweaking the Navy. "If I die when I take Junior into Haiphong, Colt will assume control."

"Out of curiosity, do you really need to risk following him into the city?" Hawke blew out a cloud of smoke. Bannister popped another stick of gum into his mouth. "You control him by radio when he's out of earshot, right?"

"Sure. But if he moves out of sight, we don't know what orders to give. We've learned that in the war games. And if the radio's damaged—"

"So he's too dumb to think for himself?"

"He's not stupid," Bannister said sharply. He saw by Hawke's grin that the captain was doing a little tweaking himself. "But he doesn't remember instructions long. Without me reinforcing them, he might wind up sitting in the jungle watching butterflies, or walking back to Da Nang and thinking it's the city he should attack."

"So the fate of the free world is riding on how well he listens to you." The captain stared at Bannister through a cloud of pipe smoke. "Better keep that flak jacket on until you're on board the Valiant."

Without another word, he walked off.

Bannister would have argued, if Hawke hadn't expressed so much of his own worries. Worries that had set his stomach churning since the truck arrived. It was real now: Within a couple of days, Junior would attack Haiphong and confront the Shrieker.

If the Son of Johnson lost that battle, America would look ineffective. Weak. Vulnerable. North Vietnam would be free to take not only Saigon but most of Indochina. Russia and China might decide their monsters could beat Junior too, and turn the Cold War hot. A hop across the Bering Strait and Nasmar and China's monster—maybe Mohvash, too—could give Communists the world domination they craved. If they thought it would work, the Treaty of Monstrous Aggression wouldn't hold them back.

America's future hinged on how well he and Junior fought.

It made Bannister wish he had the opportunity to get blind, stinking drunk.

9 May, 1973: Temple of the Champion

"Cadre, I don't understand." Anh knew that in Tringh's office she should be at attention, but instead she reached out her arms beseechingly. "If the Ape attacks Haiphong, surely the Champion must confront it."

"You have your orders."

"It is barely one hundred miles to Hanoi. If the Ape attacks our capital as its father did Japan—"

"Listen to me, child." To Anh's surprise, Tringh drew her to sit on the office's small bamboo couch. "Do you think Vietnam is cities? No, child, Vietnam is the people. Our spirit is what makes us strong, not our buildings."

"But the people in Haiphong!"

"The evacuation is already under way. All the Ape will find is an empty city. If they press onward, we will even evacuate Hanoi if it becomes necessary." Tringh's lined, nicotine-stained fingers came to rest on Anh's shoulder. "The Americans are losing. They want this battle because you and the Champion have been triumphant time after time. Haiphong is their one chance to change that: One successful bullet and the Champion is without a rider. Then the Ape can overmaster him."

"But Madam Tringh—" Anh pounded her fist against her thigh in sudden fury. "I heard the Chinese envoy speaking to you yesterday. Laughing about how inferior the Champion is to their ugly beast! If we cannot defend our own cities from the Ape, will the Chinese not continue to believe it? Perhaps decide they can conquer Vietnam once again? We must show them our strength!" Then she caught herself. "I am sorry, I know my thoughts are still incorrect."

"As are mine, child." Tringh said, earning a surprised look from the younger woman. "I despise that Chinese pig every bit as much as you. The thought of another conqueror trampling our cities horrifies me. But against that we set the risk that the Ape triumphs over the Champion. If that happens, we are lost. If we continue as General Giap directs, we win. We must swallow our pride, Anh, because only by doing so can we finally unite Vietnam."

MAY 9, 1973: Da Nang harbor

ON THE BRINK of stepping onto the 100 foot long, modified raft trailing behind the battleship, the Son of Johnson stopped and looked tentatively at Bannister, standing on the dock.

The sailors and soldiers around Bannister all tensed, clutching weapons as if they'd make a difference.

"Get on." Bannister repeated the command very clearly. After a second, the conditioning took hold: Junior reached out and set one hairy hand on the flatboat, pushing down as if testing its safety. Next, he performed a hand vault up over the muddy harbor water and came down on the raft.

It dipped under his weight, sending stinking water splashing over soldiers, reporters, and Bannister.

Paying that no attention, Junior picked up one of the dozens of crates scattered over the raft, variously containing raw steak or Reese's peanut butter cups, his two favorite foods. He swallowed the crate, wood, contents and all.

Wiping water from his face and thanking God he'd had all his shots, Bannister scrutinized the helmet pressing down on Junior's thick head of hair. It was still firmly in place: Armored and insulated against the Shrieker's deadly cry, it would hopefully keep Bannister in contact with Junior when the action started.

"Man, I don't believe this," Fox said, coming up behind Bannister and exhaling a jet of smoke. Before Bannister could ask, Fox jerked a thumb back at where Colt was laughing with reporters near the gangplank. "Somehow he's got all of them listening to him instead of photographing you and Junior."

"The pool picked someone to go on Valiant and get some film of the landing," Bannister said. "I guess that's good enough." He glanced back at Cole, surrounded by a crowd so large it was an obstacle to the dock laborers working around it. He turned back to study the raft, then Cole's laugh choked off into a scream.

Bannister spun around. He saw a Vietnamese dock worker pull the knife out of Colt's back, then drive it in again. Bannister had just enough time to register Colt's impossibly slow collapse, then a bullet taking off the killer's head, then Fox was dragging him toward the Valiant. "Fox, they got Colt, I have to—"

"You have to get on the ship!" Fox pulled him past the corpse and up the gangplank with desperate strength, not pausing to glance at Cole's body or the sailors and MPs rushing toward the murder scene. "If there's Vietcong on this dock and they get you, we got Junior out here, nobody to control him, and that's FUBAR territory! The medics will fix Colt up if he's not dead already."

They were on the deck faster than Bannister would have thought possible, then Fox barked orders at someone to open a hatch and they were suddenly below deck. Fox leaned against the wall, breathing hard, ignoring the stares from passing Navy men. "You stay here until we're away from land, clear, doc?"

"And if Junior gets restless?"

"We're only 15 minutes from departing, right? Pray he doesn't."

Abruptly Bannister reached over, pulled the pack out of Fox's breast pocket and withdrew a cigarette, then realized he hadn't asked first. "I—sorry, I just—"

"Yeah," Fox applied his lighter to Bannister's cigarette, then reclaimed the pack. "Didn't really believe you were in danger till now, did you?"

"I guess not." It could have been him, if Colt hadn't been so flamboyant about presenting himself as the top dog on the mission. "I didn't like him, but I knew him. It's a long time since I saw someone shot in combat, I guess I forgot."

He had to get a grip on himself. America was at stake. "Fox, go find Hawke, please? He needs to know about this if he doesn't already. And could you find me a towel somewhere?"

9 May, 1973: Vietnamese Coast

For the dozenth time, the Champion reached the Gulf of Tonkin and wheeled away, refusing to cross over the water.

"Please, Champion." Anh crooned in her best voice, running her hands over the silky fur. "If you destroy the Ape's ship, he and his American controller will drown ... for me, please?"

The wing-beats were leisurely, but Anh could tell his mind was made up. None of the old scrolls had mentioned his hatred—Anh could not believe it was fear—of the sea, but it was nonetheless real.

There was no way to prevent the Ape's attack, then. The military had decided not to sacrifice equipment or men to defend the city. The Chinese and the Russians had protested America invading North Vietnam without a declaration of war, but would take no further action. She had heard rumors the American president was even negotiating some sort of treaty with the scheming Chinese.

Later that night, back in the cave, she continued reassuring the Champion as he sat devouring his evening meal.

"I know you are more than a beast. If you do not cross the water, you have your reasons." Leaning against the Champion's side, she stroked his fur gently. "And even if we never battle the Ape, I know you would have triumphed over him. Perhaps Tringh and General Giap are wrong."

Anh glanced around cautiously, even though the cadre rarely came this close to the Champion. "The Americans are so rich, no matter how many weapons we destroy. They just send more. They will keep arming Thieu—he is the president of the South, you know—as long as they hope the Ape can destroy you. If you do not fight, we may never know peace."

The Champion turned back to his meal, giving an odd humming. Anh, who thought she knew all his vocalizations, had never heard one quite like it.

10 May, 1973: Gulf of Tonkin

"Haiphong in about fifteen minutes, Dr. Bannister."

Hawke jabbed the stem of his pipe at the nautical chart on the bridge, where Hawke and Fox had been invited to join him. "Your monster going to be ready?"

"Get us close enough he can walk to land and we're fine," Bannister replied. "His body doesn't float."

"We'll unload him when his head will be above water, don't worry." Hawke glanced at Bannister. "So, you've been back to the US more recently than me. Are they really protesting against this war over there?"

"Kids," Bannister said with a dismissive gesture. "A couple of college protests, but nothing big like the black power marches or the women's lib stuff. Everyone knows we've got to show Junior can stand against the Reds, otherwise what stops Brezhnev from sending Nasmar?" Bannister realized he was getting too close to airing his fears aloud. "You got a patrol boat for us, captain?"

"You sure you don't want to wait until after the monsters have their slugfest?" Hawke said. "We can get you to land damn fast."

"I'm not taking that chance," Bannister said. "We can't be sure what will happen until it happens. I'm not going to—" let Junior down, he almost said. "—screw up this mission by playing it safe.

A quarter of an hour later, Bannister, accompanied by Fox, walked over to see Junior sitting on the raft, which was empty of crates. "Well, captain, I guess this is it, huh?"

"This is it, Doc. You and your chubby buddy get to end this war." Fox clapped him on the back, but his eyes weren't as confident as his words.

"Junior," Bannister called. The monster looked up, and Bannister pointed at the waterfront of Haiphong, a mile away. "That way. Go!"

To Bannister's horror, Junior sat there, unmoving. Then he reached forward, dipped his hand into the water, pulled his hand up and watched water run off it.

To Bannister's relief, Junior slid off the flatboat and into the water. The wave he generated made the Valiant bob for a second, then Junior began walking toward the city, water lapping around his neck. An army of seagulls mewed overhead, as if unable to make sense of what looked like a moving island.

"Fox," Bannister said. He felt his stomach churning and tried not to show it. "Let's get to the boat."

By the time the boat was following in Junior's wake, carrying Fox, a sailor, a medic and Bannister, Junior was far enough ahead that it would be hard for him to hear Bannister without the radio. Bannister would have preferred to leave simultaneously with Junior, but he knew the humans would be swamped when Junior jumped into the water.

He turned the walkie-talkie on, reached back to be sure there was a spare in his knapsack. Small explosions kept going off in front of Junior, mines, obviously. They didn't disturb him, but both the sailor and Fox glanced at the water nervously.

It bothered Bannister more that they weren't seeing any other attacks. He'd expected bazooka fire, mortars, anything the Vietnamese could try to discourage the landing or kill Junior.

Was the Shrieker waiting to attack, then? No, surely it would do it now, hit Junior with his scream from the shore. Then where was it? Hell, where was the army?

"This smells like a trap," Fox said. "But there's no trap that can work for Junior, is there?"

"Only the Shrieker," Bannister said, scanning the low skyline of Haiphong, as Junior began to rise out of the water. Shoulders. Chest. Waist. The water matted his hair down tight and flowed off him like a small waterfall.

Junior set one foot onto the nearest wooden dock, which caved under him. He stopped and stared at the land, as if afraid it would collapse, too.

"Junior," Bannister said into the walkie-talkie. "Smash everything. Smash everything!" He heard the tension in his voice but couldn't keep it hidden. "Sailor, they must have evacuated. Get us to dry land, OK?"

Ahead of them, Junior brought his foot down on a small truck, then kicked, sending it flying half a mile.

His fist clenched. He brought it down on the roof of a warehouse, caving the building in.

~

"Champion, no!" Anh tugged at the Champion's hair in frustration. "Why will you not listen?"

Tringh's orders had been clear: While Johnson Junior ravaged Haiphong, the Champion would attack Saigon, proving the Thieu regime was helpless even with the Ape fighting for it. Yet as they flew south, the Champion suddenly turned, ignoring her commands and heading toward the coast.

Pleading. Commands. Nothing had swayed him.

They were a mile away from Haiphong when Anh saw the giant

on the waterfront and understood. Tringh and Giap might not care about this attack, but the Champion would defend his country.

~

PULLING up to a dock four hundred yards from the Son of Johnson, Bannister saw the winged bat-shape hurtling toward Junior and knew the trap had been sprung. A grim smile stretched across his face: If the Reds thought they had a mouse, they'd sure as hell learn differently.

Wouldn't they?

~

ANH ALMOST LAUGHED at the sight of the Ape. It looked like a hairy version of the legendary Buddhist monk, Ho Tai, too jolly and rotund to be threatening.

As the Champion approached, the Ape saw him, bent down and picked up a fishing boat. He hurled it at the Champion. Anh saw the boat flying toward her, then the Champion veered away hard to one side. The turn made Anh's hair harness snap her sharply across his body to the far shoulder.

Before the Champion could regain his momentum, the Ape flung a piece of building, then a truck, then another boat, forcing the Champion to zig-zag desperately, faster than he'd ever done before, tossing Anh from side to side. It was painful, but she refused to cry out.

Then came a telephone pole, flung like a spear. It hit the Champion right at the wing joint, sending him and Anh tumbling back through the air.

Anh had never imagined the Ape could be so powerful. For a second she hung in her harness below the overturned Champion, then back up and landing on him, then off again, so that her senses spun with her body. "Champion," she managed to say. "Do not close with the Ape! Scream!"

Standing on the docks, Bannister gasped. He'd watched the war games, studied newsreels of Johnson Senior, but nothing compared to seeing it, even at a distance. "Junior's winning, Fox, you see that, the Shrieker doesn't have the muscle to match!" He brought the walkie-talkie to his mouth as he climbed out onto the dock. "Good boy, good! Keep smashing him and we—"

Coming out of its spin with a powerful flap of its wings, the Shrieker ducked a thrown pagoda and opened its mouth. The sound washed over Junior, who flung up two hairy arms to wrap around his head.

It was powerful enough, even at that distance, that Bannister felt the world's worst migraine trying to smash his skull open from the inside. He dropped the walkie-talkie, tried to pick it up but his hands didn't seem to work well. It took everything he had to keep his eyes fixed on Junior, leaning against Fox for mutual support in their pain.

Anh felt a brief shock when she realized the Ape hadn't died. Then the Champion hurtled toward the fat monster, thrusting its rear claws forward to gouge out the American ogre's eyes. Anh couldn't suppress a howl of triumph.

At the last second, the Ape lowered its arms from its ears, reached forward and caught the Champion by the legs, swinging him around his head.

Picking up the walkie-talkie, Bannister screamed into it. "Slam him, Junior, slam him!" He couldn't hear himself saying the words, but he hoped they were coming out. "Just like in practice, Junior, slam him down!"

Junior shifted stance, preparing to turn the airplane spin into a body slam, but then the bat-winged horror opened its mouth again. Mercifully, the men weren't in the line of fire this time, but Bannister could still hear the horrible wail, like a giant violin snapping a string. Junior shuddered and hurled the Shrieker away.

ANH GRINNED in triumph as the Champion forced the Ape to let go, then she saw them heading directly for the side of an office building. In that instant she knew she was going to die.

The Champion's wings whipped Anh's hair up, beating so furiously that at the last minute its body twisted around to hit the building rear-end first, instead of on the shoulders, where she rode. The impact jarred her bones; one of the bricks showering the Champion's back struck her in the shoulder, painfully. Then the Champion rose, in control of its flight once again.

As it turned to face the Ape, Minh saw Americans standing back from the monster, on the docks, and knew who they had to be. "It is the Ape's controller, Champion!" She knotted her hands in its fur triumphantly. "Use your scream just once more and they die! The Ape is stupid, without the man we shall crush it!"

For the second time that day, the Champion ignored her. It ignored the men too, flying through the air directly at the Ape.

BANNISTER SAW Junior duck as its winged foe attacked. The Shrieker veered around, just as Junior uprooted another telephone pole, swinging it like Mickey Mantle hitting a homer. The Shrieker flew over the pole with a flap of his wings, then descended behind Junior, raking his back with its talons and tearing out chunks of flesh and sodden hair.

Junior, who was almost always silent, howled—even Bannister could hear it—and swung around punching at the Shrieker. It darted out of the way.

"Don't punch at him!" Bannister said into the radio. "Grapple. Get him and slam him!"

Junior kept swinging futilely. Bannister wondered if the walkie-talkie had broken or if Junior was too angry to obey. Then he saw the Shrieker's claws crumple Junior's helmet, and it no longer mattered. Bannister realized his worst fears about the battle might be coming true.

"The furball's losing." Hawke saw through his binoculars as the Son of Johnson threw another unsuccessful roundhouse. "Wait." He turned to his commander. "Didn't we have napalm shells brought aboard?"

Commander White nodded. "But that was only for an emergency, if the Shrieker came out over the—"

"Take a look!" Hawke jabbed at the window of the bridge. "This is an emergency. Tell the gunners to load the shells and start to fire."

"And Sonny Boy?"

"Better hope he can take it." Hawke knew if this went wrong, his career was finished. But as the Shrieker clawed a piece out of Junior's arm, he knew there was too much at stake to play it safe.

"The Ape is afraid!" Anh cried out as the Champion circled over the hairy ogre. "It knows you can defeat it. If we cut it enough, it has to die."

In agreement, the Champion descended again, thrusting out its neck, gouging a chunk out of the Ape with a single bite. The Ape squealed in anger. As the Champion winged away, the Ape leaped after it, higher than seemed possible for such a fat beast, catching the Champion by one leg and the edge of a wing.

The Champion's flight arced abruptly downward, leveling out 100 feet above the ground, dragging the Ape along behind it. The Ape's hairy body smashed into houses, pho restaurants, its legs knocking over cars and bicycles, but it still hung on.

Anh heard a strange, horrible tearing sound and the Champion screamed, not the song of destruction but a cry of pain. Turning, she saw the Ape had ripped away part of one wing.

"Up, up, Champion!" she yelled, knowing that the Ape would have to drop off or fall if the Champion could get high enough. Instead the Champion turned, flailing at the Ape with wings, claws, teeth.

This time the Ape's punch landed. It hit harder than any man-made weapon had ever struck the Champion. For a second everything went dark, then Anh came back to consciousness, aware her body ached, and that the Champion had been thrown even further than before.

The only thought she could conjure was that Tringh might have been right all along. Anh's failure to keep the Champion from the battle was about to lose the war.

BANNISTER COULDN'T KEEP down a war whoop. He half-heard Fox doing the same, then he saw the Shrieker righting itself, opening its mouth for another scream.

Something arced through the sky, landing near the Shrieker. Flames erupted under the monster; the Shrieker gave a hoarse cry of anger and darted away from the fire, into range of Junior's fists. Junior delivered a backhanded slap that knocked the creature away once more. "No," Bannister shouted, though he knew Junior couldn't hear him. "Grab it again, buddy. Wrestle it, wring its neck!"

But the Shrieker backed off as more napalm fire blossomed near it. Instead of flying higher, though, this time it swooped down, seemed to grab something, then rose up toward the sun. Bannister drew a tentative gasp of relief at the thought it was retreating.

Two hundred feet above Junior, the Shrieker let go of the two trucks in its claws.

Shielding his eyes from the sun, Junior let one truck bounce off his shoulder, swatted the other truck away, but even as he did, the Shrieker dived. Bannister saw Junior raise his fist, saw the Champion's wings spread at the last minute, braking as it smashed into Junior's arm, then his torso, hurling him to the ground, landing on top of him, then rising up again.

Junior gave an ululation of raw agony. Bannister tried to tell himself he hadn't seen the arm twist at an ungodly angle before the fall, hadn't heard a giant bone break.

Another napalm shell landed, this time right under the Shrieker's left wing. The shell exploded and liquid fire splashed over the monster, but the scream Bannister heard this time was human.

Too dazed to move, Anh couldn't crawl back under the Champion's protective fur, which left her dangling helpless from her harness. Liquid fire, splashed onto her arm, searing away her robe and her body filled with more pain than she knew existed. She screamed for a second, then everything went black once again.

The last thing she saw was the Champion staring back at her with deep, alarmed eyes.

Captain Hawke was six years old when his parents took him to see *Fantasia*. The "Night on Bald Mountain" sequence gave him nightmares for weeks.

When he saw the bat-winged demon hurtling toward his ship, for a second he was in his childhood nightmare again. Then the Shrieker smashed into his battleship, tilting it forty-five degrees, sending everyone on the bridge falling into windows that had become the floor.

The ship righted itself in an instant and they fell back. Hawke saw gigantic talons and teeth tearing into battleship steel as if it were cardboard and realized it was too close to use napalm. He tried to think of something, but nothing came, except that he was about to go down with his ship and every man on it.

"It's over water!" Fox said. "They said it couldn't fly over water!"

"I think the napalm pissed it off," Bannister said, watching in horror as the deck of the battleship gave way. "Dear God, even if Junior could—"

He'd barely noticed the tiny dark dot hanging from the Shrieker, just below its shoulder, swinging violently from the force of its attack. Then he saw that whatever it was, the attack had shaken it loose, and it fell toward the Gulf water below.

The Shrieker twisted suddenly, its wings pounding against the ship as it shifted position, reached out one rear paw and caught the falling dot. The rider, Bannister realized. It just saved its rider.

Leaving the battleship, the Shrieker rocketed back toward the land.

As it approached, Junior got to his knees, one arm hanging at a bad angle.

The Shrieker rose up and over him, regardless of its torn wing, and hurtled off into the distance.

"We won," Fox said. "Doc, I think we won!"

Bannister wasn't sure, but he realized that they definitely had not lost.

17 May, 1973: Hanoi

"Americans?" As the staff wheeled her down the hospital corridor, Anh found herself thinking clearly for the first time since the battle. She knew it was because the American drugs had killed her pain. "I do not wish to have them ease their guilt."

"This is not about you, young lady," Tringh said, walking alongside the gurney. "The American willingness to fix your scars and broken bones acknowledges your heroism in fighting against their Ape. Their Mr. Kissinger calls it a good faith gesture as we enter negotiations."

"No, no," Anh found it hard to argue. The drugs made her feel peaceful. "I am but one soldier."

"You are the symbol of our triumph," Tringh replied. "The Americans are willing to agree to a neutral government in the south, one where Thieu shares power with the Vietcong. That will do until we are certain the Americans will not return."

As the American nurses wheeled Anh into surgery, Tringh lit a cigarette, relieved she no longer had to worry about the smell offending the Champion.

Under other circumstances, she would have criticized Anh for defying her orders and sending the Champion against the Ape. But these were not other circumstances. She walked down the hall to the office where General Giap stood waiting, chain-smoking, staring out the window.

He was staring at the Champion as it circled the hospital. It had been circling since Tringh had brought the unconscious Anh to the hospital, after the monster had returned her to the cave, quivering with what Tringh could only think of as rage. Since then, it only stopped flying to scoop up food, or to land ominously on the hospital roof, just for a second, now and again.

Tringh and Giap watched until the Champion circled out of view. Then Tringh spoke. "It lost three riders before Anh. It showed no such concern for them."

"I have read your report." Giap shook his head. "Perhaps it cares for her as a puppy cares for a particular child in a family. Perhaps it is more than a beast."

"A reincarnated spirit?" Tringh stared at him in shock. "Surely you do not believe in that."

"Even the Americans and the Russians cannot explain the monsters, where they come from. What they think. Who knows what truly drives our Champion?"

He glanced back through the doorway, as if he could see all the way down the corridor to the operating table. "Whatever the reason, we must take very good care of that girl."

14 June, 1973: Johnson City, California

Unlocking the door of his office, Bannister stepped inside and glanced out the window. Down below, he could see the vast enclosed park Junior called home. The armored-glass window rattled slightly from his snores.

The table under the window was piled with the newspaper front pages Bannister hadn't gotten around to framing for the wall yet. *Son of Johnson Follows in Dad's Footsteps. Junior Johnson Turns Red Monster Yellow. North Vietnam Accepts South Vietnamese Independence.*

Of course, nobody imagined South Vietnam's independence would last, but in the flush of victory over the Shrieker, everyone in the US was happy to call it a day and go home. And with Nixon announcing a trip to China next month, diplomatic recognition to follow, Kissinger was confident China and the US could discourage Vietnam from moving against its neighbors.

Chinese Communists as allies. Bannister shook his head incredulously and wondered, for the hundredth time, if Junior didn't deserve more of the credit than the president.

He looked out the window again. Junior lay below, unmoving on his specially constructed hospital bed, his arm in what the Guinness Book of Records had just certified was the world's largest cast.

Slipping gum between his teeth, Bannister picked up his pen and resumed his letter to Fox. "—worse than my kid, tearing off the cast every time we tried to put it on, no matter what orders we gave him. Finally we hit on a way to use his own hormones, or whatever passes for hormones with him, to make him relax, sleep and stay asleep. Hopefully we can keep him under until the arm heals. With his metabolism it shouldn't take too long.

"Better news: The same discovery may lead to a way to dispense with electroshock, using the equivalent of human endorphins — It's a kind of pleasure hormone—to condition him. I know it sounds like we're turning him into a junkie, but I think it's a swell idea.

"Once he's up and well, we'll use what I saw in Haiphong to refine his combat techniques. And make sure he listens to orders, even when he's in the heat of combat. If he hadn't been in such pain from his arm, I think he'd have gone chasing the Shrieker all the way across 'Nam. No way would that have ended well. He's a hero, and he's going to be okay. And nobody's going to worry he's less of a man than his father.

"I'm glad you're heading back to the States soon. I'm sure your wife misses you as much as Aggie missed me. And trust me, Captain, people are going to be damn impressed when they realize you saw Junior in action up close. Even your kids will think you're cool!"

Smiling, Bannister signed the letter and reached for an envelope. He stuffed the missive inside as he stared down through the window at his sleeping fellow soldier.

# 7

# SOME SAY IN ICE

JAMES PALMER

*By the 1980s, the world teetered recklessly on the brink of an all-out global monster war, driven by poisonous rhetoric between the Soviet Union and the United States. Laser technology, developed by the Japanese in the late 1970s, was at a standstill following a deadly accident involving hand-held laser weapons in the US.*

*With even more monsters than ever stalking the globe, the future of the planet grows darker with each passing day.*

Some say the world will end in fire,
Some say in ice.
From what I've tasted of desire
I hold with those who favor fire.
But if it had to perish twice,
I think I know enough of hate
To say that for destruction ice
Is also great
And would suffice.

*--Robert Frost*

It was cold on top of the world.

Dr. Jack Davis shivered in his parka as a gust of wind blew across the deck. He was freezing, but he wasn't ready to go in yet. He put the binoculars to his eyes and looked at the icy waters once more. Among the floating icebergs, walruses frolicked, but nothing bigger. It had been weeks since they'd had a sighting, but Jack knew they were close. He could feel it in his bones.

The huge vessel moved slowly, knocking small bergs out of its way. The huge rig Jack designed looked out of place in the Arctic Ocean. But it was necessary to hunt the prey they were seeking. Half a mile to Jack's right, a narwhal broke the service, its huge unicorn horn of a tooth flashing briefly in the fading light. The sun was a pale disk in the cloudy sky, the air so cold it seemed that the life-giving disc was itself frozen, its heat failing to reach Jack's skin.

"You should come in. It's freezing out here," said a voice behind him. It sounded far away, and it was a full minute before Jack turned.

"It's also quiet, nothing to hear below decks but the thrumming of the engines."

"*Your* engines," said the voice.

Pamela Stewart came up to the railing to stand beside him. In their bright, government issue parkas, they looked like specks on the mobile oil derrick-size ship that had been designed and built with one purpose, for catching the giant monster that dwelled in these waters, Titanicus. That was the name the press had given it. It had no scientific name as yet. That was something Jack planned to rectify as soon as he could capture and study it. Study it and learn to control it.

The U.S.S. Searcher was the pride of the United States Behemoth Corps. The ship was a scientific and military vessel designed and built to capture sea-dwelling monsters or, failing that, kill them before another country could lay claim to them. Jack hoped it would do more of the former than the latter. Ever since he was a child, he was fascinated by the giant monsters that shared the planet. He read everything about them he could get his hands on, from Dr. Robert Fetch's *Monsters of World War II* to more recent scientific treatises on finding and controlling the enormous beasts.

They were pure forces of nature, and getting one to do your bidding was akin to learning to control the direction of a hurricane.

"You really think he's out here somewhere?"

"Yes. The sonar pings led us here. He's probably just down under the ice, so deep we can't detect him."

"Now all we need is some bait."

They were working on that. A sperm whale caught four hours ago had been cut up, and they were about to set a hook with it. Pamela had vehemently stated her displeasure, and had stayed below decks during the entire fishing expedition, as the men called it. Greenpeace wouldn't like it, but it had to be done if they had a hope of catching Titanicus.

Jack and Pamela turned as a giant crane lifted the dead whale out of the Searcher's enormous hold, which was fitted off to one side of the gigantic vessel. It lifted the whale easily into the air and positioned it over the center of the ship, which contained a rectangular opening to the sea. The dead animal hung there for a moment, and Pamela buried her head in the back of Jack's parka. Then the crane lowered the beast into the choppy blue-grey water until it was submerged.

Jack pulled a walkie-talkie from his belt. "Tell him to lower the bait to three hundred feet."

He turned to Pamela. "Let's go inside where it's warm."

"What do we do now, Captain Ahab?" Pamela asked as they walked around the rectangular opening toward the administration cluster.

Jack smiled. "Now we go fishing."

The idea was simple, on paper. Build a ship the size of three oil derricks, catch and kill a whale, and drag it through the water until something big enough to feel grabbed the line. It was an idea that had never been tested, however, and Jack's reputation was on the line.

Not only that, but the whole world was watching. Pamela Stevens was a photojournalist with National Geographic, here to capture the entire thing for the magazine. It was all a big publicity scheme. The government wanted to make a big show of strength by capturing yet another monster to add to their bizarre menagerie, showing the Russians that they could do them one better.

It was another round of back-and-forth gamesmanship in a Cold War that had raged for decades, with both sides displaying their monsters and creating an atmosphere of fear and distrust. If each country released their monsters on each other, the feeling was no one would really win, because the monsters were capable of such unheard-of destruction that nothing would be left for the victors. The basic idea was that a country could get just as much or more by not using its monster then by unleashing it.

Jack explained this idea to Pamela once more as they went inside to the relative warmth of the operations deck. A seaman moved aside to let them pass, then went on about his rounds, reminding Jack that this was first and foremost a military vessel, even though its purpose was primarily scientific.

"So you really got the idea for this rig from an old science fiction story?"

"Uh huh," Jack said. "Roger Zelazny's *The Doors of his Face, the Lamps of His Mouth*. It's about people hunting sea monsters on Venus from the decks of giant drilling platforms."

Pamela smiled. "That sounds elegant."

"It sounds crazy," said Jack. "And you can print that in your article as a direct quote from me. It took quite a few years of convincing to get enough military brass and engineers to think it was a good idea, let alone doable."

"So now that you have your big boat, what do you want to do?"

They entered a small mess hall. "I just want to study one of these monsters. I need to really see them in the wild, up close. Monsters in captivity just aren't the same. They've been fettered and tortured and tamed. I need to see them in their full, primal glory, see how they live and fight."

Pamela smiled as Jack poured her some coffee into a Styrofoam cup. "You sound like a little boy, playing with his toys."

Jack smiled. "I did plenty of that too, believe me. I have all the Johnson figures that Mattel made in the seventies. But my favorites were the Japanese figures. But we're not sailing on a toy."

Pamela poured enough creamer in her coffee to make it a different color. "And Titanicus isn't made of plastic. You think the Searcher can hold her?"

"Or him," Jack corrected. "I think so. We won't have to tow it all the way back to civilization while it struggles. Once our fish is on the line we'll drug it and cable it back to Anchorage. Or stick it in the hold if it happens to be shorter than we estimated."

"So you're certain we'll catch him. Or her."

Jack nodded, sipping his coffee. "Maybe not this trip, but yes. We'll get her. Or him. We've got to."

Pamela sighed. "I keep thinking about that poor whale."

"There are other fish in the sea," said Jack.

Pamela grinned, and groaned.

TITANICUS WAS A PARTICULARLY nasty example of genus *monstrum*. It had attacked several ships, seemingly for no reason, and no country had stepped up to claim responsibility. That meant a rogue beast, and the Behemoth Corps dispatched Jack and his new ship. They couldn't have something like that roaming their shipping lanes, unless, of course, they were controlling it.

A beast that size patrolling the oceans would assure the United States' dominance of the seas for decades. But the Behemoth Corps could not accept the consequences of a monster roaming unchecked.

"How long do you think we'll have to wait?"

Captain Pierce stared out the port observation window, his grey eyes keeping watch for any movement. The afternoon had turned grey as clouds crowded out the sun.

Jack shrugged. “We don’t know how often a creature that size gets hungry. But a dead whale will be too big a meal to pass up. I don’t suspect it’ll take longer than a couple of days.”

Captain Pierce nodded. “We don’t have anywhere else to be. We just can't stay here until winter, and the Commander in Chief isn’t a patient man.”

“I’m well aware of that, captain,” said Jack. He had been the government’s de facto monster czar since Carter, advising the past two administrations on the latest science as it relates to the country’s multi-ton killing machines. He glanced at Pamela, who was still holding her coffee cup, her hands curled around as if the retreating warmth of the liquid would soak into her fingers.

Jack wished they were chasing the beast through warmer climes. He wanted to go out on deck to smoke and pretend he wasn’t on a vessel built by defense contractors and full of soldiers. He was glad Pamela was here. Having a photojournalist from National Geographic onboard would hopefully keep things honest.

Jack's work was usually so top secret that his wife Sarah, before she left him, referred to these excursions as his classified vacations. It wasn’t so funny anymore.

“I want you to make sure your team is ready as soon as we snare this thing,” said Captain Pierce.

“We’re on it,” said Jack. He hated being ordered around like a sailor, but he took it in stride. He left the bridge, motioning for Pamela to follow.

“You took that well,” she said when the hatch was closed behind them.

“I’m used to it," he lied. "I’ve been around military types most of my career. Now let’s go somewhere much more interesting: My office.”

Jack’s office was anything but. A converted crew quarters that held a metal bunk bolted to one wall, and another foldout bunk on the opposite wall that Jack had turned into a desk, piled high with charts, maps, and books—most of them written by Jack himself—on monster biology.

Dave Westbrook was waiting for them when they arrived. Dr. Westbrook was a respected marine biologist, and the best large animal vet on the planet. Jack had him on loan from SeaWorld. The trio was old friends, having gone to the same grad school. Pamela hadn't seen him in years.

"This better be good, Jack," said Westbrook as soon as they entered the tiny room. "Please tell me I'm not freezing my balls off for another one of your wild goose chases."

"Cool it, pal," said Jack, smiling. "You're gonna love it."

"I'd love it if it was Tahiti," said Westbrook. "For now, I merely tolerate it. Hi, Pam."

"Hi, Dave," giving the tall man a hug. "I haven't seen much of you since you came onboard. How was your flight from Anchorage?"

"Horrible," Dave said, scowling. "In a rickety little puddle-jumper, I felt like I was going to die any minute. Is this how Uncle Sam treats all its consultants?"

"Just you, you old complainer," said Jack, smiling, and he shook Westbrook's hand vigorously.

Dave was roughly the same age as Jack, with frown lines making furrows in his pockmarked face. He had a head full of dirty blond hair shot through with gray at the temples, and watery blue eyes.

"You promised me a big find, and all I've seen so far are ice floes and Eskimos."

"You sound like the politicians who are footing the bill for this trip."

Westbrook nodded. "Can you draw out Leviathan with a hook, or snare his tongue with a line which you lower?"

Jack and Pamela eyed him strangely. "The Book of Job?" said Jack. "Dave, I never figured you for a religious man."

Westbrook said, "I'm not. But there are times."

He laughed and clapped Jack hard on the left shoulder. “I know you're good as your word. Besides, this is one hell of a boat. Old Noah's got nothing on you.”

"As long as it works," said Jack. "If not, I might have to get a job as one of your tank scrubbers down in Florida."

They all had a good chuckle about that. Their laughter stopped when the entire ship shuddered.

"What was that?" said Pam.

Jack looked at Westbrook. “The line!”

The three ran to the platform above, zipping their parkas as they went. Pamela stopped at her quarters to grab her camera gear. Up on deck things were humming. Men ran around shouting orders, while the metal cable dangling in the water was moving.

Jack grabbed a walkie-talkie from a metal cabinet bolted to the hull of the observation tower. “Easy on that line!”

He looked up to see someone sitting at the crane's controls, waving at him.

“Sonar's picking up something big, Dr. Davis,” said the captain's voice over the walkie-talkie.

“That's what we like to hear,” said Jack. He looked to his right, where Pamela was already snapping pictures, heedless of the frigid cold which assaulted them.

The line moved again, shooting out at almost a forty-five degree angle and striking one wall of the ship with a loud clang.

“There's something big thrashing out there!” said Westbrook, pointing. The ocean in front of them was churning, shattering the disturbed sea ice that had floated upon the surface peacefully only moments before. They watched in amazement as something broke the surface hundreds of feet from the vessel, a fin or a tail, heavy and dark against the blue of the freezing water. In a second it was gone.

“We got him!” said Jack into the walkie-talkie. “We've got him! Now let's reel him in. Slowly.”

The crane started up, the line reeling in inch by inch.

“That's it,” said Jack. “Nice and slow. We don't want him to know something's up until it's too late.”

Westbrook asked, "How do we know Titanicus won't swallow that whale like a cracker, and then do the same to us?"

"He isn't *that* big," said Jack. "Estimates put him at around eight hundred feet long. A whale should be what amounts to a decent sized meal for him."

Westbrook nodded. "I just hope he hasn't developed a taste for boat."

~

"How long is this going to take?" asked Pamela after they had retreated back inside the ship.

"Could take hours," said Jack, watching the crane nervously through a window.

"Fishing is a waiting game as much as anything," said Westbrook as he watched the ocean through a pair of binoculars, hoping Titanicus would once more breach the surface. "You have to tire the beast out first."

"That could take weeks," Pamela said.

Jack nodded. "Maybe."

"I don't have anything planned," said Westbrook. They were both in their elements now, which made Pamela feel like an outsider. She brushed an unruly strand of dark hair from her face and watched the activity outside the window.

She was used to eccentrics, explorers, scientists, and anyone else who "lived their lives dialed up to ninety" as her college roommate once said. She had made her living chronicling their exploits. But she had spent more time with Jack Davis than any of those other stories. He was different, she had decided. At least she thought he was, once upon a time.

They had been an item for about six months, after Sarah had left him. On the outside, Pamela thought she and Jack were the perfect pair. They were both married to their work, both had to suddenly leave at odd hours to go halfway around the globe; Jack to identify a giant bone or a huge claw found in some fisherman's net, Pamela to take pictures of some previously lost tribe or new archaeological find.

The truth was it was a huge wear and tear on both of them. But that was something else they had in common too. Neither of them was any good at relationships. But Jack Davis, B.S. M.S. Ph.D, was the only man who made her feel like they could try again.

Pamela watched and listened as Jack and Westbrook talked excitedly about the giant beast they had flopping around on the end of a giant hook, and wondered if he would ever let her in. Right now she felt like an outsider, the one girl ever to be allowed into the boys-only tree house. But there was one more barrier she still had to pass through. Jack's impenetrable heart, tough as the hide of the monsters he chased around the world.

There was another mighty lurch as Titanicus pulled against the line.

"I'll bet that set the hook," said Jack. "Now we'll see a show."

The grey water surrounding the ship began to churn and froth as Titanicus thrashed wildly. The Searcher listed in the direction the creature was tugging.

"I've got a bad feeling about this," said Pamela.

"Don't worry," said Jack. "The Searcher can hold her. The Searcher can hold anything." Raising the walkie-talkie to his lips, he said, "Start reeling her in. Slowly."

The Searcher bobbed atop the frothing water like a cork, but never threatened to go under. A perfect square, each side the length of an aircraft carrier, Jack's crazy ship seemed to pass muster. If there were giant monsters swimming the oceans, the Searcher would find them and catch them all.

Jack laughed at the thought, like mad Ahab after sighting Moby Dick. He wondered what Herman Melville would have thought of his monster, which would make his white whale look like a minnow.

Less than a thousand yards out, a black shape heaved out of the water, sending cold salt spray and floating ice hundreds of feet in the air. Jack was glad it was spring, otherwise the ice would have become too thick, making navigating the gigantic vessel impossible.

“We cheesed him off,” said Westbrook. The enormous tail, if that's what it was, a long chitinous limb of scalloped, razor-keen fins, fell back in the water with a mighty slap whose wake rocked the Searcher.

“Steady!” Jack yelled into his radio.

“If I think for one second that beast is going to capsize us, I'll turn it loose!” said the captain over the radio.

“I know, Captain,” Jack said. He knew the protocol. He wrote it. The winch atop the crane was fitted with radio-controlled explosives set to a special frequency. One push of a button from the captain, and the line would be severed. They would have to wait hours while the crane was repaired before they could try again.

“Do you think that cable will hold her?” Pamela asked she rapidly took more photos.

“It's got to,” said Jack. "We need that monster."

“You want to start trying frequencies now?” asked Westbrook.

Jack looked at his friend and nodded. In his excitement, he almost forgot.

“What frequencies?” Pamela asked.

"C'mon," said Westbrook. "We'll show you."

They walked down a labyrinthine passageway until they came to an elevator and climbed aboard. Jack thumbed the Up button.

“In the past, a lot of these beasties have been controlled by radio waves. Johnson and Jr., Thunderbird. Even, we believe, the Japanese and Chinese monsters. I suspect we might also be able to find a tone that will calm down Titanicus out there. At least make him calm enough to finish reeling in.”

“Sounds like a long shot,” said Pam.

“Finding the right tone could take years,” said Westbrook. "But there's no harm done in giving it the old college try now. Sound doesn't carry through water the same way it does on land.”

The elevator stopped, and the three got out. They grabbed the walls as the vessel lurched again.

“Keep reeling,” Jack called into the walkie-talkie.

They went to a small room full of radio equipment. Jack and Dr.

Westbrook sat down, donning headphones. Westbrook twisted dials and flipped switches furiously.

"This stuff is connected to loudspeakers all around the outside of the ship," said Jack to Pamela. "Even beneath the waterline. I just hope we can sing Titanicus a lullaby."

"Sounds like fornicating bats," Pamela said as Jack cranked up the volume. He and Westbrook turned and looked at her as if she suddenly sprouted a second head.

Pamela smiled. "What? Dave gets to be the only jokester in the bunch?"

"I like this one, Jack," said Dave, giving Pamela a playful wink. "Never let her go."

They all had an uncomfortable laugh at that and started cycling through frequencies again.

"These lower frequencies aren't having any effect, good or bad," said Westbrook. "Let's turn up the gain and head for the higher frequency range."

Jack nodded. He turned and looked though a tiny observation bubble at the frothing ocean below. He could sense Titanicus, just below the waves, a darker black shape against the dark grey water. He was here. He was *real.* And soon Jack would get the chance to look the beast right in the eye.

"Let's hope we don't find out which frequencies piss him off before we find the one that calms him down," said Pamela, snapping a picture of Jack and Westbrook working the radio transmitter.

"Back off, woman!" said Westbrook. "This is *science*!"

"Enough, you two," said Jack. "Something's happening."

The beast stopped thrashing. "Speed up the winch," Jack said into the walkie-talkie. "Just a little."

The cable moved faster, the dark shape beneath the water pulling closer to the ship.

"I think we found his sweet spot," said Westbrook. "Holding at nine point two oh five megahertz."

"Works for me," said Jack. "We'll have plenty of time to learn his taste in music once we've got him in an enclosure. I'm partial to The Who, myself."

"By the way," said Pamela. "Where will he be housed once you bring him back to the U.S.?"

"I'm sorry, Ma'am. That's classified." Westbrook said. "I could tell you, but then I'd have to feed you to Johnson."

"You two are just silly boys with fishing poles," Pamela smirked, hitting Jack on the left shoulder.

"She's on to us, Jack," said Westbrook. "There goes our Nobel Prize."

"Look!" said Jack. "He's surfacing!"

THEY SAW the creature for the first time. It was megalithic, titanic, like its name. Jack had imagined this moment many times, but the reality of it was much bigger.

The enormous crane pulled the monster out of the water almost effortlessly, water dripping down its black armor hide. He felt infinitesimally small next to this gargantuan killing machine.

The years Jack spent learning about and tracking this beast, then getting an assignment on the vessel designed to capture Titanicus. After all this time, was his journey almost over?

"THAT WAS EASIER than I thought it would be," said Jack. "But there he is. Look at him."

"Or her," Pamela corrected, snapping photos. "Let's go out on deck. I need a closer look at this thing."

As they climbed into the elevator, Jack and Dr. Westbrook talked excitedly. "Did you see that jaw line?" said Jack. "It's like an allosaurus."

"And the fore and hind limbs," added Westbrook. "They're clawed flippers. Excellent for swimming, but he wouldn't be a slouch out of the water."

Pamela chewed her lower lip. All she could think about was that a large, mostly unknown and completely untamed monster was now on the ship with them.

~

"Think of it," said Westbrook proudly. "The world's first known fully aquatic monster in captivity. It'll make the U.S. the best navy in the world!"

"I thought the U.S. already had the best navy in the world," said Pam darkly.

"Well, now no one will top it. What do you think of your prize, Jack?"

Jack opened his mouth to say something.

Then all hell broke loose.

Something struck the Searcher beneath the waterline with a resounding thud, and the power went out. The hum of the engines was silenced, as well as the whir of the enormous deck crane and the drone of the musical tone blasting from the ship's loudspeakers.

The creature's eyes snapped open, huge amber orbs the size of dump truck tires. The slit pupils moved around, surveying the beast's surroundings. But there was no fear in its alien eyes, only curiosity.

Titanicus thrashed and pulled at the line holding him, working the large hook loose from his mouth. It opened its jaws and dropped a few feet, lying flat across the opening so it wouldn't fall back into the sea. It issued a shriek, and the air was filled with stinging salt spray and the smell of rotting fish.

"Good Lord!" Jack cried. "What just happened?"

"We've lost power," said Westbrook. "What's running this boat anyway? Duracells?"

"Electric generators," said Jack. "Powered by diesel fuel. Nuclear was considered unsafe, given the mission." He grabbed binoculars hanging around his neck and looked out at the ocean.

"I know what happened to the power."

Grumbling, Westbrook went to a metal cabinet and, after fumbling with a tiny key, wrenched it open, pulling out a pair of harpoon guns fitted with tranquilizers. He handed one to Jack.

Pamela was focusing her attention on Titanicus, taking as many pictures of the beast as she could. The titan simply stood there, looking around, sniffing the air. As if he was waiting for something.

"Will someone please tell me what the hell is going on?"

"We threw a giant piece of bait into the water," Jack said, his eyes never leaving the ocean. "It was meant for Titanicus, but someone else came to the party."

The now dead ship shuddered and shook, bobbing like a cork on the choppy waves.

"Let me guess," said Pamela. "Titanicus's plus one?"

"So it would appear," said Westbrook. "And our big ugly friend knows it's here."

Titanicus craned its long neck, its reptilian eyes scanning the water. It alone knew what was there, just beneath the waves. It alone knew what was coming for them.

Everyone was so distracted they failed to notice one man in a parka busily climbing up the crane's steel structure.

"I need all personnel off the deck!" said Captain Pierce. Jack looked up to see him standing on the deck of the observation tower in a bright orange parka and holding a megaphone.

The helmsman fired a flare into the air, a distress signal that they were dead in the water and surrounded by monsters.

Then they saw it, arising from the water in a black stone-shaped column, seawater running down its length in rivulets. It was capped by a huge head that bent to look down at them, opening a lamprey-like mouth the width of the Holland Tunnel. Twin razors hung from the roof of that mouth, with a matching set jutting up from below. Jack thought he saw blue arcs of electricity run down its body.

Jack stared up at it, his mouth gaping. He knew he was looking at one of the largest beasts ever recorded. This was the thing that knocked out the Searcher's power. This was the thing that was going to destroy them all.

The giant eel-thing looked at Titanicus with yellow, luminous eyes. It gave an evil hiss that sent chills up Jack's spine, sliding up onto the vessel, its added weight shifting the Searcher even more to the right. Jack moved out of the thing's way as its cold, black bulk filled the space beside him.

Titanicus uttered a territorial shriek and closed with the beast, sinking its sharp talons into its inky black flesh. The eel-thing wrapped its writhing body around Titanicus. The titans danced across the deck, knocking men, equipment, and bits of the ship into the sea.

"This is bad," said Jack. "So very bad."

Westbrook scowled. "You think?" He handed Jack one of the harpoon guns.

"You sure these will work?" Jack said, snapping from his reverie.

"They have to. Otherwise the captain will bring his big guns to bear and turn Titanicus into tuna casserole."

"Man the deck guns!" said Captain Pierce into his bullhorn.

"There's no power!" Jack heard someone yell. The guns couldn't aim or fire without power. They had to get the generators and engines back online first.

"Titanicus and that giant eel are going to tear us apart!" Westbrook yelled, taking aim with his harpoon gun. He fired, the drug-filled missile bouncing harmlessly off Titanicus's scaly hide.

"Let me try."

Jack took careful aim at the eel and fired. The harpoon went straight into the thing's neck. The creature hissed, writhing in pain, and it loosened its grip on Titanicus just enough for the creature to get the upper hand. Grabbing the eel-thing's tail in his taloned hands, Titanicus hefted the monster over his head.

The eel-thing sank its fangs deep in Titanicus's neck, and he squealed in pain. His tail lanced upward, sheering off the top of the crane. The huge structure toppled to the deck, sending men and equipment flying.

"We've got to get off the deck!" Jack said, grabbing Pamela's hand and pulling her away from the battle. She was so focused on the monster duel she resisted at first. Then, realizing she was out of film, and she ran with Jack into the relative safety of the ship.

Westbrook joined them inside the hatchway that led to the observation deck.

"Well, this has gone sour," said Jack.

"You can say that again," Westbrook said, his eyes still on the fight.

"Well, this has gone sour. I'm going to have to do a lot of explaining to the Joint Chiefs."

"Maybe we can still get out of this," said Pamela. "That eel is electrified, right? He knocked out the ship's power."

"Right," said Jack.

"So why doesn't he just toast Titanicus?"

"He might need to recharge," said Westbrook. "We don't know anything about this creature's physiology. But a critter that could knock out power to Russian subs would be a terrific asset to have."

"What are you saying?" said Jack.

"I'm saying why go after one monster when you can get two?"

"For the price of one," Pamela added.

Jack looked at them.

"You're both crazy! But this just might save our bacon."

Jack went to a box mounted next to the doorway and wrenched it open. Inside was a row of tranquilizer darts. "Let's go for the eel this time. If we can get that thing subdued, then we can worry about Titanicus."

"Maybe once the power is back on, we can try our frequencies again," said Westbrook, loading several darts into the gun's chamber.

"What do you want me to do?" Pamela asked.

"Get more film and be our witness," said Jack. "We'll concentrate on the monsters tearing up my deck."

Pamela nodded and ran to her bunk. Jack loaded his gun and nodded to Westbrook.

Jack and Westbrook went back out into the cold. Titanicus and the eel had each other locked in their death grips, writhing all over the deck. Titanicus had pushed the eel-thing close to the edge of the vessel, and was on the verge of pushing the creature back into the icy water. They screeched and bellowed, each refusing to allow the other to win.

Jack and Westbrook took careful aim with their weapons, each targeting the eel creature. They fired almost simultaneously, the darts leaving the guns with a snakelike hiss.

Jack's dart flew wild, but Westbrook's seemed to find its mark. The eel didn't register the dart's entry into its skin. It continued its struggle with Titanicus. Jack readied to fire again when both creatures toppled over the size of the ship, taking the steel reinforced railing with them. They plummeted into the ocean with a crash that sent freezing salt spray up onto the deck.

Jack ran to the deck's edge, mindful of the slippery, nearly frozen water, and looked down. The eel had entwined itself around Titanicus's long neck, and the two were still screeching at each other. The titans bobbed up and down in the wake their impact had caused, and huge waves sloshed at the Searcher's sides, rocking the vessel.

Pamela appeared beside him, shivering in her parka. "They're not fighting," she yelled over the sound of the surf.

Jack looked at her, as if seeing her for the first time in his life. "What?"

"Look at them," Pamela said, pointing.

"They're not fighting. They're mating!"

They were biting each other, but it was away from fatal areas. It was playful, like puppies having a tumble through the grass.

Jack noticed the look of ecstasy in their reptilian, otherworldly eyes.

"I'll be damned," Westbrook said from behind them.

"Life has evolved some unique ways to reproduce," said Jack. "Hydra reproduce asexually. Jellyfish come from polyps. Caterpillars become butterflies. Why couldn't there be a life form that has an intermediate phase whose only purpose is to fertilize an egg?"

"We've always wondered where these big bastards come from,"

said Westbrook. "Now we get to find out." He glanced at Pamela. "I hope you're getting this on film."

As if in answer, Pamela snapped a series of photos.

Suddenly the Searcher began humming again, and Jack once again felt its comforting vibrations beneath the deck. Lights came on around them, and Captain Pierce barked orders over the radio.

"What do we do now?" asked Westbrook.

"We keep tracking Titanicus," said Jack. "See where she lays her eggs."

"I told you she was a girl," said Pamela. Jack nudged her elbow.

Jack's radio squawked to life. "Anyone care to tell me what the hell is going on down there?" said Captain Pierce.

"Just a minor miracle," said Jack. "Something we don't get to see every day."

They watched in silence as, the strange mating dance done, the eel-thing closed its eyes and died, sinking beneath the waves. Titanicus gave one last unearthly screech and followed its weird mate beneath the gray, ice covered water.

When it was gone, Jack looked down to notice that Pamela was holding his gloved hand. And for the first time in his life, he didn't want to let go.

"Fire and ice," said Jack, thinking of the ice-loving Titanicus and its electrified mate.

"What?" said Pamela.

"Isn't there a poem? 'Some say the world will end in fire, some say in ice?'"

"Robert Frost," Pamela said. "I love that poem."

"We have a world that begins with both."

"To me," said Pamela, "Frost was saying that how the world ends is no matter. It's best to live in the moment and enjoy one another."

Pamela was right. The world was as fragile as the steel platform they were standing upon, tossed in a careless sea. They'd better enjoy life while they could.

It was a dangerous world, growing more dangerous by the day. No one really knew when the saber-rattling would end and the monsters would be unleashed on each other—and trample everything underneath.

Jack pulled Pamela close and they held each other. He told himself he needed her here to give the operation public oversight, but that was wrong. He needed her here because he needed *her.* They needed each other.

On this Monster Earth, it was all that mattered.

**Contributors**

A native Toledoan, **Jim Beard** was introduced to comic books at an early age by his father, who passed on to him a love for the medium and the pulp characters who preceded it. After decades of reading, collecting and dissecting comics, Jim became a published writer when he sold a story to DC Comics in 2002. Since that time he's written official Star Wars and Ghostbusters comic stories and contributed articles and essays to several volumes of comic book history.

His work includes *Gotham City 14 Miles*, a book of essays on the 1966 Batman TV series; *Sgt. Janus, Spirit-Breaker*, a collection of pulp ghost stories featuring an Edwardian occult detective; and *Captain Action: Riddle of the Glowing Men*, the first pulp prose novel based on the classic 1960s action figure; and contributions to *Presidential Pulp* and *Black Bat Mystery Vol. 2*.

Currently, Jim provides regular content for Marvel.com, the official Marvel Comics website, is a regular columnist for *Toledo Free Press* and has forthcoming comic and prose work from Bluewater, TwoMorrows, Airship 27 and Pro Se.

Please visit him at http://sgtjanus.blogspot.com and on Facebook at http://facebook.com/thebeardjimbeard

**I.A. Watson** was bitten by a radioactive writer and became the award-winning author of the Robin Hood series *King of Sherwood*, *Arrow of Justice* and the upcoming *Freedom's Outlaw*, *Blackthorn: Dynasty of Mars* and the upcoming *Blackthorn: Spires of Mars*. He is a contributor to each volume of *Sherlock Holmes: Consulting Detective* and *Sinbad: The New Voyages*, *The New Adventures of Richard Knight*, *Armless O'Neil: Blood Prince of the Missionary's Gold*, GIDEON CAIN: DEMON HUNTER and others. He has always wanted to be a two hundred foot high monster and has a list of buildings and people he plans to crush. His website is at http://www.chillwater.org.uk/writing/iawatsonhome.htm

**Edward M. Erdelac** has been a fan of giant monsters since movies like *The Deadly Mantis* and *Gamera vs. Barugon* flickered across his TV screen via *Son of Svenghoolie*. He spent long car trips imagining immense gila monsters and tarantulas crawling over the dark Indiana countryside as it rushed by. He is the author of the acclaimed Judeo-centric/Lovecraftian weird western series *Merkabah Rider*, *Buff Tea*, and most recently, *Terovolas,* which tells the story of Professor Abraham Van Helsing's excursion to North Texas after the events of *Dracula*. He has written fiction for various magazines and anthologies, including Lucasfilm's Star Wars franchise, for which he wrote the definitive boxing story set in a galaxy far far away. An award winning screenwriter and independent filmmaker, he was born in Indiana, educated in Chicago, and lives in the Los Angeles area with his wife and a bona fide slew of kids and cats. News of and excerpts from his work, as well as reviews of his extensive home video collection can be found at http://emerdelac.wordpress.com. His favorite Godzilla antagonist is Hedorah, followed closely by Gigan.

Poet, crafter, gardener, and writer-at-large, **Nancy Hansen** lives in beautiful, rural northeastern Connecticut. She is the author of the novel *Fortune's Pawn*, and its forthcoming sequel *Prophecy's Gambit*, as well as the anthologies *Tales of the Vagabond Bards* and *The Huntress of* Greenwood for her Pro Se Press imprint, *HANSEN'S WAY*. She is Assistant Editor for Pro Se, and her short stories have often appeared in *Pro Se Presents*, a monthly digest. She has a story featured in the Airship 27 anthology *Sinbad: The New* Voyages, and the charity anthology *Lost Children*. Nancy also writes a biweekly column for http://www.newpulpfiction.com.

**Jeff McGinnis** was born, raised and has lived all his life in Northwest Ohio. He's been a film buff as long as he can remember, and a critic for the same length of time (not always professionally, of course). He graduated from Bowling Green State University in 2001 with a major in Journalism and Theatre. He would attend BGSU for a further two years in pursuit of a Masters in Theatre --a pursuit that would prove unsuccessful for a variety of depressing reasons. He writes for the *Toledo Free Press* in Ohio, where his column, "Pop Goes the Culture," appears in every Wednesday edition. He also is a regular guest on "The Morning Rush" on 92.5 KISS FM, and a panelist on the

1370 WSPD program "Eye on Your Weekend." He currently lives in Toledo.

**Fraser Sherman's** past fiction has appeared in *Realms of Fantasy*, The Drabblecast, *Allegory*, *More Scary Kisses* and *Big Pulp*. He's also the author of three film reference books—*Cyborgs, Santa Claus and Satan*; *The Wizard of Oz Catalog*; and *Screen Enemies of the American Way*. You can find him online at http://frasersherman.wordpress.com and in real life in Durham, North Carolina with his wonderful wife.

**James Palmer** is a writer, editor and publisher. He has written articles, interviews, fiction and poetry for *Strange Horizions*, *The Internet Review of Science Fiction*, *Tangent Online*, and other online and print publications. James is the author of *Slow Djinn* and the short story collection *Four Terrors: Weird Horror Stories*. His work has also appeared in *Gideon Cain: Demon Hunter*, *Blackthorn: Thunder on Mars*, and the forthcoming *Mars McCoy Space Ranger Vol. 2*. He also edited a charity anthology called *Voices for the Cure*, which benefits the American Diabetes Association and includes work by Cory Doctorow, Robert J. Sawyer, Mike Resnick, and others. A recovering comic book addict, James lives in Northeast Georgia with his wife and daughter. For more, visit www.jamespalmerbooks.net.

**JEFFREY HAYES**

www.ingramcontent.com/pod-product-compliance
Lightning Source LLC
LaVergne TN
LVHW050626100826
845148LV00011B/1747

*9780615753461*